ONE NIGHT IN THE ER

ONE NIGHT
IN THE *ER*

G. Scott McCreadie, MD

LUMINARE PRESS
WWW.LUMINAREPRESS.COM

One Night in the ER
Copyright © 2021 by G. Scott McCreadie, MD

Printed in the United States of America

Cover Design by Nina Leis
Cover Image by Jaromir Chalabala/Shutterstock.com

Luminare Press
442 Charnelton St.
Eugene, OR 97401
www.luminarepress.com

LCCN: 2020920891
ISBN: 978-1-64388-485-1

To Sue and our six wonderful children,
who have made all of my ER shifts worthwhile
and have provided so much joy
to come home to.

CONTENTS

INTRODUCTION

Everything you are about to read actually happened. Each of the patient encounters is real, and although they didn't all present on the same night shift, they could have. Of course, "the names have been changed to protect the innocent." But other than that, the descriptions herein are all of real people, with real problems, who presented to a real ER. That's the thing about emergency rooms—life doesn't get any more real than it does there.

These were all patients I saw while working as a moonlighting resident physician. I was still in training, but because I was broke and I had a wife and two kids, as soon as I had a license to practice medicine I used what limited and precious free time I had to work in a small, rural ER. Not only did that opportunity give me the ability to supplement my meager resident's salary and feed my family, it also gave me invaluable medical experience. I look back on those shifts that I pulled in that little ER as some of the best and most enjoyable of my career in emergency medicine.

I have now been practicing full-time emergency medicine for more than twenty years, and during that time I've seen a lot of crazy and interesting things. But so has every other ER doc everywhere. That's the nature of the business. The same could be said for every ER nurse, ER tech, unit secretary, and even ER housekeeper. All of the first responders, EMTs, and paramedics who transport patients to the nation's ERs have crazy stories to tell as well. Every consulting physician and floor nurse who takes care of patients after they leave the ER does as well. Although my intention was to write this for my children, I am hopeful that it finds a larger audience because I believe it contains useful information and compelling stories about real patients. I have intentionally tried to limit the use of foul language. However, that represents a certain sanitizing of the reality of emergency medicine. The ER, by its very nature, tends to be an R-rated experience.

When people learn what I do for a living, invariably the first question they ask me is, "What is the craziest thing you have ever seen?" I always struggle to answer that question. You see, if you work an average of fifteen shifts every month, and on each of those shifts you see an average of twenty patients, then after twenty years you've seen and treated more than 70,000 people. For this book, I picked a handful of those cases that I thought were interesting or stuck out in my mind. I felt that each of these stories was compelling in some way and had something to teach, good or bad, about the human condition. I first started writing this book shortly after I graduated from my residency in 1999. I have never been very successful at keeping a journal or otherwise documenting my life, but since I had young children I wanted them to have some understanding about what it was that their dad did during all of those hours he was away from home at the hospital. Because life is busy, it has taken me over twenty years to complete it.

A lot has changed in medicine in the last twenty years. I have tried to update the experience in my writing to make it somewhat more current, but the fact of the matter is that when I saw these particular patients we were still using paper charts and bulky, cumbersome plastic x-ray films that we looked at on lighted boxes. We dictated our charts and there was no reliable internet or way to look things up in real time other than referring to a handful of reference books. What hasn't changed are the patients. They still come in with the same complaints and the same experiences.

There are times when I read what I have written about these patients and I wonder how this will be interpreted. Have I been too frank? Have I been too mean, or judgmental, or have I shared too much? Some readers will undoubtedly think so. But that is not my intention. I am really interested in telling these everyday human stories from the perspective of an overworked, exhausted young doctor, working by himself, all alone on a cold, dark winter night in the middle of "nowhere, America."

Most people who don't work in the medical field have a very limited true understanding of the nuances of what occurs in the nation's ERs. But they all think they do. Maybe they've been to the ER themselves a couple of times, or maybe they have accompanied a friend or a loved one once or twice. All of them, however, have seen ER scenes played out on TV or in the movies literally hundreds if not thousands of times.

Unfortunately, what you see on TV or in the movies isn't real. It is scripted and choreographed. It is filled with stereotypes and one-dimensional characters who, although often more attractive than the real thing, are, and always will be, simply characters on a screen. Also, amazingly the depictions on the screen have the ability to wrap everything up neatly in the allotted time, even with commercial breaks. As hard as they try (and it has certainly improved over the years), these portrayals simply don't capture the sights, smells, sounds, and emotions of the real thing.

In 2018 there were 145.6 million ER visits in the United States, a country with roughly 327 million people. Think about that. That means that if those were distributed evenly, every man, woman, and child should find themselves as a patient in an emergency room once every 2.25 years. Using that math, if you are thirty-five years old you should have already had 15.6 visits to the ER in your lifetime. What is even more startling is that if you are like a lot of people, maybe you've never been a patient in an ER. If that's the case, then some other thirty-five-year-old needs to have been there more than thirty times just to make up for you.

The stories that I tell in this book are about everyday people who can be found everywhere. They may be strangers you'll never meet, but they may also be your friends, your neighbors, or maybe even you. They show up at all hours of the day or night, in every ER, in every city, town, and state, with every imaginable complaint or problem.

I consider it my greatest privilege in life to have briefly been a part of their lives and in some way to have relieved their suffering and helped them. I am just one ER doc, but there are tens of thousands of others like me across this nation and around the world who do this great work night and day.

G. Scott McCreadie MD

CHAPTER ONE →

Leaving the Mother Ship

t was 2:41 p.m. when Dr. Jim McCray, third-year emergency medicine resident, wheeled his car slowly around and down toward the exit of the hospital parking garage. He had just completed an exhausting thirty-six-plus-hour day, night, and day on his neurosurgery rotation at the university hospital. The university hospital was affectionately known by the residents as the "Mother Ship" as it was a tertiary care center where multiple satellite hospitals in the surrounding area referred patients for advanced specialty care. Jim had finally finished up rounding (seeing all of his assigned patients for the day) with the attending surgeon and had signed them out to another resident. It was the last day of his last non-ER rotations. During the night he had managed to sneak away to the call room and got two hours of fitful sleep between 4:30 a.m. and 6:30 a.m. Now he was headed home where he would try to get another couple of hours before he had to be up and on his way to Libertyville General Hospital for the night shift in the ER.

———•———

AS HE MEANDERED through traffic and along residential streets lined with trees that had long since been defrocked by winter, he reviewed in his mind the preceding night on call. It had begun benignly enough, rounding on elective surgical patients, mostly discectomies and laminectomies in otherwise healthy people. Then there was poor old Mrs. Greenberg, who a week ago had been the picture of health doting on her grandchildren. Now she was lying in the neuro ICU unable to speak or move her right arm. Her situation had begun a few weeks before when she first started to notice numbness and clumsiness in her hand. She didn't think much about it and wrote it off to old age, but when she accidentally spilled coffee on her husband, he demanded that she "go to emergency because you must be having a stroke." There was no stroke but the CT scan in the ER had revealed a large fungating mass, a tumor that had gradually enveloped a large portion of the left side of her brain. The tumor had developed a ring of swelling around it and was beginning to push the left side of her brain across the midline of her head. Because the skull is basically a box with a finite amount of space in it, this expansion had begun to compress the brain and raise the pressure in her head. This helped explained the headaches she had been waking up with for the past several weeks. Mrs. Greenberg had attributed them to caffeine withdrawal as they seemed to get better after her morning coffee.

Forty-eight hours after the ER visit and CT scan, she was on the operating table with her head open, and Jim was peering down through a three-inch-wide hole in her surprisingly thick skull. Dr. Hopkins, the neurosurgeon, was moving an ultrasonic probe around in circles gradually liquefying and vacuuming up the tumor and unfortunately, because there was not really a clearly identifiable demarcation between the two, normal parts of her brain tissue. Jim imagined her memories, ideas, and motor functions being sucked up by the vacuum. Living brain tissue has the consistency of a rather stiff Jell-O and vacuums up nicely.

As the machine whirred and consumed the brain tissue, Jim mused. There goes first grade, there goes her wedding, there goes any recollection of her husband, and there goes her ability to crochet or perhaps wipe her bottom. Like most people, Jim had mistakenly imagined neurosurgery to be the most exacting surgical specialty. He was surprised to learn firsthand that despite the million-dollar machine next to him, which helped Dr. Hopkins triangulate into the brain and remove the tumor to the margins shown on the CT scan images that flashed on the screen, it seemed it was really little more accurate than when a cook cuts a hole out of the center of a cake or the heart out of a head of lettuce. The difference between this and the cake or the lettuce was that the clumps of debris being cut out were infinitely complex brain tissue inside a living person's head.

Still this was one of the most sophisticated and accurate medical devices available for such a procedure. But it was just very difficult to tell where the tumor ended and where good brain began. To be truly accurate, this distinction was on the microscopic or cellular level, and with current technology this was an impossible level of precision. Therefore, in order to get as much of the tumor as possible, invariably a certain amount of normal brain tissue had to be sacrificed. The layperson seemed to imagine that surgery was simply a matter of opening a box, taking out the bad bits, and organizing and putting the rest back in. Jim's experience gave him much greater appreciation for just how complicated and messy things really are under the skin.

Mrs. Greenberg woke up in the neuro ICU the next day, following the seven-hour surgery. The endotracheal tube had been removed and she was taken off the ventilator. She awakened gradually as the sedation wore off, and by now she appeared to have returned to a normal or baseline level of consciousness. Unfortunately, now instead of having a weak right arm, she couldn't use it at all. It lay flaccid and nonfunctional next to her. She couldn't speak either. Outside information in the form of speech seemingly went into her ears and eyes and appeared to register and be understood by her, but the responses that came out of her mouth were simply a jumble of misplaced words. The speech she produced included fully formed words that were understandable individually, but in the particular way she would string them together they made no sense to the listener, including to Mrs. Greenberg herself. Her frustration was obvious. This once articulate, genteel elderly woman was now reduced to a one-armed purveyor of word salad.

Doctors call this condition "expressive aphasia" and it occurs when the speech center that resides on the left side of the brain in all right-handed and many left-handed people, is disrupted or destroyed. In the process of removing the tumor, which had grown into this normal area of brain tissue, the speech center had been irreparably damaged. Likewise, a portion of the motor strip that controlled the movement functions of the right arm had also been destroyed. There was simply no way to fully distinguish and separate the good brain from the bad, so speech and movement had become collateral damage in the battle against that ruthless invader known as cancer.

G. Scott McCreadie, MD

NEUROSURGERY WAS A painful rotation for Jim. He found that it consisted of countless hours standing in the operating room staring into a hole about an inch across in someone's head or spine and trying to make out what was nerve, artery, bone, brain, or disc tissue. The spine surgery was the worst. Working in that one-inch wide hole repetitively biting off tiny chunks of bone with a Rongeur, a tool that seemed to be a cross between a pair of pliers and heavy-duty toenail clippers, in order to gradually expose the pinched nerve. This was followed by unceremoniously grasping and yanking out pieces of the tough fibrous disc tissue that had escaped its normal anatomical confines and had plastered the nerve tightly against the ceiling of unyielding bone. This tiny area of dysfunction perhaps less than a centimeter across strangled the nerve and inhibited normal nervous electrical activity, which then led to unrelenting pain signals being sent to the brain as well as sensory and motor abnormalities downstream in the area the nerve controlled.

The chronic back pain patients were the worst of the worst. Neurosurgeons worked like indentured servants through eight long years of residency after medical school and then worked another eighty hours a week in practice and most of the patients they saw were "back-painers." All patients with chronic pain seemed to possess an absolutely uncanny ability to suck the very life force out of every physician they came in contact with.

Jim had experienced back pain intermittently himself for years. He knew firsthand just how miserable it was, so he did his best to empathize with patients who were suffering.

Most back pain was debilitating but temporary. However, for some patients it became chronic, and for them there seemed to be no escape. Unfortunately, a smaller subset of those with chronic pain seemed much more interested in getting their hydrocodone or oxycontin scripts filled than in actually getting better. Of course, the holy grail for these folks was permanent disability and the regular check that came with it.

In medicine there was simply no escape from such patients as every specialty had its own chronic pain patients. There were the chronic "pelvic-painers" in OB/GYN, the "chronic headache" patients in neurology, the chronic "belly-painers" or irritable bowel syndrome patients in GI and surgery, the "fibromyalgia and chronic fatigue" patients in internal medicine and family practice, and the list goes on and on. Some of these folks made a career out of doctor shopping and visiting ERs for pain shots and prescriptions.

Of course, not everyone with chronic pain was like that. In reality, probably only a small percentage were, but they seemed omnipresent and "it only takes a few bad apples…" Undoubtedly most of these patients had real and legitimate pain, but unfortunately most of it was impossible to diagnose or even quantify for that matter. Jim imagined that perhaps the greatest medical invention ever would be that of a "Pain-o-Meter," a device that could be plugged into a patient and tell just how bad their pain really was. Patients reacted so dramatically differently to pain. Jim and physicians like him had a pretty good understanding of how much something should hurt, and all of them had experienced some degree of pain in their own lives, but it remained a mystery why some patients were absolutely out-of-control-hysterical with what seemed like a fairly minor condition while others remained stoic and uncomplaining despite overwhelming injury. Pain and its management had become an enigma in modern medicine. In recent history, pain management advocates had effectively harassed and cajoled the medical community by accusing doctors of undertreating pain. They had taken to calling pain the "fifth vital sign," and had created numerical scales as well as scales with cartoon faces depicting varying degrees of suffering in order to quantify pain. Patients and even comedians had come to understand these scales and their implications. The scale was basically from zero to ten, with zero meaning no pain and ten being the worst pain imaginable. Not wanting to be undertreated, many patients assumed that their pain had to be the worst ever suffered by a human being and was therefore off the scale at eleven or fifteen or one hundred. More savvy patients who didn't want to incur the ire of their treating physician usually settled on eight, feeling this would legitimize their suffering and bring about the greatest reward in terms of pain medications without being too over-the-top.

As a rule, clinicians hated these scales and felt they were for the most part useless. The emphasis on pain management had led to the opening of clinics solely devoted to managing chronic pain and to clinicians, many legitimate but unfortunately some who were not, who took on the task of treating the population in pain. Generally, this had meant the use of escalating doses of opiate pain medications sprinkled in with a few other modalities. Much of this may have been driven by the drug manufacturers, but over time the emphasis on pain management had led to a dramatic disparity between the massive overconsumption of opiate pain medications in the U.S. when compared to the rest of the world. This seemingly had created new diagnoses for unexplained pain such as fibromyalgia, chronic fatigue syndrome, tertiary Lyme disease, irritable bowel syndrome, interstitial cystitis, chronic migraines, and others. All of these undoubtedly had some legitimate underlying basis, but they were incredibly difficult to quantify or prove with conventional medical investigations and testing.

With each of these conditions there was thought to likely be a component of unrecognized or unappreciated depression, anxiety, or other components of mental illness, including the residual effects of childhood trauma or abuse. All of this was further aggravated by the obesity epidemic and the general decline in human happiness and the functionality of modern human society. The easy availability of prescription opiates had not only led to their widespread abuse but also to their diversion from legitimate medical purpose and illegal sale.

When patients were suspected of being over-consumers or addicts and were cut off abruptly, they had no way to cope. The receptors on the cells of their bodies specific for pain medications had, over time, been gradually upregulated. Now that the supply was cut off, they began to experience the agonizing symptoms of withdrawal. This led to a vicious downward spiral that many patients found themselves trapped in.

Even in his short career in emergency medicine, Jim had already dealt with this on a massive scale. He had treated so many patients who were consuming an enormous amount of pain medicines but were still in pain. They were physically and emotionally dependent on these medicines, and when anything disrupted the flow they often found their way to the ER, claiming they had run out of medicine, used it up too quickly, or that it was stolen. On and on went the stories of why they needed more pain medicine immediately. By contrast sometimes they arrived in the ER because they had overdosed. Many overdoses survived but tens of thousands did not, and more were dying every year. The great opiate epidemic was sweeping the nation, but the reality was that it had actually been an epidemic for decades.

Because of the nature of opiate addiction and the body's inherent escalating need for more medicine for the same effect, many patients progressed from relatively safe prescription pain pills to needing something more and something stronger. This led some to turn to illicit drugs such as heroin or the more recent explosion of the use of nefarious fentanyl manufactured in labs and available on the street and on the internet. Frequently, patients who were unable to find opiates, or at least enough for their needs, substituted alcohol or habitual marijuana use or any number of other substances in order to numb their pain, both physical and emotional. The cycle continued and the number of patients seemed to be essentially infinite.

The vast majority of patients who came to the ER were there because of pain in one form or another. Patients hated it because they felt that doctors treated them like "drug-seekers" and doctors hated it because they struggled to separate the legitimate from the addicted. Jim, like most residents and for that matter most doctors in practice, was constantly exhausted. Exhaustion led to irritability, and irritability was manifest in contempt for people who abused the system. People who really needed a reality check rather than a million-dollar medical work-up.

———————•———————

JIM'S MIND DRIFTED away from neurosurgery and dead-beat patients as he pulled into the driveway of the tiny two-bedroom house he shared with his wife, Susan, and their two small children. He stepped out of the car into the cold but sunny daylight still dressed in his OR scrubs and white lab coat that was badly in need of washing and ironing. He stepped carefully over the scattered toys and around the little plastic cars that littered the deck. Winter was beginning to lift and Jim's three-year-old son had a bad case of cabin fever. Now that the weather was improving, he dragged everything he owned onto the deck, yard, or driveway.

Jim opened the back door and called out, "Daddy's home." This was always the best part of his day. He sank to his knees and waited a split second until Tyler, an overgrown and surprisingly muscular three-year-old, rounded the corner and ran full speed into his chest.

Tyler threw his arms around Jim's neck and screamed "Daddy, Daddy" with the sort of ebullience that can only be exhibited by a child who truly loves his dad. Jim closed his eyes and drank in the smell of his son and felt the warmth of his solid, wiggling body. The timing was just right, and when Jim opened his eyes again his little girl, Anna, just over a year toddled toward him, her eyes shining, her face seemingly about to burst due to the size of her smile. She clambered onto his knees and nuzzled against his neck with a fraction of the force of her brother. These were precious moments that seemed so rare as Jim's life was consumed by the hospital.

As he pondered on this, he remembered a time when he was an intern in the ICU and he had been up all night caring for a group of patients among whom the youngest was seventy-eight. Each had lived a full life. All were dying of illnesses resulting from the inescapable ravages of age or self-inflicted by lifestyle choices. At home lay his infant son, Tyler, seven months old, burning up with a fever and coughing through the night. Jim took calls from the ICU nurses to adjust ventilator settings and to order medications for his patients in the unit as well as calls from Sue who was up all night with Tyler, who was too hot and miserable to sleep. Jim recalled the overwhelming nature of his feelings and of stifling a deep, aching, primitive urge to flee the hospital and race home to care for his boy. His boy had a future and the inherent will to live of an organism that had not yet begun to fulfill its potential. This was in stark contrast to the exhausted, burned-out shells of formerly productive people who inhabited the ICU. These people were trying hard to die but instead they were propped up by breathing machines and by medicines that were dripped into their veins to pound on their tired hearts, as well as by potent antibiotics that struggled to thwart the microbial angels that in the past took such people home to meet their various gods.

To Jim, the ICU was like a vegetable garden where one fed and watered a group of humanoid/houseplants with the hope that they might open their eyes or move some muscle. This was the paltry fruit of the gardener's costly labor. That's not to say that intensive care, or as some said, "expensive" care, medicine wasn't interesting and exciting. In fact, it was one of Jim's favorite rotations; it was life and death, the sickest of the sick. This was where the cutting edge of medicine was most evident with lots of invasive procedures, devices, and new, novel drugs. It was rewarding, particularly when patients were snatched back from the brink of death after an exhausting fight championed by doctors and nurses using science and skill. However, more often than not, the outcome was death or a life greatly diminished and of questionable value. The outcomes were often a foregone conclusion, easily and accurately predictable when the patients first arrived, and long before tens or even hundreds of thousands of dollars were spent. In the ICU, the money got spent but the lingering question often remained: For what?

Jim loved the ICU, but in the end it was too impractical. He related this back to his own dichotomous experience of using all of his skills and spending countless hours and dollars trying to save people with no productive life left, while his little boy lay at home with only the care of his mother, scorched by fever and infection, but with limitless potential.

Jim returned from his thoughts as Sue entered the room following the children. She looked tired but content and beautiful. They had married when Jim was just finishing his first year of medical school. Sue had a degree in psychology but gave up grad school in order to work and put Jim through the remainder of medical school. They married after a short engagement, grateful to have found each other, each having grown tired of single life and each having recently gotten over a painful breakup. Medical school had been uneventful. Susan worked while Jim studied. There was little time for anything else. It was a simple life and they had little else between them to encumber or distract them. This time together had helped them to bond deeply. During this time the rest of life was simply put on hold pending the completion of training, when the hope was that the schedule would be reasonable and the paychecks respectable. In the meantime, they worked and waited.

As medical school graduation loomed and Jim was about to start his internship and residency, they decided they had waited long enough for some things. Both desperately wanted children, and Susan now was pregnant. Knowing it would be difficult but hoping it would be worth it, she quit her job as a secretary and they packed what they had and moved across the country to where Jim would begin his internship. Jim's salary as an intern was almost exactly the same amount that Sue made as a secretary so there was no real change in their financial situation. A few months into Jim's intern year, Tyler was born.

Jim didn't see much of his little family over the next couple of years, and when he was around, he was often too tired to stay awake. Twenty months after Tyler, Anna was born. Jim's life was absorbed by the hospital and Sue's by the children. But their love remained strong and constant. Each was strengthened by the thought that they were engaged in something noble and with the vision that the land of "milk and honey" was growing closer each day. Now graduation from residency was only four months away. Winter was slowly beginning to lift and with the coming spring there would be new growth and greener pastures for Dr. Jim McCray and his young family.

Jim had already signed with a group of emergency physicians back on the West Coast. In July they would be going home and Jim would start working in a moderate-volume emergency department in a typical community hospital. If everything went well, the group he signed with had promised that within a year he would make partner.

But for now, he still had four months to go to complete his residency. Winter held a tight grip on everything around him and Jim knew he still had plenty of work ahead before summer.

After the first year of residency, or internship as it was called, Jim passed part three of the Medical Board exams. When he finished his second year of residency, he became eligible for his state medical license. Jim didn't waste any time applying because he wanted to moonlight. Moonlighting residents were an ancient tradition in medicine. In the past it seemed like residents in every specialty moonlighted. Gradually over time it seemed that emergency medicine residents were the only ones left who moonlighted in small ERs. There was some talk of eliminating all moonlighting. Jim was glad that he would be finished with residency before that happened. He had moonlighted every month since getting his license over a year and a half ago. Although it meant more work and more time away from his family with his already exhausting schedule it also meant money. By picking up just three shifts a month Jim could double the amount he made as a resident. With a wife and two small children this extra income was hard to live without.

As it turned out Jim found he didn't mind the extra work, in fact he relished it. Moonlighting was fun. Jim enjoyed the exhilaration of seeing patients when he was solely responsible for their care. It was scary at first, but over time he had gained greater confidence and saw a lot of great cases. As a senior resident at the university hospital he had a lot of autonomy but he still had to run everything by an attending physician. Also, at "the U" there was an inexhaustible supply of back-up where specialists of every variety were readily available for consultation.

That wasn't the case at Libertyville General Hospital. When Jim was there, he was the only show in town. Jim swelled with pride when he thought that for the twelve hours of his shift anyone seriously ill or injured in the 125-square-mile catchment area of the little hospital came to him. At night when he worked there and all of the doctor's offices were closed, he served as the sole provider and protector of the health of the entire community.

That was why essentially only emergency medicine residents moonlighted like this anymore. They were the only physicians in training who really possessed the diversity of skills necessary to adequately manage the variety of cases that came into the emergency room. Medicine had become too complex. Expectations for rapid diagnoses and treatment were now the standard of care. In the past a patient may have been admitted by their doctor to the hospital for a week for a "work-up" to sort out what was wrong with them. Now patients came to emergency and the entire process was condensed. The patient was "worked-up" in real time by the emergency physician. Rapport had to be developed quickly, and in a few hours lab results, x-rays, CT, MRI, and ultrasound were all completed. Most patients had their diagnosis, if one could be had, before they left the emergency department. Treatments were initiated and they were then either discharged home or admitted if their management required surgery, more time, monitoring, or further evaluation. Most in-patient physicians who took over a patient's care while they were admitted to the hospital had the expectation that the emergency physician would have essentially completed the work-up and have at least a working diagnosis and treatment would be underway. The admitting physician would see the patients in the ER or later on the floor after they had been neatly packaged and prepared almost to the point where the ER doc left a bright line in Sharpie pen on the patient's skin saying "cut here." If the ER was too busy and the patient went upstairs without a complete work-up it was not uncommon to hear frustration and complaints from the admitting physicians. This was in part because the ER was streamlined to get a lot done in a hurry. If a patient made it out of the ER and onto the floor without a complete or nearly complete work-up, time suddenly had a way of slowing down and any further investigations seemed to take much longer.

Emergency physicians had become the experts in rapid diagnosis. The tricky part was that emergency physicians often had to juggle the investigations and treatments of multiple patients, sometimes ten or more, simultaneously. These patients were often on the extremes of age and could have any number of possible problems. Worst of all was the constant worry about an impending disaster that could come through the door at any minute and thereby completely destroy the somewhat controlled chaos that the emergency physician was trying to manage.

Jim learned early on that the most important patient was the department itself. One had to keep the flow going and keep the patients moving along. It was imperative to adapt and adjust constantly or else the whole place would become so constipated it would be gridlocked and there would be no room for the crush of new patients arriving at the door. There was no slowing down and no closing the doors. The emergency department didn't have the luxury of scheduling, or of rescheduling if something came up. Frequently when the ER was full and all hell was breaking loose there was no reprieve and there were more patients on the way. When overwhelmed and when people became increasingly irritated and angry because of the wait, Jim would try to assuage their anger and refocus them by saying, "I'm sorry it took so long to get to you, it's crazy busy, and try as I might I just can't get people to schedule their emergencies."

There was always a point, at which there were simply too many patients, and it was just too busy, and it was then that it became unsafe. At that point, corners invariably got cut and important things were forgotten, neglected, ignored, or missed. There was no way around it. Most emergency departments were frequently overwhelmed. It could happen in a matter of minutes, and there were limited mechanisms to ramp up quickly to adjust for it. You just had to work harder and faster and hope that no one died because you were just too damn busy.

Essentially, only emergency medicine residents were equipped to moonlight in the chaos of the modern ER. Other residents were good at what they did but were too specialized. A surgical resident might be great at sorting out belly pain but wouldn't have a clue about how to manage the kid seizing in the next bed. The pediatric resident might be great at managing kids but give him a seventy-five-year-old with chest pain and you had a recipe for disaster.

Part of the reason that Jim chose emergency medicine was the fear of the unknown. He feared being caught not knowing what to do. He wanted to know how to do everything. He desperately wanted to be all things to all people. It didn't take long before he realized that this was impossible, of course. Although his knowledge was broad, it was of necessity shallow. Yes, he could treat all-comers, but there was always a specialist who knew a lot more about any given problem than he did. The specialist's knowledge was deep but narrow in scope. Medicine in its entirety was far too vast for any one person to even come close to mastering. There were myriad diseases for each individual cell type and organ in the human body, and often disease entities affected multiple organs at once. Additionally, each of the cells and organs were affected differently at different stages throughout life.

This was the great paradox of emergency medicine. Emergency physicians were trained to take care of anyone, with any condition. At least at first. The expectation was a work-up and a diagnosis but sometimes it was reduced to glorified triage. (Triage is the assignment of a degree of urgency to an individual patient in order to decide the order of treatment when dealing with multiple patients at once.) This had become less of an issue with the advent of faster tests and results. When Jim was in medical school, he mentioned to a pompous plastic surgeon that he was thinking about emergency medicine. The retort had annoyed Jim and had stayed with him.

"Do you want to treat patients or triage them?" the surgeon said.

On average, 80 percent of patients leave the ER with a diagnosis and with treatment initiated. The other 20 percent were admitted into the hospital for further treatment or work-up. Emergency medicine was a generalist specialty. Emergency physicians didn't do any more triage than any other generalists such as those in family practice or internal medicine. Of course, this comment was made by a guy whose entire medical practice consisted of providing healthy people with boob jobs and face-lifts.

Over time, Jim had found that emergency medicine fit him well. He had a short attention span and he enjoyed the variety and the fast pace. Sometimes he wished he could have the long-term relationship of seeing a patient over and over again over a period of years. But most of the time he was glad he wouldn't have to see the patient again anytime soon. Jim remained fearful, but it had changed from a fear of not knowing what to do for an individual patient to the fear of losing control of the whole department.

The federal government had long ago mandated that the nation's ERs were a safety net. It was against the law to turn anyone away from an ER. It didn't matter if you were too busy that day or that the patient couldn't or wouldn't or didn't have a way to pay for the care they received. The patients in the ER often came from the fringes of society. They may have waited too long because of the fear of the cost and let their disease get out of control. They may have had no access to health care or no interest in it. They were often drunk, high, psychotic, violent, or all of the above. Frequently they had to be restrained or sedated, or they were led in bound in shackles by the police. The presence of these types of folks was unthinkable in a tidy doctor's office waiting room with its regular schedule, magazine racks, and relaxing background music. By contrast in the ER this was routine and such patients were a permanent fixture every night, everywhere across the country. These were the thoughts that filled Jim's head as he drifted off to sleep in the afternoon. His body was exhausted and melted into the mattress, his mind buzzing with a blur of patients. He was tired but he was happy, and he was proud of what he did.

CHAPTER TWO

Entering the Arena

A couple of hours later, Susan sat on the edge of the bed in the darkened bedroom and kissed Jim's forehead to wake him up.

"C'mon lover, it's time to get up, dinners almost ready," she whispered.

Jim's eyes slowly blinked open. For a second, he was disoriented, thinking he had slept all night and it was morning. Then his brain adjusted and he remembered he had only napped, and soon it would be time to get up and drive to Libertyville for his night shift.

"What time is it?" Jim asked.

"Five thirty," came the reply.

He quickly made the calculation: Forty-five minutes to drive to the hospital left him with forty-five minutes to shower, eat, and play with the kids. Jim shook the last remnants of sleep out of his head and suddenly, infused with energy, jumped out of bed in his underwear. He grabbed Susan in a playful embrace and danced her around the room and then dropped her onto the bed laughing.

"I love you; wish I had time to...*love* you!!!" He sang as he stripped naked and bounded for the shower.

Twenty minutes later he emerged from the bedroom

showered, shaved, and dressed from head to toe in clean blue scrubs with a graying lab coat draped over his arm. He laid the coat aside and sat down at the dinner table and surveyed his family.

"What's going on people?" he said.

Tyler and Anna, who had already begun eating, both erupted into large smiles and nervous giggles.

"Daddy go to work?" Tyler asked. It was half question and half statement of fact.

"Yup, Daddy goin' to wuhk," Jim repeated, imitating his son's three-year-old speech. "What else is new, eh?"

They finished dinner quietly, or as quietly as is possible with two toddlers, and then Jim briefly wrestled with the children on the living room floor amid their screams and giggles. Reluctantly, Jim extracted himself from their grip and put on his warm winter coat, grabbed his lab coat, and headed for the door. There Susan met him, they embraced and kissed. The children grabbed his legs desperately trying to hold him there.

Susan bent over and picked Anna up. "Can you two say thank you to Daddy for going to work?" She said. Together the children exclaimed their thank-yous.

"I love you all and I'll see you in the morning," Jim said, and then a moment later he was out the door into the cool evening air.

It was six fifteen and winter dark. Jim slipped behind the wheel of his beater station wagon and headed out of town. He was oddly proud of this car although it was a complete wreck. Sue drove a relatively new minivan, which was safe and reliable to haul the kids around in. Jim's car, in contrast, was fifteen years old and he had driven it for the last three years after buying it for a thousand bucks. At the time of the purchase there were already more than 200,000 miles on it. When he test-drove it in the middle of the summer and the engine was warm it ran quite well. It wasn't until the cold of winter that the steering problem became noticeable. The car turned to the left just fine but any right turns were done without the assistance of power steering. This wasn't a big problem in and of itself, as Jim had once owned a truck that had no power steering at all. But Jim had learned that with this car at slow speeds you used full-arm-strong steering to go right and easy power steering to go left. However, it was unpredictable because sometimes the power steering would kick in intermittently during a turn where Jim was using all of his strength and the sudden lack of resistance would cause him to dangerously oversteer. This was like trying to pull open a door when someone on the other side is holding it and then they suddenly let it go. Sue refused to drive the beast because she wasn't strong enough to make it go right, but Jim enjoyed the challenge of predicting the steering problem and wrestled it like a cowboy wrestles a calf to the ground.

The other problem with the car was the oil leak. Jim kept twelve-packs of oil in the trunk to routinely fill it up. He had long since given up on the dipstick as a means for monitoring oil consumption. Instead he used the oil light or the intensified tapping sound of the valve lifters as they dried out. Jim felt bad about this, knowing that his car was a mobile environmental disaster and probably on the EPA's top-ten most-wanted list. But he justified it because it wasn't worth fixing, and if he could just limp it along for four more months, he would get rid of it and buy a responsible car. Then maybe in the future he could pay his debt to the environment by volunteering to wash ducks and seagulls the next time an oil tanker spilled after it ran aground.

Before long Jim was off the freeway and entering the town of Libertyville. There was nothing unique about it. Libertyville was cast from the same mold as a thousand other little towns in Middle America. Its only claim to fame was a midsummer fair that attracted some has-been rock bands as well as thousands of their faithful followers, who drank and fought and passed out in the July heat overwhelming the little ER where Jim worked. Jim intentionally avoided working during fair week. He was paid by the hour so it was advantageous to avoid busy shifts. However, degree of busyness was notoriously difficult to predict. Weekends and evenings tended to be bad. Long weekends and when events came to town were even worse.

Numerous studies had been done to see if full moons or other phenomenon really increased emergency department volumes. As a medical student, Jim had even done a study looking at the days following the distribution of welfare checks, the so called "Welfare Wednesday" phenomenon. These studies all seemed to conclude there was no measurable or predictable correlation between these events and ER patient volume. Jim's study did reveal an interesting spike in heroin overdose deaths in the two days following Welfare Wednesday however. Despite all of the studies, everyone who worked in the field of emergency medicine held a loosely formulated belief that certain events such as full moons certainly made the place weirder if not busier. In general, it was hard to predict and the nature of the busyness included random unforeseeable events that would occur without warning; the proverbial "bus full of hemophiliacs going off a bridge."

IT APPEARED THAT this was just the sort of night that Jim was in for. As he entered the hospital parking lot, he could see the drive-up ramp to the ER. This is where ambulances pulled up to unload patients and where occasionally a private car would speed up and dump out a dead or nearly dead body and then slip away into the night. If Jim arrived and the ramp was empty, he felt he had a pretty good chance of having a good night. Tonight, it wasn't empty—in fact, it was as full as he had ever seen it.

At the top of the ramp sat an ambulance, and behind it there was a police car and a fire engine. The police car's emergency lights were on and threw pulsing red and blue shadows onto the side of the building. Jim steeled himself as he had done so many times before. There was no turning back now. No matter what happened he was "the man" for the next twelve hours in this place. The only comforting thought he held onto was that no matter what came through that door and no matter what the world threw at him tonight, there was no one who could stop the clock.

Jim walked out of the cool night air through the automatic sliding doors into a blur of bright fluorescent light and a cacophony of noise. Anxious voices were mixed with the wailing of infants and the beeping of monitors. This was a small ER by anyone's standards, but a lot of sick people crammed into a small space on a cold night made for a scene of commotion and chaos. Jim felt a familiar tightness develop in his chest and a mild wave of nausea flowed over him. He always got this feeling when he first arrived at work. Sometimes he woke up with it when he had been dreaming of being at work and something had gone tragically wrong. He even felt it when he watched TV shows or movies that depicted ER scenes. He had never been able to sit through an entire episode of "ER." This was in part because he couldn't stand to let work invade his leisure time, and he couldn't stand how dramatic and serious everything always seemed to be when there were actors pretending to do what he did in real life.

This feeling of anxiety was mildly unpleasant but it wasn't overwhelming. He had the same feeling as a teenage athlete just before a game. Jim suspected there must be some evolutionary reason for it. Perhaps it was the brain's way of focusing attention on the task at hand, or perhaps it was related to the release of stress hormones preparing the organism for "fight or flight." It generally was at its worst during the anticipation phase prior to starting a shift but once he started actually seeing patients and he was actually in the arena, ready to do battle, the sensation gradually subsided.

Tonight, the arena was full and it quickly became apparent to Jim the reason for the ambulance, fire truck and police car. Perched on top of a sagging ambulance gurney was the largest woman Jim had ever seen. She looked frightened. Around her were a half dozen paramedics and firefighters holding pressure and pushing on her various body parts to keep her from spilling off the gurney. Nearby, two nurses were strapping two regular hospital beds together in an attempt to provide a suitable landing pad for this enormous piece of human cargo, which was about to be delivered and would be the first patient of Jim's night.

Behind the desk at the nurses' station stood Dr. Lindstrom, a squat, middle-aged, single woman whom Jim knew from the university hospital. She was part-time faculty there but only worked nights. In fact, Jim could not recall ever seeing her during the day. She motioned Jim over, obviously anxious to get out and turn the mess over to him.

"You've got six patients and four more to come back," she started without even saying hello. "Bed two is a kid with a cough; three is a dislocated shoulder—he's in x-ray. Four is a CHFer who's had Lasix and nitro—his labs are cooking. Five is a psych patient who should be a slam dunk admit. She's obviously psychotic—Mental Health is in seeing her. There's a vag bleeder in the pelvic room and you have seen the leviathan that just arrived for bed one. She apparently has a fever."

"Looks like you had a busy day," Jim said, trying to sound upbeat despite his contempt at being left a department full of partially worked-up patients.

"Not really," Lindstrom said. "It wasn't bad until an hour ago when all hell broke loose. Have a good one, I've gotta run. I've got a night shift at the U tomorrow."

Without another word she had her bag and her coat and was out the door. Jim could tell by eyeballing the triage times that she had strung these patients along doing the minimum until Jim arrived to take over so she could get out right on time.

Typical, thought Jim. She was well-known at the university hospital as a work avoider, always riding the residents to do all of her work.

Jim took a deep breath, his nausea lifted and he dove in. Almost instantly he began to feel that swelling sense of pride as he took control to make order out of chaos. He was a conductor directing an orchestra and pulling together notes and tones and sounds and tying them together into one beautiful flowing piece of music. He started with the coughing two-year-old in bed two. She was the source of the crying that had first met his ears. She had a low-grade fever, a cough, and mild wheezing, and was receiving a breathing treatment that she didn't like. She had a typical mild childhood viral respiratory infection and was discharged with an inhaler and instructions to control her fever. Bed four was in congestive heart failure but was responding to Lasix, a diuretic. His chest x-ray showed a backup of fluid accumulating in his lungs due to the inefficient pumping of his tired heart. Diuretics are medications that prompt the kidneys to produce more urine, thereby drawing fluid from the bloodstream, which subsequently has to be replaced by fluid shifted from the patient's water-logged lungs. This eased his breathing and helped to shrink his swollen legs. He was admitted to the medical service.

By this time, the staff had the heavy woman signed in and everyone was ready to move her off the gurney and onto the bed, or rather, beds. Her name was Violet, and she was thirty-nine years old. She weighed something over 600 pounds. She lived with her twenty-one-year-old son who was mildly mentally handicapped. She had no other family and few, if any, friends or other contacts. She almost never left her home as she couldn't really walk any distance. She sent her son to the store regularly to buy cigarettes and food. The ambulance was called when a neighbor happened by and found Violet lying on her bed in the garage. She slept in the garage because the other doors in the house were difficult for her to get through. There were three space heaters in the one-car garage to keep it heated despite the uninsulated garage door. The space heaters were going full blast and apparently were working well because the medics reported that it was about ninety degrees in the dank space.

Violet was found lying in her bed, which was filthy and soaked with urine, and she was delirious with a high fever. The firefighters were grateful she was in the garage however, because it meant they didn't have to cut the house apart to get her out. Even with that advantage, it had still taken four volunteer firefighters and two paramedics an hour and a half to get her out of the garage, into the ambulance, and to the ER.

———•———

TONIGHT, THERE WERE two nurses on duty in the ER, as well as a tech and the house supervisor. The house supervisor, or house sup, was a nurse who managed the whole hospital at night, including all of the floor nurses. When it was busy, she would come down to the ER to help out. The two main ER nurses were Carol and Marcie. Carol was fiftyish—she had been a nurse for almost thirty years and had seen it all. She was desperately trying to stay young and hip to keep up with her younger colleagues, and had recently gotten a tattoo of a butterfly on her ankle. Marcie was twenty-four. She was one year out of nursing school, but what she lacked in experience she made up for with street smarts. She was savvy and could handle anybody. In general, the ER seemed to attract a higher quality of nurses. Only the most confident were interested in the fast pace and the variety. The lazy ones were quickly weeded out, and the stupid ones were usually driven out by intolerant physicians, patients, or other nurses.

Knowing he had Carol and Marcie tonight gave Jim confidence. Even the nurses at the U had difficulty comparing to these two. Good ER nurses made the physician's job so much easier, whereas incompetent ones made it into a nightmare of constantly checking their work, which took up valuable time. The tech tonight was Ginger, who was in her mid-forties. As an ER tech, she made a little over twelve dollars an hour. She had finally gotten rid of her deadbeat husband after paying his gambling debts for years. In addition to that, she had somehow raised four kids on her meager wages. She was smart and capable, and had she chosen a different path through life she certainly could have become a nurse or even a doctor, for that matter. She was pretty much angry at the world all the time. She essentially hated all of the patients, but she absolutely adored the doctors and nurses in her ER.

She would man the phone, place orders, draw blood, start IVs, apply splints, and generally provide an extra set of hands. She had limited formal medical training, but after working for twenty years in an ER she had seen almost everything and was an invaluable addition to the team.

Vinny was the x-ray tech and at night he could also do head CT scans. Only heads though, none of "that fancy chest, abdomen, pelvis stuff." Ultrasound and other CTs were available but a tech had to be called in from home for those. There was no MRI at Libertyville. The last piece of the puzzle was Thea, who ran the lab and helped draw blood when necessary.

Also, in the ER on busy nights, there always seemed to be a stream of medics and cops, who liked to hang out long after they had dropped off their patients. There were also mental health social workers who would come in when called to help evaluate and place psych patients. Occasionally you would even see consultant physicians, although they seemed to prefer to see patients on the floor after they had been sent up. That way they wouldn't have to actually set foot in the ER, running the risk of there being other patients that the ER doc might ask them to see.

The consultants at Libertyville were mostly family doctors and internists who did the bulk of the inpatient work and managed most of the admitted patients. There were also two general surgeons in town who alternated call and an orthopod who took call every night as he was on his third wife. Lastly, there was a radiologist who read films during the day. That was the extent of medical care in Libertyville. If you needed something more specialized, you got shipped to the U.

THE GURNEY THAT held Violet's mass was wheeled adjacent to the two strapped-together beds. There was no way of picking Violet up and moving her over, although the firefighters thought there should be. The paramedics, firefighters, and nurses began by positioning themselves around her and then attempted to lift each gigantic limb and pull her over. This proved impossible, however, as the central core of her weight, her center of gravity, was her trunk with its giant apron of fat that cascaded down her front to below her knees. This portion was simply immobile and immovable.

Finally, after witnessing the struggle, Violet took control of the situation herself and with one forceful thrust; she twisted her body over and spilled from the gurney onto the beds. The beds, hastily strapped together, shuddered but held. One medic who had hold of one of her legs was thrown aside and almost to the ground. She came to rest nicely centered in the beds with her enormous naked backside facing up. Slowly the wave-like oscillations of her fat dissipated, and one of the nurses threw a sheet over her to cover her up. Jim and nine others stood around the bed in shocked silence as they contemplated what they had just witnessed. It was mesmerizing, like watching a twisted version of a Discovery Channel documentary with "never before seen footage" of some colossal beast.

A second later, the silence was broken by a muffled cry from Violet's mouth, which was buried in a pillow at the head of the bed. "*Stand back*," she cried. A few seconds later the warning came again but clearer this time. "*Stand back.*"

Everyone looked around questioningly. Finally, Carol approached Violet on the right side and bent down next to her ear.

"What's wrong, dear?" she whispered.

Violet struggled to lift her head off the bed and proclaimed in a voice that was audible but strained, "I gotta fart."

Instantly, a foghorn-sized bellow erupted from her rectum, momentarily tenting the sheet. Jim and the others struggled to stifle their laughter. Jim had to leave the room. He felt guilty that he was laughing at the plight of this poor woman, then he realized he wasn't laughing at Violet's flatulence, but rather at the whole bizarre scene and at how his life had become so warped and yet somehow enriched by these sorts of experiences; these wonderfully strange, spontaneous events that occurred frequently and naturally in the ER.

CHAPTER THREE

Wounded Warrior

Jim's mixture of disgust and reverie was soon disrupted when he heard bed two coming back from x-ray. This was the dislocated shoulder that Dr. Lindstrom had mentioned. Rolling past on the gurney was a thick, muscular man in his thirties with close-cropped hair and an anguished look on his face. Tears were cascading down his cheeks. Pushing the bed from behind was Vinny; the x-ray tech. Vinny wore a look of bored contempt. He didn't tolerate wimps well. Vinny deposited bed two back in its slot and sauntered out of the room. As he did so he intentionally wandered over to be within earshot of Jim.

"Biggest pussy I ever seen," he mumbled as he passed Jim in the doorway.

Jim had already reviewed the triage note in the chart, and with an almost imperceptible grin he acknowledged Vinny and entered the room.

"Hi, I'm Dr. McCray." Jim tried to sound official but caring at the same time. "Looks like you banged up your shoulder eh...Brad, is it?" Jim said as he glanced at the chart that read:

Name—Brad Johnson
Age—30
Employer—US Navy

"How'd you do it?" he asked.

"Skiing, Doc, and damn it hurts, pardon my French, but you gotta give me something for this pain," Brad moaned, elevating the volume until he climaxed on the word pain so that everyone would know that this was serious. Then he began to cry again.

Brad's wife, or female significant other, who had been standing just behind Jim having followed the gurney carrying Brad back from x-ray, rushed past Jim to Brad's side. She cradled his head in her arms and buried his tear-soaked face in her long blond hair. Jim stood back and surveyed the scene. It seemed oddly familiar to him. Brad was a large muscular man, he had those all-American, captain-of-the-football-team looks, but currently he lay on the bed whimpering and carrying on like a forlorn child. His wife was comparatively tiny with fine features, a lithe figure, and straight blond hair. She only lacked the mini-skirt and pom-poms to be the prototypical cheerleader. Brad was large, she was small; they looked like different species: "Beauty and the Beast." Tonight, the beast had a thorn in his paw and was coming unglued.

"Well, it looks like the paramedics gave you fifteen milligrams of morphine on the way here," Jim said and asked simultaneously.

"Yeah, well it didn't do shit," Brad snapped back, briefly lifting his head off the cheerleader's shoulder and emerging from her veil of blond hair.

"OK," Jim said, purposefully ignoring Brad's confrontational tone. "We'll see if we can get you something a little stronger and get that shoulder fixed up."

Clearly Brad was not at his best. Pain had a way of bringing out the worst in people, and pain was the most common reason people came to the ER, which made for some unpleasant interactions at times. Jim wished again for his "Pain-o-Meter," a device that could determine just how much pain a person really had, as individuals and their responses varied so greatly. Likewise, the individual response to pain medication also varied enormously.

Jim approached the bed and began to examine Brad's right shoulder. He could tell from the doorway that it was dislocated. As he got closer, he saw that Brad was holding his arm across his body with his elbow flexed at about thirty degrees. The left hand was supporting the right forearm. Jim examined the deltoid, or shoulder muscle, and noted the obvious hollow under the skin. On this spot was a tattoo of an eagle in flight. In its talons it carried a banner with the letters USN. The banner appeared slightly crumpled now as the skin sagged. The head of the humerus had shifted down and medially out of the socket leaving this indent in the skin. Above this a ridge of bone pushed up, tenting the skin from the inside. This ridge was formed by the acromion process and the glenoid rim, portions of the scapula that form the socket where the ball-like head of the humerus fits into the joint. Now the ball was lying anterior and medial against the ribs and the edge of the large pectoral muscle of the chest.

Jim began to carefully rotate the humerus or upper arm outward by gently rolling the lower portion of the arm and hand away from Brad's body. He wanted to assess how much movement Brad could tolerate. Some patients with good pain tolerance could be talked through the pain and Jim found he could often gently support the arm and slowly move it until the shoulder dropped back into its normal position. This was advantageous because it meant the patient wouldn't have to undergo "conscious sedation." Conscious sedation or procedural sedation involved using medications to control the patient's pain and sedating the patient to the point of near unconsciousness so that painful procedures could be performed. The idea was to use the right pharmaceutical agents in the right amounts so that the patient would not stop breathing, but would be relaxed and pain-free enough to tolerate the procedure. This stopped short of general anesthesia and did not require intubation and ventilation, which meant placing a plastic endotracheal tube down the patient's throat to control the airway and then breathing for them.

"Owww!" Brad yelled.

Jim had barely begun to move Brad's arm when it became clear that he couldn't tolerate any movement at all.

"OK, well it looks like I'm going to have to give you some medicine, which will make you really relaxed and sleepy so we can get this thing back in. It's definitely dislocated. Have you ever had any problems with anesthesia or pain medicines before?" Jim asked.

Brad shook his head no.

"All right," Jim said. "In order to fix this, we'll need to hook you up to some oxygen and a heart monitor. Then we'll give you two different medicines in your IV. One of the medicines is called Versed. It relaxes you and it also causes amnesia so most people don't even remember the procedure. The second one is called fentanyl. It's a pain medicine sort of like morphine, only it's a lot stronger. It's also shorter acting so it wears off quickly after we're done. You may have heard of fentanyl before…"

Brad suddenly looked up. It seemed like he had only been peripherally hearing what Jim was saying, but as soon as Jim mentioned fentanyl, he was suddenly alert and on edge.

"Fentanyl, don't people overdose on that all the time?"

"Yes, that's the one, it seems to be in the news all the time these days. Unfortunately, it is frequently abused and pretty dangerous if you don't know what you're doing," Jim replied.

"I vaguely remember…" Brad said, "…something about Russian commandos pumping it into the air vents of that theater where those terrorists were holed up with all of those hostages."

It had been many years since that event, so Jim was impressed that Brad had recalled that it was indeed fentanyl that they used in an aerosolized form.

"Wait a second, didn't like a hundred people die in that raid? And they said it was the gas that killed them," Brad said nervously.

"Yeah, it's the same stuff. We use it all the time. Except we don't make you breathe it; we shoot it straight into your veins," Jim said, watching with sly satisfaction as Brad became slightly pale.

"Don't worry it's very safe; we control the dose so it takes away the pain. Most people think it feels really good. Of course, with the Versed on-board you usually don't remember any of it.

"Now any time we put you out to do a painful procedure there are certain risks, which I need to tell you about. The biggest risk is that the medicine makes you so relaxed that you forget to breathe. Fortunately, we have another medicine called naloxone or Narcan that can instantly reverse the effects of the fentanyl. It's the same medicine that we give to heroin addicts when they overdose. It's really amazing; they go from unconscious and barely breathing to wide awake and swinging in a matter of seconds. If we don't use that, we can always just breathe for you for a few minutes until the medicine wears off. But we prefer not to do that because sometimes some of the air goes down into your stomach and sometimes you throw up and because you're unconscious you can potentially breathe the vomit down into your lungs and that's a bad thing."

"Doc, you're not making me feel too confident about any of this," Brad said.

"Well, we can always leave your arm out of the socket if you'd like," Jim replied, realizing that he was probably having too much fun at Brad's expense.

"No, no, that's OK. I'll take my chances with the Russian highball," Brad said.

"Great, I'll go take a peek at your x-rays and make all of the arrangements. And don't worry, I've been yanking your chain a little because you seem like a tough guy and can handle it, but it's actually very safe and most people fly through it without any problems," Jim said reassuringly and then winked at Brad's wife.

This slight stroke of Brad's ego made his bravado resurface. "If I can land an F-14 on the deck of a carrier I think I can handle this," he said.

"Are you a pilot?" Jim asked politely, intentionally taking the bait.

"You know it, US Navy," Brad said, motioning to the tattoo on his shoulder.

Jim backed slowly out of the room. He smiled at Brad. "Cool," he said.

As he returned to the nurse's station, Jim ordered the medications in the chart and smiled to himself as he imagined Brad shot down over enemy territory spilling all sorts of national secrets after the slightest torture.

CHAPTER FOUR

Principles of Triage

J im next saw the woman with vaginal bleeding. She was hardly a woman, barely sixteen years old and pregnant for the first time. She was accompanied by her mother and her boyfriend, who was presumably the "baby daddy." He had a greasy look, and his face was deeply pocked with acne scars. He was twenty-two years old and naturally he worked as a fry cook. Jim wondered if their age gap meant for some potential legal ramifications. He couldn't remember exactly, and it had become such a common thing to see that he let the thought pass through his mind.

The patient's mother was about thirty-five although her face looked about fifty, and her T-shirt would have been snug on a ten-year-old. Whenever Jim met people like this—close to his own age but who looked much older due to the effects of years of hard living—he always wondered if he looked that old. He had to assume that was not the case as he was frequently told by patients that he looked too young to be a doctor.

Mother had a muffin-top belly with stretch marks extruding from underneath the T-shirt, which had the "Taz" Looney Toons character emblazoned on it. Jim had come to appreciate this creature, although now maybe a bit old-school, as one of many different cartoon or comic book symbols most appreciated by the "white trash set."

Melanie was the patient's name. She was eleven weeks pregnant and was inwardly delighted that she might be having a miscarriage. She had already been considering an abortion when she began spotting a few days ago. She hadn't mentioned this to her mother, however, who seemed ecstatic that her daughter, a C student and sophomore in high school, was pregnant. In her eyes this child was tantamount to the second coming of Christ or perhaps some equally famous professional wrestler.

"Hi Melanie, I'm Dr. McCray. When did your bleeding start?" Jim began as he squeezed into the small exam room stepping over the fry cook's long, gangly legs.

"I don't know, a couple of days ago I think," Melanie replied, looking bored.

"The triage note said that your last menstrual period was eleven weeks ago, is that right?" Jim asked.

Melanie nodded.

"Have you been to the doctor yet?" Jim asked.

"Not yet, but I was planning on it," Melanie replied.

"How did you find out you were pregnant?" Jim asked.

"You know, one of those home 'pee test' thingies," Melanie replied.

"Is this a wanted pregnancy?" Jim asked.

Melanie's face broke into a partial smile.

"Umm, I guess so."

Grandma "Taz" began to squirm uncomfortably in her seat. The fry cook remained motionless.

"Well, when you're pregnant and you have bleeding, that can mean that you're starting to have a miscarriage and you may lose your baby," Jim said as he began his regular miscarriage speech.

"Miscarriages are actually incredibly common, especially in first pregnancies. A lot of times a woman may not even know she is pregnant and may just experience what she thinks is a heavy or late period. If a miscarriage occurs in the first trimester, or first twelve weeks, it's almost always due to something being genetically abnormal with the baby, and as it can't survive it is just nature's way of taking care of it. You are eleven weeks, which is still in the first trimester. So, one of two things is likely to happen: You may stop bleeding and the pregnancy will continue on, or the bleeding will worsen and you will begin to pass what we call the 'products of conception,' that is, the baby, the placenta, membranes, and stuff."

Melanie nodded understanding.

"Are you having any pain?" Jim asked.

"Yeah it feels like hard cramps down there," Melanie said, pointing to her lower abdomen.

"That's pretty common. When you have a miscarriage, your uterus begins to clamp down and push on its contents in order to expel them just like a miniature version of labor so you have similar pains, although usually not quite as severe," Jim said.

"So tonight, here's what we need to do," Jim began. "First, we need to draw some blood and do a test called a quantitative beta HCG. It's a pregnancy test, but rather than just tell us if you're pregnant or not, it actually gives us a number to tell us how far along you are. That way if the pregnancy continues, we can repeat the test in a few days to see if it is going up like it should. If the number goes up that indicates the baby is growing. If it goes down that means the fetus has died and a miscarriage is inevitable."

Melanie nodded again.

"Do you know your blood type?" Jim asked.

"Umm no," Melanie said, looking at her mother to see if she knew.

"OK, we'll check that too. If you are Rh negative, we will need to give you a Rhogam shot. That's a medicine that clears up the antibodies that your body will make if the baby's blood mixes with yours and the blood types don't match up. The antibodies don't actually affect this pregnancy, but during a subsequent pregnancy they would attack the new baby's blood like it was a foreign invader and cause all sorts of problems. That's one of the reasons you used to have to get your blood tested before you got married and also one of the reasons you were weren't supposed to marry close relatives. Of course, that was back in the old days when people actually got married before they had children. Nowadays we have Rhogam so you guys needn't worry about all of that," Jim said.

"Mmm, mmm, nothing spells lovin' like marryin' your cousin," the fry cook said as he grunted and laughed.

"That's sick," exclaimed Melanie as she flung a chubby white leg out from under the sheet in an attempt to kick him.

The fry cook dodged the kick and laughed again.

The moment passed and Jim continued. "We'll also need to do an exam and see what your cervix looks like. We'll see if it is open and if any of the fetus or products of conception are being expelled."

Jim winced inside as he said this, worried about how it might sound, but no one seemed to care so he continued on. "Most likely we will do an ultrasound as well."

Jim had been burned before by ordering the ultrasound upfront before confirming the patient was actually pregnant only to find out there was no actual pregnancy to look at.

"All right," Melanie said, looking bored again.

Looking bored as only teenage girls can. The kind of teenage girl who has an undeniable but unspoken belief that she has the world entirely figured out. That she already knows everything she needs to know when in reality she knows almost nothing about the world, childbirth, motherhood, or medicine.

"Do you have any other medical problems Melanie?" Jim asked.

"Not that I know of. Mom, do I have any medical problems?" Melanie turned to her mother.

"No, she's been pretty healthy," her mother said.

"Have you had any sexually transmitted diseases?" Jim asked.

"No, that's gross," Melanie said.

"Have you ever been tested for sexually transmitted diseases?" Jim asked.

"Not that I know of," Melanie replied.

"Well, have you ever had a pelvic exam?" Jim asked.

"What's that?" Melanie said, looking uncomfortable.

"It's where the doctor looks inside of your vagina to look for infection and to check your cervix. Sometimes they do a test to look for cervical cancer and then the doctor puts his fingers in to feel your uterus and ovaries," Jim said.

"No. Nobody's ever looked in there, that's disgusting," Melanie said.

"Melanie, how many sexual partners have you had?" Jim asked.

Melanie thought for a moment. "Seven, I think, or maybe eight. I can't remember."

Mother dropped her head and twisted slightly in her chair. The fry cook grimaced.

"Well, have you ever used any birth control or condoms or anything like that?" Jim asked, trying to remain professional. He'd had this identical conversation many times with young girls who had multiple partners and had not given even the slightest thought to birth control or prevention of disease and then seemed incredulous when they came in with complications of pregnancy or a sexually transmitted infection. He realized that there had to be an equally large population of young men with the same sexual habits, but they didn't end up in the emergency room as often so he rarely got to talk to them.

"Melanie, when did you start having periods? Jim asked.

"When I was about thirteen, I think," Melanie said.

"Well you didn't waste any time getting to use this stuff did you," Jim remarked with a not too subtle reference to Melanie's well broken-in reproductive organs.

"With that many partners and no protection, you are at a pretty high risk for sexually transmitted infections, and believe it or not…" Jim paused for effect. "Pregnancy…I hope that doesn't come as too much of a shock," Jim said, trying not to sound too preachy, but with a measured portion of contempt.

For a few seconds he wanted to launch into a tirade about how obtuse and irresponsible she was, and how she was destined to be a teenage single mother without even a high school education living off welfare for the rest of her life, and how unfair it was to bring a child into the world under those circumstances. But as always, Jim held it in, realizing it was politically incorrect, would lead to a patient complaint, and was probably pointless anyway. Melanie knew all of that already but she just didn't get it, and who knew what other extenuating circumstances existed in her life. Jim did not want to damage the tenuous doctor-patient relationship he had developed.

"OK," Jim paused to let it sink in and then continued. "They'll come and draw your blood and I'll be back in a little bit with the nurse to do the pelvic exam."

Jim turned and slowly left the room. It was a struggle to not be judgmental of people like Melanie. He didn't think of her as a bad person, he had just seen so many young women in her situation who seemed basically clueless. He saw them throughout their lives; as teenagers they seemed so empowered by their emerging sexuality, but they were careless and indiscriminate, oblivious to placing any rational restraint on their behavior. They were often preyed upon by older men (if you could call them that) like Melanie's fry cook. By the time they were thirty-five they were dealing with their own pregnant daughters and perhaps already had grandchildren. By that time, they were almost universally overweight, depressed, sporadically single, and working for minimum wage, if they were working at all. By that time, they were certainly less clueless, with vast stores of experience from "learning the hard way." They were old before their time, used up and worn out. Most had realized the opportunity for a good life had long since passed them by. The cycle perpetuated itself over and over again from generation to generation. Three such generations awaited Jim's return to the pelvic room.

JIM WENT BACK to the nurses' station and began putting the orders for Melanie into the computer. While at the computer he clicked on the tracking board, which listed all the patients in the department, including those who had been seen and those still waiting to be seen. The number waiting to be seen had not diminished any. In fact, it looked as though it had grown by three or four. It was now 7:45 p.m. Jim had been working for forty-five minutes and had already seen five patients. The national average for emergency physicians was to see somewhere around two patients per hour. This doesn't seem like a lot, but with the variety of patients and the fact that many of them take several hours to work-up, treat, and come to a disposition decision on, it's plenty. Jim was well ahead of that average pace at this point. It was typical early in a shift to see a lot of patients quickly and then to gradually slow down as the shift progressed and as patients began to stack up waiting for test results, x-rays and other imaging tests. Jim knew he would probably see ten or more in the first couple of hours and then things would begin to back up. He had a finite amount of space to work with—the number of beds in the department that could be filled with patients. Once all of the beds were full, he would be slowed down until he could "dispo" patients in order to make room for more.

Dispo was short for disposition and meant one of three things. Admitted, meaning the patient was admitted to the hospital for further care. Transferred, meaning the patient was sent to another facility with greater or different capabilities, or discharged, as in "OTD" or "out the door." If the beds filled up and the patients couldn't be dispo'ed, the department became gridlocked. It was at this point the waiting room would begin to fill up with the "walking wounded."

Everything in emergency medicine was based on the principles of "triage." Triage is an 18th-century French term meaning to sort according to quality. The military had adopted the term for assessing the wounded on the battlefield. Triage meant that patients were seen, not in order of arrival, but rather based on the severity of their illness or injury. Life-and limb-threatening illnesses obviously received priority, as did those who arrived by ambulance. This was a major source of frustration to the patients in the waiting room. Most of society operated on a first-come, first-served basis. So, for people to be sitting in a waiting room feeling sick or injured and to see others who arrived after them being taken back ahead of them was infuriating. Many people simply couldn't imagine that anyone else's emergency could possibly be more serious than theirs. This sometimes led to angry outbursts directed at the triage nurse, whose job it was to prioritize and sort them all out. Tensions could run high in an overcrowded waiting room full of people in misery; screaming, crying, whimpering, barfing, or simply suffering in silence with their worried family members.

This was one of Jim's greatest frustrations and greatest sources of stress. Fixing each patient's medical problem was often easy compared to the agony of dealing with the patient's anger over being made to wait. The first few minutes of the doctor-patient interaction were often taken up by apologies for the delay and attempts to calm an exasperated patient and to develop rapport. Some patients were understanding of the circumstances. But others were often irate and accusatory, convinced that the doctors and nurses were intentionally dragging their feet, perhaps eating doughnuts or watching TV. Some felt there must be some source of revenue or monetary gain being had by the doctors that led to the prolongation of their suffering. Others just couldn't seem to grasp why that guy with chest pain got right in while they had to wait two hours with their screaming three-year-old who had an earache.

Jim would simply apologize and resort to his standard line: "If I could just get people to schedule their emergencies." He felt like he must have said that a million times. The incongruous thought of actually writing on your calendar or putting a reminder in your phone for the date and time to get hit by a bus, have a heart attack, or pass a kidney stone, sometimes brought people back to reality and reminded them of the nature of the business. After all it was called an "emergency" room for a reason.

———•———

JIM'S RESIDENCY DIRECTOR always said the most important patient wasn't a patient at all, but rather it was "the department." In other words, the emergency physician must always be aware of the entire department and not get bogged down with an individual patient. This meant juggling multiple patients, sometimes ten or more all with different problems and in different stages of their work-up. Other physicians rarely appreciated this aspect of emergency medicine. They could schedule their office and know based on the schedule basically what the patient's problem was and set aside a corresponding amount of time to deal with it. Naturally they would get behind or be delayed by unforeseen problems that would arise, but even at its worst they rarely had to juggle more than two or three patients at a time. They could also schedule lunch breaks, and office hours were daytime hours. Lastly, many of the patients were well-known to the doctor and were there for simple rechecks or prescription refills. That was never the case in the ER where almost every patient was new to Jim. This meant that he had to start from scratch with every one of them. Each required a full assessment with no prior knowledge of the patient, their condition, lifestyle, or previous treatments. There was no way for Jim to schedule anything. He could never just close the doors or say the schedule was full. When doctor's offices were unable to accommodate patients, they could just put them off until the next day, or if they absolutely had to be seen, simply tell them to go to the ER. This of course, just added additional stress on the ER.

Jim liked to be busy as it made the time go fast. But he hated to be overwhelmed. Overwhelmed was dangerous. It required corners to be cut and greatly increased the risk of missing something and sending someone home with a serious ailment.

Tonight, Jim was busy but not overwhelmed. He had learned to organize his time to care for the most important patient, the department. He stayed focused and organized to provide good care to each individual patient by balancing the time for assessments, exams, and procedures as well as the time it took to interpret labs and imaging, and give sound advice and move people through the system. Sometimes patients just needed to be there long enough to allow for the "tincture of time," that critical period of observation during which Jim could decide if the patient was "sick" or "not sick," not in the layperson sense but in the doctor sense. That "gestalt" or gut feeling that nagged at the doctor and made him think, "I'm missing something" or "It doesn't add up" or "There is something else going on here."

Not all emergency physicians were equally good at keeping multiple balls in the air, but Jim felt this was one of his strongest attributes. He had "the knack" and the nurses appreciated it because they were often the ones who felt the pain most acutely when the doctor couldn't keep up and the place got bogged down and gridlocked. Jim could "move the meat" as his residency director was fond of saying.

Jim's residency director was a "lion" for emergency medicine. He came from an internal medicine background but had gone back and completed an emergency medicine residency back when the specialty was in its infancy. He had found his way into academia and now guided thirty-plus residents through their training. He never used the term "emergency room" and never let anyone say it around him without correcting them.

"Does this look like a room to you? It's got forty-five beds," he would say, referring to the university hospital emergency department. "Doesn't that make forty-five emergency rooms, this is an emergency *department*, an ED, not an ER."

He almost came unglued when the drug companies began selling the public drugs for "ED," the cool new abbreviation for erectile dysfunction. Viagra and Bob Dole made "ED" a household term, but it had nothing to do with emergencies, although some undoubtedly would argue otherwise.

———————•———————

THE USE OF the abbreviation ER never bothered Jim much, however. It was accepted and it had history. Originally, it was just *one* room, usually staffed by a nurse who would look over those who straggled into the hospital needing treatment. She would then notify the doctor on-call who would decide if it was something he needed to come in for. He, because in those days almost the entire profession consisted of men. Nowadays most medical schools actually graduate a majority of women by a small margin. Emergency medicine still attracted more men than women generally, but that was gradually changing and now over 30 percent of emergency physicians were women.

Back in the old days the doctors on staff at the hospital would alternate ER call, some nights it was the family doctor, and on others it was the general surgeon. On some nights it could even be the urologist or the ophthalmologist. If you came in with appendicitis on the night the general surgeon was on, you were lucky. If you came in on the same night with a heart attack, you were lucky to survive. Gradually ERs became busier and patients' expectations grew. ERs were staffed by general practitioners or generalists trained in family medicine, internal medicine, or general surgery. They tended to be doctors who had an interest in emergency medicine or liked the schedule, but there was an enormous variability in both knowledge and skill. Then came the formal recognition of emergency medicine as its own medical specialty, and that was followed by specific emergency medicine residency training programs. Around that same time the world entered the era of both fast food and fast medicine. Large hospital ERs became essentially enormous diagnostic and treatment centers staffed twenty-four/seven with multiple physicians simultaneously working alongside an army of nurses, therapists, techs, secretaries, and social workers. These mega-departments are closely attached to the hospital's full-service laboratories and radiology departments, and specialists of every kind are available on-call for consultation and to continue with more specialized care once the emergency physician completes the work-up or establishes the need for a patient to be admitted for further management.

Jim liked being on the frontlines of medicine and being the guy to see people first and to never turn anyone away because the office was full. He liked the variety of seeing patients for their emergencies from cradle to grave; male, female, or otherwise; physical or emotional; day or night. It was stressful and exhilarating, emotionally draining and physically exhausting, frustrating and fulfilling. Best of all, when he was done, he was done. Each shift had a finite number of hours and no one could stop the clock. Also, he didn't have to worry about pagers, office staff, or overhead.

Although the specialty of emergency medicine had evolved out of the "room" into the department, Libertyville General was still a pretty small department, just six beds, easy to fill up, gridlock, and overwhelm.

———————•———————

JIM SCANNED THROUGH the charts on the computer track board looking for the chief complaints: low back pain, twisted ankle, index finger laceration, and headache. Well, at least all of these were relatively quick and easy. All were common complaints and fairly straight forward. Of course, that was on first blush, and only the exceptionally naïve would not recognize the hidden dangers in each of these seemingly innocuous complaints. The back pain could be a simple muscle strain or it could be an aortic dissection, a condition where the wall of the aorta, the massive artery that arches away from the heart carrying blood to most of the body, begins to tear apart. If it tears through, the patient bleeds to death in a matter of minutes. The twisted ankle may be just a simple sprained ligament or it may be a complex fracture requiring immobilization, sedation of the patient, and skillful manipulation to reduce the pieces back into anatomical position and preparation for subsequent surgical fixation. The finger laceration must be carefully evaluated for a foreign body, or a tendon or nerve injury, both of which might require repair by a hand surgeon and if missed could result in long-term disability. A headache may be a simple migraine or tension headache, or it may be the first sign of meningitis, a life-threatening infection of the covering of the brain and spinal cord. Or it could be due to a subarachnoid hemorrhage, which occurs when a weakened bloated portion of an artery, known as an aneurysm, ruptures and begins to bleed into the area surrounding the brain.

Jim's job and that of every emergency physician was to be suspicious of every innocuous complaint, and to consider the worst-case scenario, as well as all of the other potential causes, in every patient, until he had sorted through the possibilities and was satisfied that he had ruled out the bad stuff and knew the reason for the patient's symptoms. This was the real reason that doctors spent so many years getting their education. Anybody could diagnose and treat a headache—"Take two aspirin and call me in the morning"—and most of the time they would be right. But doctors spent a long time learning to think about all of the other things "it could be." This process was called developing a "differential diagnosis." The "differential" was a laundry list of possible causes, starting with the most likely and paying special attention to the conditions that could kill. Because emergency physicians like Jim went through this mental exercise on every patient, he had to know something about everything. This allowed him to sort out every conceivable complaint about every different organ system.

No one understood his limitations more than Jim because it was simply impossible to know that much. Although in malpractice cases plaintiffs' attorneys and their expert witnesses gave the impression that they knew everything and inferred to the jury that the defendant doctor should as well. At least if he was any good. The reality however was that sometimes the best that Jim, or any emergency physician, could hope for was to know enough to know the patient wasn't going to die, at least not right away. This was one of the frustrations of dealing with patients who got on the internet and self-diagnosed before they came in, or with overconfident paramedics and nurses. Sometimes people knew just enough to be dangerous but not enough to know that they were. Jim knew as much as anybody in the world at his level of training and experience, which was considerable, but the most important thing he knew was his limitations. This was humbling, and any doctor worth his salt ought to be humble.

Perhaps the first question Jim had been trained to ask himself in the doorway to a patient's room whenever he laid eyes on a patient was: "Sick or not sick?" The vast majority of ER patients were "not sick." They didn't have true emergencies, conditions that could kill in a matter of minutes or hours. The absolute sickest were the "ABC patients." ABC stood for airway, breathing, and circulation. Serious compromise of any of these resulted in death in a matter of minutes. Jim, like all emergency physicians, was an expert in managing airways and restoring breathing and circulation. Thus far tonight Jim had not had any true emergencies, but the night was still young.

CHAPTER FIVE →

Satisfying Sedation

No sooner had this thought passed through Jim's mind than he heard the familiar tones ring out from the radio on the desk at the nurses' station. Carol looked up from her computer, and she and Jim listened together to see what the call was about.

"Sixty-year-old woman with chest pain and decreased level of consciousness," the dispatcher said.

The medics radioed back that they were on their way and Jim could hear the siren begin to sing in the background. Then the radio became silent again. Thus far it had not been a busy night for ambulances, just the one that brought Violet and her enormous infected leg. Jim quickly calculated that he had a minimum of twenty minutes before the medics could get to the patient's location and back to the hospital. This would give him enough time to fix Brad's shoulder if he moved quickly.

"Carol, let's get the shoulder in bed three done," Jim said. "Are you ready to go?"

"Yeah, he's on the monitor and I've got the drugs right here," Carol said, pointing to the empty vials and full syringes she had drawn up and placed together in a plastic kidney-shaped emesis basin on the desk next to her. She had neatly taped the vials to the syringes so she knew which of the drugs was in each of the syringes. Many a patient had been given the wrong medicine due to the sloppy work of doctors and nurses who had picked up an unmarked syringe and injected it thinking the clear liquid inside was one thing when it turned out to be another.

Jim walked back to bed three and slid back the curtain. Brad was lying there, right where Jim had left him, still whimpering, and the cheerleader was still doting and dabbing his face with a wet washcloth. An ice pack was strapped to Brad's dislocated shoulder and thin wires snaked off of his chest, behind the bed and up into the cardiac monitor mounted on the wall above him. A nasal cannula rested on his face and the end of the clear plastic tubing was attached to the oxygen valve on the wall. Finally, a pulse oximetry probe ran from the tip of his left index finger and back to the monitor.

The monitor showed the electrical discharge of Brad's heart as a green lighted line, which slid up and down and across the monitor in a steady rhythm; seventy-six beats per minute. Beneath it, the red pulse oximetry line lifted up and down synchronized with his pulse, indicating that his blood was 99 percent oxygenated.

"Well, Brad, are you ready to get this thing fixed?" Jim said as he passed through the curtain and into the room.

"Ready as I'll ever be, I guess Doc. Just don't hurt me too bad," Brad said, looking as small as a man his size could.

"It's not that bad, a lot of people don't even remember it," Jim said reassuringly.

Jim opened a screen on the computer work station that had been wheeled into the room. On it he brought up Brad's x-rays. In the old days, x-rays and other imaging studies were printed on thick plastic films that were stored in large envelopes and had to be placed on a lighted view box mounted on the wall. With the advent of computerized imaging systems everything was now stored on a computer. This made life a lot easier because the radiology computer programs had lots of built-in features that allow the viewer to zoom in and change the lighting and the contrast, among other things. Also, the patient's entire file and often images from other facilities could be imported instantaneously in order to make comparisons. No longer was it necessary to store enormous files of films in dusty storage racks.

Jim showed Brad the x-rays and explained to him the appearance of the bones and their current versus normal position. He pointed out to him and the cheerleader how the humeral head or the ball end of Brad's humerus was lying against his ribs instead of up in the now empty socket of his shoulder joint.

Next, Jim took two neatly folded bedsheets from a cupboard on the wall and placed them on the bed next to Brad. Jim reviewed with Brad the risks and benefits of the procedure and the use of the medications. He took a quick look in Brad's mouth to see if there would be any difficulty intubating him if complications arose and he were to stop breathing. When Jim did this kind of procedure at the university hospital, there was always a respiratory therapist at the head of the bed whose job it was to monitor and manage the patient's airway and breathing. However, in a tiny hospital out in the sticks, it would be just Jim and Carol. Together they would administer the drugs to sedate Brad, monitor his vital signs, put the shoulder back in place, and then wake him up, all while reassuring his wife, who chose to stay in the room at his side.

Jim picked up one of the sheets and folded it along its length until it was about eight inches wide. He gently slid it under Brad's chest obliquely from the armpit under the injured shoulder and across to the good shoulder. The remainder he laid across the front of his chest until the two ends came together on the bed above the good shoulder with Brad inside the loop. The other sheet he folded until it was six inches wide and then wrapped it loosely around his own waist and tied it in a square knot. He slid the knot to the back so that the sheet resembled a cheap and somewhat loose cummerbund against his blue scrubs. Brad and the cheerleader watched, slightly bewildered.

"There are lots of ways to put a shoulder back in," Jim said. "I am going to use something called the modified Hippocratic method. This has been used for thousands of years, but thousands of years ago they didn't have the advantage of drugs to relax your muscles."

"They probably got you good and drunk and hit you on the head or something," Carol said.

Brad smiled.

Jim continued. "The key is to get you nice and sleepy so you don't resist too much when I pull on your arm and then as your muscles relax, they let the bone go and it slips right back in place."

"Why do they call it modified?" the cheerleader asked.

Jim was impressed by the question; obviously she had both the looks and the brains in the family.

"Well, that's where the sheet comes in," Jim said. "When I start pulling, I will pull you right off the bed if we don't have some sort of counter-traction. So, Carol will hold onto the sheet that is around your chest. In the original Hippocratic method, the doctor pulled on the patient's arm and put his foot in the patient's armpit to provide the counter-traction. But there are a lot of important nerves and blood vessels that run through the armpit and with that method those can sometimes be damaged. It looks bad if we put your shoulder back in, but you can't move your arm because we tore up all of the nerves."

Brad and the cheerleader both nodded in agreement.

"OK, are we ready to go?" Jim motioned to Carol.

"We're ready," Carol said.

"OK, give him fifty of fentanyl and one of Versed," Jim said.

Carol pushed the plungers on the syringes and the medicine flowed invisibly through the IV tubing and into Brad's vein.

"It will probably take a few doses to get you good and sleepy," Jim said.

"I don't feel anything yet," Brad said.

A short time later, Jim said to Carol, "OK, another fifty and one."

Again, she pushed the medicine into the IV. She checked the monitor, and the automatic blood pressure cuff began to inflate to take Brad's blood pressure.

Jim watched Brad closely for signs of sedation. He gently lifted Brad's right hand and keeping the elbow flexed began to slide it under the sheet that was tied around his waist so that the back of Brad's forearm rested against his abdomen between his scrubs and the sheet.

"Wwwait," Brad said, groggily.

"Don't worry," Jim said. "I'm just getting you in the right position. I won't do anything until you're good and sleepy."

However just the fact that Brad had allowed him to move his arm as much as he did let Jim know that the medicine was working and he would be sedated soon.

"Another fifty and one, please Carol," Jim said. He smiled at Brad's wife who looked worried, but relaxed slightly.

He had now given Brad one hundred and fifty micrograms of fentanyl and three milligrams of Versed. At this point most people would begin to experience at least some degree of sedation. There were many combinations of drugs that could be used for procedural sedations such as this. At Libertyville, the usual cocktail was fentanyl and Versed. This was considered "old school" but it was the policy at Libertyville. At the U, Jim typically used a drug called propofol, which was nice as it was a single agent and didn't cause as much respiratory depression. Propofol didn't work out well for Michael Jackson, however.

Fentanyl was a super short-acting opiate analgesic. It was essentially a synthetic variation of opium or morphine, but the particular tweaks to the molecule made it much more potent and gave it a much shorter duration of action. The fact that it was short-acting made it nice because if too much was given and the patient was overmedicated it wore off much more quickly than other opiates. Unfortunately, however, the shorter acting an opiate is, the greater its abuse potential. That is why long-acting opiates such as methadone are used to treat heroin addiction. The longer the half-life of a drug, the longer its effects take to wear off and the less the body notices its absence, and therefore the less likely it will cause withdrawal and addiction. IV fentanyl, with its high potency and short duration of activity, meant that it could be highly addictive, and that was why it was a favorite for abuse by health care workers.

Shorter-acting, more potent drugs were also more difficult to titrate with regard to dosing and therefore much easier to overdose on. An opiate overdose killed the person by sedating them to the point that they simply lost the drive to breathe. Jim remembered when he was in college reading in his hometown newspaper about an anesthesiologist at the local hospital who died in the middle of an operation. He apparently put the patient under anesthesia and excused himself from the case to go the restroom while the surgeon worked on the patient. When he didn't come back the surgeon became annoyed and sent a nurse to find him. They found him dead in the bathroom with a syringe in his arm neatly labeled "fentanyl."

In more recent years the use of fentanyl had shifted from the illicit use by medical personnel who diverted it from the hospital supply, to rampant use by people from all walks of life. Fentanyl was being made offshore in clandestine chemistry labs and was widely available both on the street and on the internet. Its availability and use had skyrocketed as had the number of tragic overdose deaths.

Versed was the other drug Jim was using to sedate Brad. It was a sedative in the class of benzodiazepines similar to Valium, but again with a much shorter half-life. As Jim had mentioned to Brad, it had the unusual effect of causing amnesia to events surrounding the time it was given.

JIM REMEMBERED HIS first experience with the effects of this drug. He was barely three months into his first year of medical school. Every Wednesday afternoon the medical school class was broken up into small groups and students took a break from all of their didactic lectures. They went out to various hospitals and doctors' offices and had a chance to practice their physical exam skills on real patients while being supervised by practicing physicians.

On this particular day Jim and a group of five other fresh-faced first-year med students were at a large teaching hospital in the endoscopy suite. Their preceptor was a venerable colorectal surgeon named Dr. Atkinson. He was known around the hospital, not to his face of course, as the "Rear Admiral." Today the Admiral was going to teach the students the fine art of the rectal exam. There was always a degree of anxious anticipation among medical students leading up to the first highly invasive interaction with patients, such as the first pelvic exam or the first rectal. The unfortunate patients, however, really got the worst of it as they were subjected to a series of fumbling, inexperienced fingers intruding into their most private orifices. Today, the victim was an attractive forty-year-old woman who had the unfortunate circumstance of having a sizable polyp in her rectum that had come to her attention because of blood on her toilet paper.

Dr. Atkinson had scheduled her for surgery but prior to that wanted to take a look at the lesion with the sigmoidoscope and had convinced the woman that allowing the medical students to examine her backside would greatly enhance their education. So, there they were with Dr. Atkinson, six bright-eyed young medical students in ill-fitting white lab coats, surrounding a table on which sat an uncomfortable businesswoman clad only in a hospital gown. She had spent the preceding night on the toilet after her bowel prep making sure she was cleaned out for the procedure. The room lights were lowered so that everyone could see the inside of her rectum as it was projected onto two video screens. Dr. Atkinson explained the procedure to the patient and explained that after he removed the scope, he would supervise each of the medical students as they probed her rectum with their finger to feel the polyp. He also explained that he would give her a sedative known as Versed in order to relax her for the procedure. The patient looked at the students somewhat bewildered. She looked back at Dr. Atkinson who was smiling confidently down at her. She nodded in agreement and mumbled something about it all being "in the name of science," and then she lay down on the table on her right side with her knees pulled up to her chest.

Her buttocks were exposed. A nurse monitored her pulse and oxygen level and administered the Versed through her IV. When the patient was sedated nicely and seemed oblivious to what was going on, Dr. Atkinson adeptly inserted the lubricated end of the flexible two-foot-long fiberoptic scope through her anus and into her rectum and the lower part of her colon. The super bright white light at the end of the scope briefly glowed red as it passed through her nethers and then disappeared inside her. The image on the monitors revealed the glistening orangey-colored walls of an empty rectal vault and a plump red polyp the size of the end of your thumb dangling from the ceiling. Dr. Atkinson maneuvered the scope around assessing the situation and discussing it with the students, pimping them with questions about anatomy and colon polyps, and then he extracted the scope and placed it carefully in a plastic bin.

It was now the medical students' turn. They had seen the prize in vivid color on the monitors and it was now up to them to reach in blindly with their index fingers and feel for the first time, clinically at least, what a rectum and a mass that shouldn't be there felt like.

The patient remained nicely sedated and one student after another took their turn. Finally, it was Jim's turn and he positioned his gloved hand with his index finger extended, at the patient's anal verge. He had some jelly on his finger, although she was already well lubricated as this was her sixth exam in the last five minutes. He used his left hand to gently lift her buttock out of the way. He felt his finger slip through the tightness of the sphincter and into the void. He then probed the wall of the rectum until at the very tip of his finger he could feel the soft, fleshy polyp. Just as he reached the polyp the woman began to raise herself off the table with her arms. She twisted her body with Jim's finger still inside her. This forced Jim to duck downward and when he looked up, he was staring up into her face: Her eyes were full of fury and question.

"What the hell do you think you're doing?" she said.

There was an uneasy silence between them as the groggy woman seemed to slowly contemplate why on earth this man she had never seen before had his finger in her ass. Jim didn't know what to do. He was caught with his hand in the cookie jar.

He stammered, "I'm doing uh, uh, a rectal exam."

At that moment Dr. Atkinson intervened and said calmly to the patient, "Lie back down, it's all right."

Simultaneously he pushed more Versed into the IV and the patient, still looking bewildered, laid back down and drifted off to sleep.

Jim pulled his finger out and removed his gloves. His face shone red and a few nervous giggles spread among the students.

Dr. Atkinson turned to the nurse and remarked, "I guess we let her come up a little bit, didn't we?"

He then explained to the group how Versed causes amnesia, which is why the patient had accused Jim. Although she was fully informed and aware of what she was in for ahead of time, during the procedure due to the effects of the drug she had no recollection and therefore no idea what was going on.

"The good news," Dr. Atkinson said, "is that when it's all over and she's fully awake, she won't remember any of this. Including you, Dr. McCray."

It was a hilarious event that spread quickly through the class. That had happened almost seven years ago now in Jim's training, and he could hardly believe, looking back on it, how green he was then and how new everything seemed. Since that time, he must have done a thousand rectals, but none were quite so memorable as his first.

———————•———————

"GIVE HIM ANOTHER fifty of fentanyl and one of Versed, Carol, and then I think we should just about be there," Jim said, as he began to gently lean backward while holding Brad's arm, bent at the elbow and tight inside and up against the sheet around Jim's waist, effectively applying a gradual lengthwise stretch to Brad's upper arm. As Jim pulled, Brad's torso began to slide toward him, so simultaneously Carol began to pull back from the head of the bed applying counter-traction using the sheet wrapped around Brad's chest. Brad's eyes fluttered open and he groaned slightly.

"Well, we're still not quite there," Jim said to Brad's wife. "With a big muscly guy like this we want him totally relaxed so he won't be resisting me.

"One more time Carol, fifty and one."

Carol pushed the meds and they waited another thirty seconds or so. Brad clumsily lifted his left hand and scratched at his nose. Jim had seen patients do this many times before with this combination of drugs and it seemed to him that it often was a sign that they were becoming fully relaxed. Carol noted it also and instinctively tightened her grip on the counter-traction sheet. Jim leaned back again, holding Brad's hand in his. Brad's arm was bent at ninety degrees and the sheet around Jim's waist went around it just distal to the elbow. Jim allowed his body weight to gradually overcome Brad's muscles as he leaned back like he was water-skiing, using Brad's arm as a rope. Suddenly the muscles let go and the humeral head disengaged and there was a satisfying clunk as it dropped back into its normal anatomical position. Jim stepped forward, releasing the pressure off of the sheet. Brad's shoulder once again looked filled out and the tattooed eagle's breast puffed up to its original proud size. Brad's wife let out an audible sigh that Jim perceived as a cheer.

Jim placed a shoulder immobilizer sling around Brad's arm and stuffed a pillow between his arm and the bed rail so it wouldn't fall while Brad was still sedated.

"OK, we will just let him wake up a little and then we will get some post-reduction x-rays to make sure everything is back where it's supposed to be," Jim said to Brad's wife.

Jim left the room to order the x-ray while Carol remained to monitor Brad as he woke up.

Marcie met him at the door. "You better come see this one right away," she said.

CHAPTER SIX

Speed it Up or Slow it Down

Jim took just a few steps in the tiny ER and went behind the curtain in what was the trauma/cardiac room. This was the area reserved for the sickest patients. Lying on the gurney he saw a short, obese woman who appeared pale and was groaning softly. Two paramedics were in the room, and along with the house supervisor they were rapidly changing the patient's cardiac leads from those of their portable EMS cardiac monitor/defibrillator to that of the fixed hospital unit. Jim moved around to the side of the bed to look at the patient more closely. She was barely conscious and her skin was pale, almost to the point of being gray, and it was covered in a fine mist of perspiration.

"What do we have going on here?" Jim asked.

Benny, the lead paramedic whom Jim had known for quite some time and thought highly of, responded. "Well this is June; she is sixty and has a long heart history. She was at home tonight and complained to her daughter that she had chest pain and felt like she might pass out. When we got there, she looked pale and diaphoretic. We put her on the monitor and this is what we found." Benny handed Jim a long narrow strip of paper that had been produced by the heart monitor.

Jim looked at the tracing closely and saw immediately that June's heart rate was exceptionally slow and that the P-waves, which indicated the electrical impulse of the atriums of the heart, were frequent but uncoupled from the slow QRS waves that resulted from the electrical activity of the ventricles.

"Third-degree heart block," Jim exclaimed.

"Yeah," Benny replied. "We threw a line in her and gave her a dose of atropine. With that her rate came back up into the sixties for a little while and then we just 'scooped and ran' to get her here as soon as possible."

"Did you try pacing her?" Jim asked.

"Briefly in the back of the rig, but when her rate came up with the atropine, she was awake and talking and she didn't tolerate the pacer well," Benny said.

By this time the nurses had June undressed and she was now on the hospital cardiac monitor. Two large pacemaker pads had been applied to her chest, one over her sternum and one on her left lower ribs. Numerous wires snaked away from these large pads and the smaller leads and went up into the heart monitor suspended from the wall behind the bed. Jim reached his hand under the hospital gown and pushed his fingers deep into June's groin feeling for the pulse of her femoral artery. It was faint and slow. He watched the monitor, which was ringing with a loud alarm bell. He could see the heart rate on the monitor was twenty-two and he got the same information from his fingers pushed against June's femoral artery. The automatic blood pressure cuff began to inflate again as it didn't seem to like its initial reading of 70/32, which was flashing on the screen. The monitor alarmed continuously as these pulse and blood pressure readings were not compatible with life for long.

"Marcie, turn on the pacemaker and get another milligram of atropine," Jim said calmly.

June was still breathing but her low cardiac output secondary to her slow heart rate and low blood pressure was not adequately perfusing her vital organs with blood. This was most evident in her decreased level of consciousness as her brain was starved of blood and the oxygen it brought.

In real life emergency rooms, critical situations like this where a patient is literally dying before your eyes were rarely punctuated by the drama and emotional yelling depicted in the movies or on TV. For the most part things happened spontaneously. Within a very short time June had been moved onto the bed, hooked up to all of the monitoring devices, blood was drawn, IV fluids were running and oxygen was flowing. The nurses were experienced and they knew what needed to be done and did it instinctively, anticipating Jim's orders.

Marcie turned the external pacemaker on and set the rate at eighty. Tiny bright green lines began to march across the monitor screen eighty times a minute. Beneath this were the larger lines representing June's actual heart beat moving more slowly at a rate of twenty. Marcie gradually dialed up the power on the pacemaker until the pacemaker lines began to overlay June's heart rate, which gradually increased until the two were locked in sync and the artificial pacemaker had captured or overridden the electrical function or conducting system of June's heart.

Each area of the heart has its own intrinsic rate of contraction. Embedded in the upper two pumping chambers called the atria resides an area of specialized cells known as the sinoatrial node. This is a collection of nerve fibers that send out tiny electrical impulses that normally coordinate and tell all of the cells of the heart muscle to contract in a rhythmic and organized pattern. This SA node is called the "pacemaker" of the heart as it sets the pace. When the pacemaker is functioning properly the heart is said to be beating in sinus rhythm. The resulting electrical activity can be mapped on an electrocardiogram or ECG, sometimes also referred to as an EKG after the original German. The ECG tracing is made up of a flat line when the heart is resting between beats and no electrical signal is being sent. When the sinoatrial node discharges and the atriums contract, the resulting wave is a small bump on the EKG tracing known as a P wave. There is then a tiny pause as the electricity passes through the heart's conducting system and into the ventricles. The ventricular discharge and subsequent contraction are represented by a tall spiked wave known as the QRS complex. This is followed by another small hump called the T wave as the whole system repolarizes and resets in anticipation of the next beat. Each heart beat is represented electrically by the PQRST over and over again. The morphology or shape, height, and width of these waves may all be altered by changes in the heart function or chemistry.

In June's case some sort of damage had uncoupled the pacemaker in the atrium from the ventricles, blocking the propagation of the electrical impulse into the ventricle. This led the ventricles to fend for themselves without direction from the pacemaker. The result was that the ventricles contracted very slowly at their own intrinsic rate somewhere in the low twenties while the sinoatrial node continued to send impulses that went unheeded into the atrium and the rest of the heart. The ECG tracing that this situation produced had a characteristic slow, wide rhythmic QRS complex with numerous P waves marching through but the two were totally unconnected. This phenomenon is referred to as a third-degree heart block and is perhaps the most serious and life threatening of the heart blocks. The resting heart usually beats somewhere between sixty and eighty times per minute in the average adult, so a heart rate of only twenty means a serious decrease in the amount of blood being pumped. This can result in "shock," a condition of hypo-perfusion at the cellular level. Shock seemed to be a commonly used term by laypeople and was generally thought by them to be some sort ethereal condition of badness both physical and emotional, frequently associated with pain.

"When I broke my arm, I went into shock," someone would say.

However, this is far from the medical definition of shock, which is that for some reason, often associated with an inadequate flow of blood, the cells of the vital organs—the brain, heart, and kidneys—as well as every other cell in the body, are not receiving an adequate supply of oxygen and other vital nutrients. This also results in inadequate removal of waste substances. Shock can be the result of numerous different insults such as blood loss; resulting in an inadequate volume of blood and fluid in the circulatory system. This is referred to as "hypovolemic shock." "Septic shock" occurs when an overwhelming infection dilates the blood vessels so severely that circulatory collapse occurs as the amount of blood in the body is inadequate to fill and maintain the pressure in the enlarged system. "Neurogenic shock" occurs after severe brain or spinal cord injury when there is a loss of communication between the brain and the circulatory system.

June's problem was known as "cardiogenic shock" and had occurred due to an injury to the heart that had reduced its pumping capacity. In her case this was primarily related to the decreased heart rate. There was plenty of blood in the system and the pump was strong enough, but as cardiac output is the sum of the volume of blood moved with each beat times the heart rate, June's output was essentially diminished by a factor of four. The evidence of this was her low blood pressure, which was only seventy millimeters of mercury (seventy mmHg), barely enough to deliver blood and oxygen to the organs. This lack of blood supply led to her being on the brink of unconsciousness and caused the severe pallor of her skin. Less easy to see were the effects on her other organs such as her kidneys, which were struggling and had ceased to make urine or clean the blood, as well as her heart itself, which was becoming weaker as it was starved of fuel. Left unchecked, this condition would rapidly deteriorate and as the cellular insult and injury worsened, it would soon lead to total organ failure and ultimately to death.

To Jim, this was unacceptable and he needed to fix it. In cardiology, there is an old adage: "If the rate is too slow, speed it up. If it is too fast, slow it down." The heart has a rate at which it is most efficient, and much like the rpm of a car's engine it works best when the rate is in concordance with the demand being placed upon it.

The external pacemaker was now delivering a rhythmic, intermittent electrical charge directly across June's chest, which was telling her heart to contract eighty times each minute. This dramatically improved cardiac output and June's blood pressure began to respond. The automatic blood pressure cuff that was set to go off every three minutes now measured 87/49. As June's brain began to be filled with blood again, she began to wake up and she didn't like what was happening. She was not awake enough to communicate but she was awake enough to feel the repetitive bee stings of electricity as they surged through her chest eighty times each minute from the external pacemaker. Her chest muscles twitched with contractions with each electrical discharge. Unable to stand or understand the pain, she began to thrash about on the bed.

"Marcie, give her five mg of morphine and two mg of Versed," Jim said calmly.

Marcie had already opened the resuscitation drug box, which was stocked by the pharmacy for patients just like this. From this box she had access to all of the necessary drugs right away. Jim knew that the morphine and Versed would give June some pain relief and sedation to tolerate the shocks, but they would also lower her already dangerously low blood pressure.

Soft restraints were applied to June's arms and legs to keep her from pulling the pads and monitor leads off of her chest as she desperately struggled to stop the continuous stings of electricity that were keeping her alive. Rarely did patients tolerate external electrical pacing for very long unless they were unconscious. To make matters worse, because June was obese and had a thick layer of insulating fat over her chest, a higher degree of electricity was necessary to penetrate her chest wall to get to her heart. Jim knew that he would have to do something fast, but it was something he had never done before.

He turned to the house supervisor, who had come from upstairs to help, and said, "I am going to need to place a central line and float a pacer. Can you get me the kit?"

"Benny, when you gave her the atropine, how long did her rate stay up for?" Jim asked, turning toward the paramedic.

"Well, it was a pretty quick trip over here and her rate dropped again when we hit the doors so I would say maybe five minutes," Benny said.

"And you gave her one milligram?" Jim asked.

"Yeah, one," Benny said.

The house supervisor handed Jim a Cordis central line kit and slid a Mayo stand (a small stainless steel table on wheels) next to the head of the bed. Jim retrieved a sterile gown and gloves as well as a mask from a set of shelves in the room that held all of the resuscitation equipment.

"OK, here's what we will need to do. There is no way I am going to be able to get this central line in with her moving all over the place with these shocks and I'd rather not have to intubate her and use paralytics. So, we will get set up and then turn off the pacemaker and give her more atropine. If she tolerates that and her blood pressure remains adequate, I will put the line in and float the internal pacer. She has already had one milligram of atropine so she can only have a total of two more before we run into problems," Jim said while the others nodded agreement.

Jim then leaned over and explained in simple terms what he was about to do directly into June's ear. It was unclear if she understood but she seemed to thrash a little less.

Jim opened the Cordis kit (or percutaneous sheath introducer kit. Cordis was actually a trade name and much easier to say.) carefully in order to keep the contents sterile. There were several different types of commercially available pre-packaged central line kits. These were all basically giant IVs that could be inserted into the jugular vein, the subclavian vein, or the femoral vein. Each of these veins were huge, the diameter of a finger, and enormous volumes of blood flowed through them. The central line was a long, flexible plastic catheter that could be placed inside the lumen of the vein and then was sutured or taped in place in order to secure it to the skin. Central lines came in two basic varieties. The Cordis type was shorter and stiffer and had only a single large lumen. This could be used to pour large amounts of blood or fluids into the circulatory system very rapidly during resuscitation. These were also used as a sheath through which pacemaker wires or Swan-Ganz catheters could be placed. It was this type of catheter that Jim would place in June's neck. The other type of central line had two or three ports and individual lumens that were combined into a single large catheter allowing it to be used to deliver multiple different fluids or drugs at the same time.

Jim donned his sterile gown and gloves and opened the sterile package of Betadine swabs that came in the kit. He had already positioned June on the bed in Trendelenburg position. This meant that she was on a slope with her head down. This position would help to engorge the veins in her neck to make them larger and easier to hit. June's head was turned to the left exposing the right side of her neck and clavicle or collarbone area. The best place to put in a central line for a pacemaker was in the right internal jugular vein. This provided the easiest and straightest shot down into the superior vena cava and directly into the right side of the heart.

Jim looked at June's fat neck, or at least where her neck should have been if she had one. June had the appearance of one of those lovable grandmothers who baked all day and sampled way too much of what she baked. He could just imagine her in the kitchen wearing her apron with the smell of fresh baked cookies. She was almost as wide as she was tall, a plump cherubic grandmother with chubby cheeks. Her fat was cute and comfortable when cuddling grandkids, but it was her enemy tonight. Jim prepped a wide swath of skin on her neck and chest with the Betadine knowing that if he had to abandon the jugular vein, he would have to try to cannulate the subclavian vein instead. He unfolded the sterile paper drapes from the kit over the top of her, covering her head and chest leaving exposed only a small triangle of skin from the corner of her jaw out to her shoulder. Jim began to feel her neck to find the carotid artery. Standing at the head of the bed he placed his fingers against her fleshy neck feeling for the hard cartilage of the trachea and then he slid his fingers laterally off the side of the trachea feeling for the artery pulsing in her neck. His objective, the jugular vein, lay just superficial and lateral to the carotid artery. Normally, Jim would use an ultrasound machine to help him locate these vessels but a tiny hospital like Libertyville didn't have one in the ED. He would have to do this simply by feel. However, with June's chubby neck and with her receiving shocks from the pacemaker eighty times a minute, which resulted in all of her muscles twitching, it was impossible to distinguish what was pulse from the artery and what was a muscle twitch from the pacemaker's electric shock.

Jim finished setting up the equipment on his tray so he would be ready to go when they turned off the external pacer.

"OK, give her one milligram of atropine," Jim said. He waited while Marcie pushed the plunger on the syringe and the medications flowed into the IV line and into June's vein through the peripheral IV. He waited thirty seconds, giving the medicine time to reach the heart and begin to have an effect.

"OK, turn off the pacer," Jim said turning to Benny who was closest to the defibrillator/pacemaker.

They all watched the monitor as the pacer spikes disappeared. June's heart rate actually began to go up a little into the nineties. Marcie pushed the button and the blood pressure cuff began to fill with air around June's arm.

"June, I am going to inject some medicine into the skin of your neck so I can put in a big IV, this will sting a little," Jim said as he began the procedure.

June was awake, but sedated from the effects of the morphine and Versed.

"I need you to hold really still," he continued, as he injected lidocaine into the skin of June's neck to numb up the area. He did this with a relatively small needle. Most of the nerves that sense pain reside in the surface of the skin, and therefore that is the area that can be best anesthetized. After injecting a few cc's into the skin, Jim plunged the needle deeper to try to find the jugular vein. The vein sits just lateral to the carotid artery in the neck and by keeping the fingers of his left hand on the pulsing artery Jim could move the needle adjacent to the artery to search for the vein. This also helped him know where the artery was so he didn't accidentally hit it instead. He aimed the needle downward at a roughly forty-five-degree angle and in the general direction of the right nipple. Unfortunately, not everybody's anatomy was exactly the same and not all nipples were predictably in the same place. These were general guidelines only. By using the smaller gauge needle of the lidocaine syringe Jim could search for the vein by gently pulling back on the plunger. When he hit the vein there would be a sudden decrease in resistance and dark blood would flow into the lidocaine. Once he found the vein with the narrow-gauge needle, he could follow its path with the much larger needle for the central line and place it directly into the vein. This avoided damaging structures with the large needle and worst of all accidentally plunging the large needle into the carotid artery. You could normally tell when you hit the artery because the oxygenated blood in the artery came out bright red and under pulsatile pressure. Hitting the artery was a known complication of this delicate procedure and Jim had unfortunately done it before.

Jim methodically moved the needle up and down, searching for the vein and its tell-tale flash of blood, from as close as he dared go near the carotid artery under his fingers and away from it laterally. Despite going where he thought the vein should be there was no flash. June's pulse rate began to drop into the seventies and her blood pressure was 90/50.

"I can't find the vein; her neck is just too fat. I can't feel the landmarks and I can barely feel the carotid pulse. I am going to have to try the subclavian," Jim exclaimed with frustration.

Marcie and Benny nodded in agreement. Jim had already prepped the area of June's right upper chest with Betadine and had arranged the drapes in such a way so that if he had to change position he would not have to start all over again but could maintain his sterile field and use the same catheter kit and gloves. He moved from the head of the bed to the right side. He could feel sweat begin to bead-up on his forehead and temples. He could feel it begin to run down his back. There was perhaps nothing more stressful in emergency medicine than performing a lifesaving procedure on a patient, when that patient's life hung in the balance, and for whatever reason, it wasn't going as planned.

The placing of a central line was a challenging skill to master and the circumstances often made it more challenging. Whether the complicating circumstances were trying to hit a moving target in a patient who was thrashing around, or anatomical differences, or patient body habitus (aka: obesity), there always seemed to be something that made it harder than the textbooks suggested. It was also a procedure that was rife with serious complications. At this stage of his training, Jim had now done this kind of central line procedure many times. Like anyone who did this a lot he had also caused all of the known complications.

He did his first one as a third-year medical student in a massive forty-bed ICU, but tonight he realized this was the first time he had done it completely alone, without any supervision or backup. Tonight, there was no attending physician and no senior resident or fellow close by to help out if needed.

The subclavian vein lies, as its name implies, under the clavicle or collarbone. As with most large veins, it is paired with an artery, in this case with the same name. As it lies under a bone the pulsations of the artery cannot be felt, so finding and cannulating this vein was done simply on the basis of pointing the needle where the vein anatomically should be and hoping that the individual patient's anatomical landmarks lined up where they were supposed to. June was chubby, and unfortunately fat made everything more difficult. Finding landmarks that were covered in a layer of blubber was like trying to identify objects by feeling them through a thick down comforter. This time Jim would not have the luxury of first finding the vein with the smaller gauge lidocaine needle as it was not long enough to reach all the way under the clavicle.

"Another sting here, June," Jim said, as he began infiltrating the skin of June's chest just below the midportion of her collarbone with the local anesthetic.

June groaned softly and moved a little. Jim looked at the cardiac monitor, the pulse had dropped to fifty-six. He took the four-inch-long, large-bore needle and loosely affixed it to a ten-cc syringe. He had learned to line the bevel of the needle up with the numbers on the syringe. He plunged the needle through June's skin and moved it medially until it came in contact with June's collarbone where the bone naturally curved down toward her sternum. June groaned again as the needle hit the bone and its sensitive covering or periosteum. Jim quickly marched the needle deeper toward the chest along the collar bone until it cleared the underside and could be slid beneath it. The trick now was to advance the needle forward under the bone without angling too deep and passing between the ribs and puncturing the lung.

The two most serious complications of this procedure were puncturing or "dropping" the lung and thus causing a pneumothorax where the lung deflates like a leaking balloon and air rushes out of it into the chest cavity. The other was passing through the vein and cannulating the artery. Putting a large needle hole in the subclavian artery could lead to severe bleeding as the artery, lying protected under the bone, cannot be compressed to control the bleeding. This was a high-risk procedure and every doctor who did it had at one time or another caused these complications. Jim had actually once caused both at the same time to a thirteen-year-old girl during his pediatric ICU rotation. At that time everything seemed to go well until he looked at the chest x-ray afterward and saw not only was the lung collapsed but the tip of the catheter was sitting in the knob of the patient's aorta. Jim had been mortified at this double blunder, but after the initial feeling of guilt and remorse he was grateful for the opportunity to then place a chest tube to correct the pneumothorax. He thereby accumulated another important emergency medicine procedure.

The stakes were higher today. In the peds ICU, Jim had the backup of the attending pediatric intensivist if he had a problem. Here, however, he was all alone, and if he didn't get this line in without complications, he knew that meant Grandma June would have baked her last cookie. Jim continued to push the needle deeper into her chest under her clavicle. Time was running short if he didn't find the vein soon.

Jim mumbled a silent inner prayer. "C'mon Lord, I'm all alone here and I could really use some help."

Just as the words passed through his mind, he felt the release on the plunger and the syringe began to fill with dark blood. He was in. Next, he gently held the end of the needle so it wouldn't move from its position in the vein and carefully loosened it from the plastic syringe. Dark blood dribbled from the hub of the needle onto June's chest. He placed his gloved thumb over the hub to stop the flow and prevent air from entering the needle when June breathed in. As the chest expanded it created a negative pressure to pull air into the lungs but it would also pull air into the end of the needle and directly into the vein creating a potentially dangerous air embolism.

Jim then reached for the coiled-up wire that he had separated from the kit on the Mayo stand, and he began sliding it carefully through the needle's bore. The wire was a springy flexible type about eighteen inches long and it was snaked down through the end of the needle into the subclavian vein, and then followed its course leading into the brachiocephalic vein, then the superior vena cava, and eventually all the way into the right side of the heart.

One could often tell when the wire reached the heart as it caused irregular electrical impulses to show up on the heart monitor as the metal irritated the myocardium. Occasionally the wire turned north at the brachiocephalic and went up into the jugular vein of the neck and into the head. This was another embarrassing complication that Jim had the unfortunate experience of having caused in the recent past. In Jim's mind, however, the worst complication of all, which fortunately Jim had not had, was to lose the wire entirely through the skin and leave it floating inside the confines of the vascular system inside the patient's chest and heart. This was dangerous and required an invasive procedure to recover the wire.

Jim slid the wire in about a foot and then pulled the needle back out of the skin over the wire. For the first time he could relax just a little as at least now he knew he was in the vein. This brilliant system of passing the wire through the needle and then passing the flexible catheter over the wire was called the Seldinger technique, undoubtedly named after a Dr. Seldinger somewhere in medical history. Jim picked up the scalpel from the kit and made a nick in the skin next to the wire.

"Her pulse is dropping. Do you want the other atropine, Dr. McCray?" Marcie asked.

Jim looked at the monitor; the heart rate was now thirty-eight.

"Yeah, go ahead and give it to her, run another blood pressure, and then start opening the pacer kit," Jim said.

He pulled the Cordis catheter from the kit and placed it over the top of the introducer. The introducer was a stiff tube of plastic sharpened at one end that would push the tissue out of the way in order to get the softer, floppier catheter into the vein. He pushed the two together as a unit over the wire until the wire came out the other end. Then with firm steady pressure he slid them down into June's chest following the path of the wire into her subclavian vein. He was careful to make sure he held the end of the wire and that the wire slid easily inside the introducer and catheter so that the wire would not become kinked. Once the catheter was in to the hub, he pulled the wire out and then pulled out the stiff introducer leaving just the large-gauge Cordis catheter inside of June's chest. Using a syringe that he attached to the catheter he found that dark red blood could easily be drawn up through the line indicating that it was indeed in the vein. Marcie held out the end of the plastic IV tubing that Jim then screwed onto the IV connector that came off the side of the Cordis.

The second dose of atropine pushed the pulse back up to one hundred and June's blood pressure responded, rising to 95/60. Marcie next opened the package with the pacemaker leads onto Jim's sterile field on the Mayo stand. Jim pulled out the leads, which were two thin wires wrapped in a rubberized coating coming together into a single wire on the business end, where there was also a tiny deflated balloon. Jim had never actually placed a pacemaker before but he had seen it done. In medical training, there is an old saying, "See one, do one, teach one." Jim didn't expect that his "do one" would be all alone with no one who actually knew how to do this within forty miles.

Jim inspected the bundle of wire and tubing and then tested the balloon by using a syringe attached to the port on the end opposite from the balloon in order to blow up it up with one cc of air. Once inside the patient's heart, when the balloon was inflated it would allow the tip of the catheter to float in the blood coursing through the heart until it was in the correct position. It was imperative to only inflate the balloon when the wires were inside a large vein or the heart itself. Inflating the balloon in a smaller lumen vein would potentially damage the balloon but more importantly ran the risk of rupturing the vein from the inside leading to severe bleeding.

Normally at this stage Jim would have taken the time to secure the Cordis to June's chest by suturing it to her skin. Also, he would have obtained a chest x-ray to confirm the tip of the Cordis was in the right place before attempting to float the pacemaker. But tonight, there was simply not enough time. He just had to hope it was in the right place. He felt confident that it was. Perhaps that was the advantage of not having a senior resident, fellow, or attending physician standing over his shoulder. He could cut corners when he had to and usually you could get away with it. Tonight, he had already given both doses of atropine and in another minute or two June's heart rate and blood pressure would again be too low to sustain her vital functions. He would cut this corner and hope the Cordis was where it was supposed to be.

Jim placed the protective plastic sleeve over the pacemaker wire, which would help keep it sterile, and then he began sliding the pacemaker wire with the little balloon on the end through the little rubber diaphragm at the top of the Cordis and down into June's vascular system and ultimately into her heart. Once he knew the catheter was in twenty centimeters by following the marks on it, he handed off the lead wires to Marcie who plugged them into the pacemaker control box. By this time June's heart rate was beginning to drop again. Jim could see the P-waves on the monitor as they danced along as well as the wide complex ventricular waves. These were waves that represented the beats, the very contractions of June's heart, as they gradually slowed down and the distance between each of them grew longer and longer. The automatic blood pressure cuff began to inflate again searching for June's pulse. They had used all the atropine they safely could and now it was up to the pacemaker to do the job.

"OK, turn it on please, Marcie," Jim said.

Jim pushed the plunger on the little syringe to inflate the balloon. He then visualized in his mind the tiny round balloon on the end of the white rubber-coated wire being buffeted gently in June's blood stream while emanating tiny electrical discharges into the blood and the surrounding tissues. Jim slowly pushed the wire further into the Cordis and deeper toward June's heart. He could see the tiny electrical spikes from the internal pacemaker now beginning to show up on the monitor. They were moving along regularly eighty times each minute. June's actual heart rate was now down to twenty-four and her blood pressure could not be detected, which caused the alarms on the monitor to continuously ring and started the blood pressure cuff recycling again trying to find a pressure. It was now or never. Jim pushed the pacemaker wire even further into the Cordis and the slow, tall, wide waves of June's heart gradually began to sync up with the pacer spikes. As they began to sync, the impulses from the pacemaker captured the electrical conducting system in June's heart and her heart rate jumped to eighty good, solid beats per minute. Jim placed his fingers on her neck and could now feel a strong, consistent pulse. The monitor stopped alarming and the blood pressure readout showed a very satisfactory 115/70.

June began to stir under the drapes. Jim quickly sutured the central line in place tying it to June's skin and then he pulled the drapes away from her face. She was awake and staring up at him. Her face and hair were sweaty and she still looked a little pale.

"Thank you…" she said with a weak smile, "…and thank God."

"You're welcome," Jim said, as the intensity of the situation washed over him. In his mind, he also thanked God for the help.

"Ginger, would you order a portable chest x-ray for line placement and call cardiology at the U and call the helicopter for critical care transport," Jim said.

A few minutes later, Jim had pulled up the x-ray, and to his satisfaction he could see the Cordis in the correct place with the pacemaker wires snaking into June's chest and resting in position inside her heart. The lungs were also inflated normally, no pneumo.

Ginger looked up at Jim from behind the desk. "There's a Dr. Morris from Cards on line two."

Jim knew Dr. Morris well; he had spent hours with him rounding on patients during his coronary care unit (CCU) rotation. Morris was a heart specialist, or cardiologist, with additional fellowship training in electrophysiology. This made him an expert not only in heart disease but more especially in conditions that involved the electrical conducting system of the heart. Interventional cardiologists are the ones who place balloons and stents in clogged arteries to open up the pipes and get the blood flowing again. They are the "plumbers." Electrophysiologists are experts in managing the conducting system of the heart. They are the "electricians."

"Hi, Dr. Morris," Jim said. "Yeah, it's Jim McCray. I'm working up in Libertyville tonight, and I've got a sixty-year-old lady named June Johansen. She has a history of coronary artery disease, and today she developed chest pain and decreased level of consciousness. When the medics arrived, she was very hypotensive and she was pretty much out of it. Her twelve-lead EKG showed a third-degree block with a rate in the twenties. She responded to atropine for a little while but couldn't tolerate the external pacer."

"Well, she needs an internal pacer," Dr. Morris interrupted, sounding impatient.

"Yeah, I know," Jim said. "So, I just floated one in. She's pacing at eighty with a blood pressure of 130/70 and she's sitting up looking at me."

"Well, then you just saved her life," Dr. Morris said, sounding both relieved and slightly surprised.

Jim continued. "I don't have the cardiac enzymes back yet to know if this was precipitated by an MI (myocardial infarction) but I would like to send her down to you on the helicopter."

"That sounds good..." replied Dr. Morris, "...and Jim, nice save."

Jim completed the call and hung up the phone. He looked at June and smiled, feeling a swelling of pride in his chest, knowing that he had really made a difference here tonight for her. June smiled back.

CHAPTER SEVEN

Managing the Flow

D espite having just completed a complex medical procedure and saving June's life, there was little time for Jim
to bask in his glory. The helicopter would be here in
fifteen minutes, and they had to get June packaged for the
trip. Also, Brad, the shoulder dislocation, was wide awake
and wanting to go. Melanie the vag bleeder was ready for
her pelvic, and Violet the obese woman had labs back to
review. In addition, the waiting room was filling up. Several
patients who didn't need rooms were placed in chairs. Jim
would evaluate and treat them from the chairs. The two
remaining beds had been filled, one with a shoulder injury
and the other came by ambulance with a chief complaint of
"glass in rectum." That should be interesting, thought Jim. He
rapidly scanned through all of the charts and ordered quick
tests such as x-rays and blood work he knew he would need
in order to keep things moving along until he could actually see each of the patients. He also typed up the discharge
paperwork and prescriptions for the shoulder dislocation,
and after the required post-procedural sedation wake-up
time, he said goodbye to Brad and his wife.

Next, he arranged with Carol to meet him in the gyn
room in order to do Melanie's pelvic exam. Jim entered the

room and closed the door behind him. The fry cook was gone but mother was there next to the head of the bed holding Melanie's hand. Melanie lay on the bed covered with a sheet. Carol began positioning her for the exam.

"Her bleeding has really increased a lot in the last half an hour," Carol said as she slid a blood-soaked disposable absorptive towel called a Chux pad out from underneath her and replaced it with a fresh one.

"Yeah, it just started coming out like crazy," Melanie said to Jim.

"Is there any more pain or cramping?" Jim asked.

"No, it's about the same, but I feel really cold."

Jim noted that the IV bag that was hanging from the IV pole was almost empty. He looked at the monitor which showed Melanie's vital signs. Her last blood pressure read 93/45. Carol had noticed the amount of blood loss and the low blood pressure and had initiated giving Melanie some IV fluid to keep her blood pressure up and replace some of the fluid volume she was losing due to the bleeding.

"Sometimes the IV fluid can make you feel cold when it goes in fast," Jim said reassuringly.

Sometimes losing a lot of blood makes you feel cold also, he thought to himself.

The bed on which Melanie was lying was a convertible gyn bed. It looked like a normal stretcher but it had stirrups that could be pulled out from underneath and the end of the bed where the feet normally were could be broken down and moved out of the way. Carol broke the bed down and put each of Melanie's feet up in the stirrups with her knees and hips bent and her legs spread apart. She was careful to maintain Melanie's modesty and keep her covered with the sheet. Jim put on some gloves and sat down on a wheeled stool and rolled it over until he was positioned at the end of the bed between Melanie's legs. He lifted the sheet and exposed Melanie's external genitalia. Her pubic hair was completely shaved off and she had a decorative stainless-steel stud that traversed her clitoral hood. Her entire perineum was smeared with blood. Other than that, she looked pretty much the same as every other woman from this angle. There was nothing inherently sexy or alluring in these exams. After having done hundreds or perhaps thousands of them, Jim found them to be one of his least favorite patient interactions.

"OK, just let your legs relax apart and let your muscles go loose," he said.

Carol was on Melanie's right side near her foot, and she had a Mayo stand with all of the necessary instruments on it. Jim picked up the plastic speculum and smeared clear jelly lubricant on the end of it. He used his left hand to gently spread Melanie's labia apart and then inserted the speculum and twisted it into position. He opened the jaws of the speculum, which made an audible clicking sound. The speculum was disposable but had a place for a light in the end of it, which illuminated the now widely patent vaginal canal. All Jim could see was blood that streamed out through the open speculum over his hands and onto the floor. Carol having anticipated this had laid several disposable towels on the floor strategically placed to catch the cascade of blood.

Pregnant women markedly increase their blood volume in response to pregnancy. This was necessary for just this sort of problem. Some of the blood was from the fetus and placenta and some of it was Melanie's. A unit of blood given as a transfusion and also the amount one donates at a blood drive was around 250 cc's. Jim estimated that perhaps close to a unit had just spilled onto the floor in addition to what was in the pads that had been under Melanie. Once the frank red blood had stopped draining, Jim still couldn't see anything in Melanie's vagina as there were several large formed clots sitting low in the vault. These looked similar to large chunks of uncooked liver but with slightly less structure and substance. Jim took a pair of ringed forceps, which are similar to a long pair of hot dog tongs except the rings on the ends are smaller, and he began to gently pull out the clots. Carol positioned a basin under Jim's hands into which he dropped each of the clots. He quickly looked at each clot to see if there were any formed elements such as membranes or fetal parts. The blood continued to flow and Jim continued to pull out more clots. Finally, he had them all out and he could see that at the mouth, or os, as it is referred to in medical terms, of Melanie's cervix there was a mass that was the size, shape, and color of a purple plum. The surface of it was glistening and tense.

This was the gestational sac, and it was being delivered whole and intact through Melanie's cervix. Jim gently reached down into the depths of Melanie's vaginal canal with the forceps and carefully grabbed onto the end of the sac. He closed the forceps and began to gently pull. This was the pregnancy, so essentially Jim was completing the spontaneous miscarriage or abortion that had been naturally occurring.

This pregnancy was well beyond the point of no return. Although it was technically possible that the fetus inside of the sac was still alive, it had probably been dead for some time and now the body was simply expelling the detritus. If it were still alive there was simply no way for it to survive the impending complete loss of its blood supply. On a personal basis, Jim was opposed to the idea of performing an abortion on a fetus that was minding its own business and simply growing away in a uterus. But this was different. Jim was now simply expediting the natural and inevitable process of miscarriage and in so doing he was relieving the suffering of the mother and reducing the chances of life-threatening bleeding. If Melanie continued to bleed at the present rate, she was at significant risk of bleeding to death. But, the delivery and removal of these products of conception would allow the cervix and uterus to contract and slow the flow of blood. As Jim pulled, the sac tore open and collapsed and out spilled a cascade of clear amniotic fluid, and in the midst of the gush was the tiny body of Melanie's unborn child. Jim retrieved the fetus with the forceps and placed it in a small specimen container that Carol was holding at the ready. He then reached back in and pulled out all of the membranes and remaining tissue. With this removed the hole in the center of the doughnut shaped cervix immediately collapsed on itself and the bleeding slowed to a trickle. Jim mopped up the remaining blood with some folded-up pieces of gauze placed in the grip of the ringed forceps. The vaginal vault was now empty and dry with only a slight ooze of red blood from the os.

"Well, Melanie I am sorry to say that you have lost the baby," Jim said.

Melanie's mother groaned audibly.

"Can I see it?" asked Melanie.

Jim looked up from between her legs at her face. She seemed smaller in the bed but somehow older and more grown up.

"If you would like," Jim said and motioned to Carol, who brought the specimen cup to the head of the bed for Melanie to examine its contents. As she peered into the container tears began to well up in her eyes and she looked away.

Jim patted her gently on her leg as he covered her back up with a sheet and reassembled the foot portion of the bed.

"Your bleeding should slow down now," Jim said. "But we will still need to get an ultrasound to make sure that your uterus is completely empty and I will be giving you some medicine that will help your uterus clamp down and shut off any further bleeding. Sometimes it causes a little cramping but probably no worse than you have already experienced."

Jim turned to leave the room while Carol cleaned Melanie up and changed her sheets. As he did so he felt his attitude toward Melanie soften. He felt for her loss, even as ill-conceived as it was, it was nevertheless a loss.

———————•———————

JIM WENT BACK to the computer and placed the orders into Melanie's chart. He then switched into Violet's chart to review her labs. He returned to Violet's bedside where he found her sitting up slightly now and breathing heavily. Everything about Violet seemed oversized. She was probably only about five-foot-five but lying semi-reclined in the bed she looked like a mountain. Her face and neck and arms and chest were puffed up to comic size. The fat of her enormous sagging arms cascaded down her bulk where they then emerged from the tent sized hospital gown and tapered into surprisingly dainty, small hands and fingers tipped with bright red nail polish.

"Hi Violet, how are you feeling?" Jim said.

"Not so good," replied Violet with a soft whispering voice.

Jim began his examination, first checking her ears and throat, and listening to her lungs and heart. He palpated her giant belly and then examined her legs. He knew from the doorway that her legs were the source of her infection. Violet's enormous pannus of skin and adipose tissue layered down from her abdomen and extended to her knees. From the knees down on the front of both legs her skin was a deep, angry red with the texture of a rough orange peel. Hairy stubble emerged from the bumpy surface and clear yellow edema fluid leaked from cracks in the skin. The visible portion of her legs from the knees down were like misshapen tree trunks and they ended in her tiny feet. The surface of the skin was hot with infection and for a moment it reminded Jim of sizzling bacon frying in its own grease. The left side was clearly worse, but both legs looked sick.

"Well it looks like you have an infection in the skin of your legs. It's called cellulitis," explained Jim.

"Cellulite?" asked Violet.

"No…Although you've got a little of that, too," Jim replied as he smiled cautiously.

Violet smiled also, and then she turned her head away slightly and demurred. At this instant Jim felt her humanity for the first time. She wasn't a circus freak after all but a real woman with tender emotions and feelings.

"Cellulitis is an infection that is usually caused by a type of bacteria that lives on our skin. If we have a break in our skin such as from a small cut or a crack the bacteria can find their way in and then spread along the layers of skin. You are more prone to this if you are a diabetic or if your circulation is not very good," Jim said.

"The infection causes the fever and that can lead to

confusion and delirium and the infection will continue to spread and can get into your blood and really make you sick and potentially kill you," Jim said as Violet nodded understanding.

"Your fever has come down now, are you feeling a little better?" Jim asked.

"Yeah, I felt a little out of my head earlier," Violet said.

"Your white blood cell count is about 23,000, that's more than twice what it should be. That's an indication that your immune system is really ramped up to try to fight this infection. I am going to treat you by giving you some IV antibiotics to help fight the infection and kill the bacteria. You will need to be admitted to the hospital for a few days."

"Did this happen because I'm fat?" Violet said.

"Who said you were fat?" Jim said, feigning surprise.

Violet smiled.

"Well, it certainly doesn't help any," Jim said. "Being overweight affects your circulation as does smoking and your whole immune system is negatively affected."

"Violet, if you don't mind me asking, how did you get this big?" Jim said as he stepped back and surveyed her entire bulk.

"One cheeseburger at a time," Violet said.

"If you can believe it, I weighed 120 pounds when I graduated from high school, but I've got bad genes and I had a bad marriage and I don't get much exercise unless you count opening potato chip bags."

Jim really liked Violet, which never entered his mind when he first saw her. She was frankly physically a little revolting but she was also delightful, honest, self-deprecating, and a pleasure to talk to. He felt a strange affinity, and although he pitied her, he very much wanted to help her.

They continued their conversation for a few more minutes and then he excused himself and went back to the nurses' station where he entered her admission orders in the computer and discussed her case with the internal medicine hospitalist doctor on call who would care for her once she was moved up to the floor.

G. Scott McCreadie, MD

CHAPTER EIGHT →

Aeromedical Transport

Jim reviewed his progress for the night. He was only a few hours into the shift and he was still behind, but he was making progress and anticipated that the patient flow would begin to taper off after 11 p.m. The helicopter had arrived for June. The crew, which included two nurses and the pilot, sauntered in rolling a specially made gurney with their monitors and gear strapped to the top of it. Jim met them at the door. Given that the flight crew wore moderately sexy form-fitting flight suits and swooped in and out of small-town hospitals in their $10 million helicopter, they had the swagger of Hollywood action heroes. Jim knew the power of the flight suit because all senior emergency medicine residents could opt to do two shifts a month as the flight physician on the helicopter transport team. When a resident was along for the ride this meant there was a fourth crew member in the cramped confines of the helicopter and with the addition of the patient it made for some very tight accommodations.

Jim had worked with all of the nurses and all of the pilots. They were a tight-knit group. Some of them liked the residents, and some of them hated them and their presence in their domain. Generally whether they were liked or loathed by the flight crew depended on the individual resident and their personality. Nurses in general seemed to be territorial. The worst, in Jim's opinion, were obstetrical nurses and after that, pediatric nurses. Jim suspected it was related to some sort of primordial maternal instinct as in those two areas they were almost exclusively women. It was actually an admirable quality, but it could make it difficult for a resident who might only rotate through a given service for a month, to garner any respect in that short time. Although OB and peds were also almost entirely dominated by women, the emergency department in contrast attracted a lot of male nurses.

When it came to the flight crew, if the resident was unsure or lacked confidence, the flight nurses, who were exceptionally well trained often having worked for years in the ER or ICU, would simply run over the resident. Added to that was the fact that the space was tight and patients were often very sick and very complex, so the mood in the chopper could be very tense. For this reason, some of the residents had opted out of the helicopter program and spent those two shifts in the ED instead.

Jim however, loved his flight shifts. He had proven himself and had become good friends with many of the flight nurses and pilots. Plus, it was a great break from the emergency department and an opportunity to see how medicine was practiced in other small towns that routinely shipped patients back to the university hospital. Most of the patients on the helicopter were either cardiac or trauma, and they really needed the advanced care that could only be provided at a big teaching hospital. Occasionally there would be a pediatric patient or an OB patient, and every so often the helicopter would be called out to the scene of a bad accident for direct transport. Sometimes the patients were stabilized and the flights were uneventful, but at other times it was a real fight trying to keep a patient who was "sick as hell" alive in the tiny confines of the helicopter.

Jim admired the flight nurses for what they did. Personally, he never felt comfortable taking care of sick people in the back of the helicopter primarily because he just felt he was physically too big to contort himself into the positions necessary to be able to see and hear and assess what needed to be done. The equipment was limited by space, the environment was incredibly noisy, and with turbulence and weather and blood and vomit and three people trying to work on a fourth in a space the size of the interior of a compact car. It was exhilarating but daunting. Jim never felt as large and oafish as he did when he was in the back of the chopper. He was especially conscientious about his feet, on which he was required to wear heavy black leather boots and, on his head, a huge helmet with a radio that was tethered by a coiled cord plugged into the ceiling.

The flight nurses on the other hand clearly self-selected as they all seemed similar, with muscular compact bodies. The heaviest was perhaps 140 pounds fully dressed in a flight suit with boots and helmet. This kept the weight down on the helicopter, and their strength and athleticism allowed them to move around and contort themselves like gymnasts while caring for the patient.

The residents were not nearly so uniform in size and although it had never happened to Jim, if the patient was exceptionally large and the combined weight of the flight crew and the patient exceeded the weight that the helicopter could safely transport, then it was the resident who got jettisoned at the pick-up location and had to find his or her own way home. This was hard on some of the residents' egos and that flight suit wasn't nearly as glamorous or sexy when the helicopter flew away without you and you had to sit in a bus station waiting for a ride home.

This humiliating experience had led some of the residents to opt out of the program. Knowing the personalities involved, Jim wondered if the weight limit were actually exceeded or if the pilot, perhaps at the urging of the nurses, had intentionally dumped off some of the less well-liked flight physicians. Jim understood why some of the residents opted out. The learning experience wasn't that great, and there were a lot more patients to be seen in the ED during the course of a shift. Perhaps more importantly, in the ED the residents were clearly in charge and had the backup of the attending physicians. But for Jim, he continued to enjoy his flight shifts mainly because he loved the helicopter. In fact, he had become really good friends with the pilots and had a standing invitation to ride in the copilot seat on the outbound leg and if the patient was stable, on the return trip as well. It was an enormous rush to ride shotgun in this ultracool helicopter as it lifted off, screamed over the treetops and houses and then set down on the pad. People couldn't help but look.

One time, Sue had arrived at the hospital with Tyler and Anna and they were standing at the fence next to the landing pad with their hair blowing out of control in the rotor wash as the chopper hovered and then descended to the ground. The kids' eyes nearly popped out of their heads when they saw their dad open the helicopter door from the inside and step out onto the ground.

The crew tonight did not include a flight physician. The flight nurses were Janie and Kat, both in their early thirties, both exceptionally bright and also quite easy on the eyes. They were good friends outside of work and often arranged their shifts together. The pilot tonight was Devin; he was perhaps forty and had never married. He was the playboy type. He was the only one of the four pilots who had not learned to fly in the military. He had been bankrolled by his wealthy parents to take flying lessons and once told Jim he estimated that it cost them $300,000 in helicopter rental fees for him to get enough hours to qualify for a commercial license and to get the job he had now. Jim liked all of the pilots, but Devin was his favorite as he was the least disciplined and the most "cowboy." This was likely due to his lack of military training.

Devin loved to show off in the helicopter and flew it like it was a sports car. Jim had flown with the exact same crew a few months earlier when they had been called out by the sheriff's department to help search for the body of a missing person. The sheriff's department did not have its own helicopter and had been searching the river with divers for two days trying to find a man they had arrested but who had subsequently escaped.

Two nights earlier an officer patrolling the highway had picked up a driver for a DUI who had outstanding warrants. The suspect was in his twenties and only wearing flip flops, jeans and a T-shirt despite the winter weather. It was two in the morning and the man was handcuffed in the back of the officer's car as they came into town and neared the jail. The officer had just crossed a low bridge over the river and stopped at a red light when the man somehow managed to open the back door of the police cruiser, jump out, and begin to run.

When he realized what had happened the officer also jumped out of the car and gave chase on foot but the suspect ran back along the sidewalk toward the bridge and then down past the bridge railing over the bank and down to the water's edge. With the officer only a few feet behind him he splashed into the frigid river with his hands still cuffed behind his back. The officer radioed for help and scanned the black water with his flashlight but never saw the suspect resurface or make it to either shore. Although the river was not large or fast moving it was dark and bitterly cold and the suspect was both drunk and handcuffed. The sheriff's department was now desperately searching for him, suspecting he had drowned but not knowing if he may have escaped.

Jim and the rest of the flight crew were having a slow day and the sheriff's department had called and asked if they wouldn't mind bringing the helicopter down and scanning the river from above with the hope that a bird's-eye view might bring better luck than the divers who were now on their second day in the water. Jim rode in the copilot seat next to Devin with Janie and Kat in the back. They flew up and down the river downstream from the bridge at least a dozen times scanning the river with four sets of eyes looking for anything that remotely resembled a human form. Although the river was not particularly deep, it was difficult to see anything in the dark green water set off against the drab gray winter surroundings. It was possible to occasionally make out a light-colored rock or submerged dark-colored log on the bottom. If the helicopter got too close to the surface the water became obscured by waves whipped up by the rotors. If they flew too high, they simply couldn't distinguish anything on the river bottom. After a half an hour the crew was ready to give up, especially since law enforcement wasn't even sure the guy was in the river. For all anybody knew he could have escaped the river and was sitting at home in the warmth of his living room watching the whole search effort on the news right now.

The four crew members in the helicopter agreed to make one more pass and then call it a day. They slowly hovered over the bridge and then moved down the river flying over the sheriff's office Zodiac boat from which the divers were working. They moved down the meandering course of the river for about a half a mile and then turned 180 degrees and began flying back up stream. Jim strained his eyes to see the bottom. He wanted badly to find something, but he didn't want to sound a false alarm unless he really thought there was a body there. That's when he saw a shape come into view. From his vantage point high above the river he saw a pale, roughly rectangular shape that was perhaps three feet long and at the end of it a dark shape also roughly the same length.

Jim spoke over the intercom in the helicopter. "Hey guys, do you see that light shape and dark shape below us about a third of the way across from the south shore?"

Devin stopped the helicopter's progress and backed it up slightly and hovered.

"I think that looks like a guy's back and the dark part could be his legs in dark pants," Jim said, trying not to sound too excited.

"I don't know," Janie said, sounding skeptical.

She was seated directly behind Jim and had the best vantage point next to his.

"Although, the more I look at it, I think you might be right."

Devin opened the radio mic and called to the sheriff on shore and gave the details. The crew watched intently from the hovering helicopter as the information was relayed to the dive team and the Zodiac roared to life and then zipped down the river until it slowed to a stop directly beneath them. Two divers dropped over the side of the boat and one surfaced again a few seconds later waving the "thumbs up." Radio traffic went back and forth, and then the sheriff's excited voice sounded in the flight crew's headsets.

"Thank you, Air Med! We have confirmed we have found what we were looking for!"

The flight crew let out a collective whoop and congratulated each other and especially Jim whose "eagle eye," as he was later called by the crew, had spotted the body. Devin took the helicopter into a steep bank and flew downstream a few hundred yards before he turned it around and dropped down to just over the tree tops. He then opened up the throttle and screamed back up the river waggling the chopper back and forth in salute as they flew over all the law enforcement people and bystanders who were cheering below.

Later, Jim learned that the escaped man had apparently drowned shortly after entering the river and had floated downstream about a quarter of a mile from the bridge before his handcuffed hands had become hooked on some branches and debris on the bottom. The current had lifted his T-shirt over his head exposing the pale white skin of his torso, which Jim had first spotted. For all of the live patients Jim had worked on while in the helicopter, his most memorable flight crew experience had been the time he found the dead guy.

"Hello, Dr. McCray," Kat said cheerfully as she led the team into the tiny emergency department. "What have you got for us tonight?"

Jim pointed behind her to her right where June was now sitting up in bed and looking pleased.

"This is June," he said, motioning for the flight crew to follow him into her room.

They wheeled the transport gurney in and stationed it next to her bed while Jim gave the details about June's history, presentation, and what had been done to stabilize her. As he spoke, Janie and Kat rapidly and methodically went about doing their assessment, switching her to their cardiac monitor and sliding her off the bed onto their gurney. Within five minutes they had her packaged up and were ready to go. Jim and Marcie were standing together at the nurses' station as the flight crew wheeled June toward the door and out to the helicopter pad. Jim could see the rhythmic spikes of the pacemaker on the cardiac monitor as it directed June's heart to beat. They had June bundled up against the cold night air but she was sitting up. She was able to free her hand from the blankets and she waved to Jim.

"Thanks again doctor, you saved me. I really thought this was it."

Jim smiled at her. "Take care June. I'll try to stop by and see you in the CCU."

The team moved out through the sliding door followed by Devin who slapped Jim on the shoulder and said, "When are you coming flying again Eagle Eye?"

"It should be soon. Take care, Devin," Jim said.

Devin turned on his heels, gave a fake salute and sauntered out behind the two nurses.

CHAPTER NINE

Work-Related Injury

J im turned back to the computer to see what was next, leaning over Marcie to look at her screen. Marcie pointed to the name of the next patient in line to be seen on the electronic track board.

"You're going to love this next one," she said and then lowered her voice to a whisper. "She's a stripper. Oh, but wait the best one is the one after that, she's from the state hospital and she shoved broken glass up her butt."

Jim turned to look at Marcie whose smile of devious glee nearly ruptured her cheeks. Jim just rolled his eyes.

"It gets even better; she says she knows you," Marcie said.

Jim pretended to be shocked and then bent down and whispered in Marcie's ear.

"Which one?"

"The crazy one with the glass in her ass," Marcie said, pleased with her rhyme.

"Well, that's probably better for me," Jim said, and they both chuckled.

Jim chose to see the stripper first. Of course, on her chart under occupation it didn't actually say stripper, it said "dancer." It always said dancer. Jim suspected one day he would actually meet a patient whose chart said dancer and she would turn out to be a prima ballerina, but so far dancer had always meant stripper. Perhaps there just wasn't enough space on the line to include the descriptor "exotic." "Dancing" seemed to be a somewhat dangerous occupation because Jim had seen his fair share of dancers over the past few years. Mostly they had simple orthopedic injuries such as twisted ankles from falling over on five-inch stilettos in dark bars or sprained knees from twisting into awkward although provocative positions. Jim's experience with strippers in the medical setting was certainly not fully inclusive, but the ones he had met seemed to be fairly similar. They were typically in their mid- to late-twenties, they were uniformly thin, and usually with obviously surgically enhanced chests. They were almost always smokers, and they always seemed to have a somewhat hardened, weathered look to their faces. This made them appear older and angrier than they actually were. In the ER, they tended to give off a vibe that was anything but alluring or sexual. Perhaps this was a protection from the occupational hazard of inviting lustful stares that was encouraged in their workplace but generally not acceptable in other arenas and certainly forbidden in the doctor's office. In Jim's experience, they were usually suspicious and always a bit pissed off. Of course, Jim's experience was typically limited to a single visit for a single complaint, and he had never developed enough rapport in these short interactions to know what these women were really like. He hadn't been one to visit their working environment so they remained a bit of an enigma to him, like beautiful but dangerous wild animals to be observed through the bars at the zoo but never to really know or understand their inner lives.

Jim looked at the chart in front of him. The name read Antonia Vancelli, age twenty-three. Hmm, an Italian stripper, Jim thought.

Occupation: Dancer.
Employer: The Mermaid Lounge.

Jim had driven by this establishment a hundred times. It was a rundown one-story bar with a flat roof. It was away from town a bit and it was set back from the road with parking in front. There was one main door in the middle and no windows, or at least none that allowed in any light. Elevated at the edge of the road there was a large sign that consisted of a neon mermaid who lounged inside a neon martini glass, her tail was draped over the side and appeared to swish back and forth as the light switched on and off.

Jim slid the curtain open and stepped into the room. He was taken aback by what he saw. There, sitting upright on the edge of the bed sat one of the most strikingly beautiful women he had ever seen. She was wearing only the hospital gown, which she had tucked tightly and neatly around her body. She sat poised and alert with her bare legs and feet hanging off the bed and reaching toward the ground. Her back was straight and her head erect. Antonia it seemed had accomplished the impossible. She made a hospital gown look good. Her shape pushed the drab fabric in precisely the correct directions with just the right dimension and combination of both curve and angle. Jim suppressed the urge to stare and finally spoke. "Hi, I'm Dr. McCray."

"Antonia," was all she said.

As she did so, she turned her head slightly and looked up at Jim and smiled a most disarming smile. She lacked the usual stripper hardness and edge. Her skin was a glowing olive with just a hint of color, which contrasted nicely with her thick shoulder length hair that was almost black and glistened under the fluorescent lights. Jim had heard the term raven hair and here it was. It had that iridescent sheen like the back of the bird in sunlight. Her eyes were almost as dark and they were deep, bottomless.

"What can I do for you today?" Jim asked

"It's my right shoulder," Antonia said as she motioned to her shoulder. "I have a pain in it."

"Let me have a look," Jim said as he moved to her side.

He reached out and took her outstretched arm in his hands. His skilled, efficient hands suddenly seemed coarse and clumsy as he held her thin, finely muscled, nearly hairless arm. He couldn't see her shoulder as it was covered by the hospital gown. So, he lowered the arm and instinctively reached his left hand up behind her neck and under her glossy mane to untie the gown, which fell forward slightly. Antonia swung her head in such a way that her hair fell off to the side allowing Jim easier access to the tie. Now came the tricky part. He had to have her pull her arm back while he pulled the gown forward until the two could be separated, and then he would swing the gown under her arm and tie it again leaving her shoulder exposed for the exam. This maneuver would or could briefly expose her breasts. Presently the front of the gown was strained and elevated as it struggled to contain her. It would be almost unavoidable during this maneuver to pull the gown forward just enough to uncover her.

For a split-second Jim struggled, weighing the inclination to look, against his training that dictated he maintain her modesty and expose only the injured shoulder. It wasn't like Jim didn't see plenty of naked body parts. In fact, hadn't he just finished digging around in Melanie's crotch across the hall? But there was a distinction and he knew it. He understood that he had a primal inclination to peek at Antonia. Over the last several years he had seen thousands and thousands of patients in various degrees of undress. He had touched them and poked them and cut into them, all in the interest of helping them and fixing their disease. It was part of being a doctor. But every once in a while, he came across an Antonia, where in addition to a clinical need there was also a tiny spark of chemistry that could, if allowed to ignite, blur the boundaries of propriety. He knew others who had fallen into this trap. It seemed easy to do and almost justifiable. After all, in Antonia's case, didn't she make her living taking off her clothes for leering men?

Jim regained his composure, steeled himself and gently pulled the gown away from the arm and slipped it under her arm and tied the knot again all the while safely shielding her modesty. It was a victory. She had no idea there had been a battle. He relaxed and began the exam.

"Show me where it hurts," Jim said.

Antonia pointed to the top of her well-defined deltoid muscle. She lifted her arm and said. "When I am at work, I use this arm a lot and it hurts."

"What kind of work do you do?" Jim asked.

He had now recovered and was not feeling as unbalanced by her beauty. His impulses were back in his control.

"I'm a dancer," Antonia said.

"What kind of dancer?" Jim asked.

Of course, he knew the answer but he wanted to hear her say it, explain it. He was back in his element now. He would be asking the questions. She had no inkling of the transient internal struggle she had precipitated in his mind a moment before. Of course, she understood the power she had over men. Any beautiful woman with a little experience quickly learns how to read the subtle signs and cues when the power of their form and presence has disarmed a man.

"I'm a stripper," she said.

She had no malice or anger when she said it. There was no apology in her voice. There was also no pride. It was matter of fact; it was what it was.

"I use a pole and when I swing around the pole, I go in a clockwise direction holding on with my right hand. Last night I was swinging particularly fast and my momentum kind of got out of control and it seemed to really pull my shoulder. Now whenever I lift my arm above my head, it really hurts."

Jim picked up her arm and pushed on the structures of her shoulder, carefully palpating each area. He then brought her arm out to the side and internally and externally rotated it. Antonia grimaced slightly with the movements. He checked her pulse at her wrist while her arm was dependent at her side and when lifted above her head. He checked her sensation, her strength, and her reflexes, then gently set her arm back down at her side.

Jim pulled a rolling stool that was in the corner over to the bed and sat down so he was at the dancer's eye level to discuss his findings.

"Well, I think you have a muscle strain," he said. "I don't think there is anything broken and I don't think you have a rotator cuff tear, although sometimes that is very hard to tell. The most important thing your shoulder needs right now is rest. You shouldn't use it very much for a week or two. It needs time to heal. If you go back and do what you have been doing, you run the risk of developing an overuse injury, and that can become chronic and can really take a long time to heal."

"Will I be able to work?" Antonia said.

"Well, you can't swing on the pole anymore, at least not clockwise. How are you at going the other direction?" Jim asked with a smile.

His smile was returned. "I'm not as good, not as smooth. I'm right-handed."

"The best strippers and the best doctors are ambidextrous you know," Jim said, smiling again.

Jim spent the next few minutes explaining the mechanics of muscle strains and the importance of rest, ice, and anti-inflammatories. He explained that if it wasn't better after a couple of weeks with that, then it might be time for an MRI to look more thoroughly at the internal components of her shoulder. Antonia relaxed and took it all in.

She listened intently, occasionally asking a question. For those few moments, a connection between them developed. Antonia clearly enjoyed the attention of an educated, intelligent man. She apparently didn't run into those often in her line of work or at least didn't see that side of them. Jim remained awestruck by her beauty. He was surprised at his feelings because admittedly he normally looked down on people like her. But she didn't have that hard worn-out look of most of the strippers he had met. She didn't have that unmistakable "rode hard and put away wet" vibe. Antonia seemed so innocent, almost angelic. But there was no mistaking what she was. Maybe she was just doing it to put herself through college. Maybe she could dance before the slobbering masses and yet remain unstained. Jim's mind bumped up against all of his preconceived notions, his conservative upbringing, his puritanical self-righteousness. Yet who should be judged more harshly here: the college girl using her God-given gifts to make a few bucks to pay tuition, or the doctor, who was bound by the moral code of his profession to not take advantage of his position, who found himself struggling to stifle his baser instincts.

This issue was of course an epidemic in medicine and throughout the modern workplace, although truth be told it was really an enormous part of the human condition, or for that matter the animal condition, and had been since the very evolution of sexual reproduction. The recent explosion of this issue in the media was really only the most current examples shining greater light on the interactions between people in general with regard to sex. It wasn't just in the workplace and it wasn't just between men and women. It extended throughout society and across ages and genders and sexual orientation. The bigger picture seemed to involve the interaction of those with authority or power and those who were subject in one way or another to that authority or power. In whatever its various forms were, people had been abusing their power over others for their own sexual gratification since the beginning of time.

Jim had seen this among physicians, nurses, and others working in the hospital. He had seen it go both ways with patients. He had seen physicians, nurses, and others accused of inappropriate behavior with patients. Certainly, there were the well-documented, horrifying cases where a trusted physician was a serial abuser of unwitting patients in his care.

However, in the ER, Jim had been more appalled at the

outrageous sexual things that he had heard patients say or do, directed toward nurses or other staff. Usually the staff were young attractive women and the perpetrators were male and often intoxicated or under the influence of drugs. The fact the perpetrators were patients and were intoxicated somehow turned the power aspect on its head and somehow rationalized and excused their behavior.

Jim was a handsome man and had endured many comments and advances from patients. Generally, these were from little old ladies who were effusive in their admiration for the "handsome young doctor." Only occasionally did these interactions become uncomfortable or seemingly cross a line. Jim typically laughed these things off, recognizing they were harmless. But when the dynamics of the interactions change, they still presented a minefield that had to be carefully traversed.

Jim's brief thoughts about Antonia were, for better or worse, the natural consequence of biology. Antonia was a beautiful young woman and Jim was a handsome young man. She had come tonight for his help and advice, and he had an obligation to interact with her, examine her, and treat her. He knew his position and his responsibility to her and to all of his patients and also to his coworkers. Fortunately, he had a strong sense of right and wrong, and he knew where the line was and carefully guarded himself for fear of ever crossing it. In the words of the poet Emily Dickinson, "Behavior is what a man does, not what he thinks, feels or believes." Jim didn't know if he agreed with that completely, but he certainly understood the sentiment. Unfortunately, you didn't have to look far in modern society to find many examples of those who blurred the lines and behaved badly.

Jim wondered at the contrast between Antonia and

Violet. They were both women. Both had essentially the identical genetic blueprint, the same female parts. They both had pleasing personalities. Yet one repulsed while the other enticed. One evoked sympathy and revulsion, the other desire and lust. The only real difference was packaging.

As Jim completed his discussion with Antonia, he stood up to leave. She stood also and reached out her hand to take his.

"Thank you, doctor," she said looking intently into his eyes with a pleasant smile.

Jim left the room to complete the chart and then moved on to the next case.

CHAPTER TEN

Of RFBs

J im returned to the nurses' station to complete Antonia's discharge instructions and then prepared to see the next patient in line. This was Mary, whose chief complaint was "rectal foreign body" or RFB. Jim read over the notes briefly trying to remember who she was and why he should know her. She had been transported by ambulance from the state hospital. The state hospital was a huge inpatient psychiatric facility that had been in use for over a hundred years. In its prime it housed over 2,000 patients with various and sundry psychiatric disorders. Many were lifers who, once they were admitted, never left the confines of the hospital until they died. Even then they didn't really leave as those whose bodies were not claimed by relatives, which was most of them, were buried in a cemetery on the hospital grounds.

Over the years, changes in psychiatric philosophy, public perception, and the development of better drugs had led to the mentally ill becoming more integrated into society. Most patients were managed in large mental health programs that monitored the patients, managed their medications, and brought them in for therapy sessions. When an individual patient became acutely psychotic or suicidal, they were generally brought to the nation's ERs where they were evaluated and if deemed a "danger to themselves or others" or "gravely disabled" they were again admitted to an acute psychiatric bed. This could be done voluntarily for those who were with-it enough to know they needed help and could express a desire to cooperate and be treated. Or they could be involuntarily held against their will by state mental health professionals who could take away their rights and could order them detained. The detention would then go before a judge who would either uphold it or release the patient. It was a difficult mixture of medicine and law, and surprisingly hard to accomplish.

Over the years Jim had seen many people who in his opinion were floridly psychotic and completely unable to make rational decisions, but who were not detained and were simply released back into the public despite the best efforts of the emergency physicians and mental health professionals who evaluated them in the ER.

Facilities like the state hospital still functioned but on a much smaller scale, and usually were reserved for the sickest patients who were completely unmanageable as outpatients or were simply in and out of ERs and hospitals so much that it was safer to keep them in a long-term facility. There were very few lifers anymore as even those at the state hospital were usually only kept there for a few weeks or months. The population at the state hospital was now down to just over 400 patients. That is still a large and busy facility, and because the patients didn't stay as long, they were constantly turning over with new admissions and discharges. The sickest were in the locked wards or units, but those who were less dangerous or less likely to try to escape were gradually integrated into the population on the open units.

Of course, the mental health system throughout the country was chronically overburdened and underfunded. Patients with chronic mental health issues often lead very disorganized lives. They almost never had real incomes or insurance. Most were on some sort of social assistance. They invariably had substance abuse issues, and with the closure of beds in long-term institutions many were homeless. Mary was one of the lucky ones as she had been an inpatient at the state hospital for the last three months.

Jim recognized her as soon as he walked into the room. Mary sat upright on the bed in a hospital gown and with a sheet covering her from her abdomen down. She was a plump and jovial thirty-year-old woman with short dark hair that stuck out of her head at all angles.

She smiled and laughed. "Hello Dr. McCray, it's nice to see you again. I didn't know you worked here."

"Hello Mary, it's nice to see you also. How have you been?" Jim smiled back, resigned to his fate.

He had seen Mary on several occasions at the University Hospital. She was famous there for swallowing all sorts of indigestible objects and stuffing them into every orifice that she could reach. Jim went to the side of the bed and lifted the sheet off of her abdomen.

"How are you healing up?" he said.

Mary's protuberant abdomen was crisscrossed with multiple long surgical scars. For the most part they were well healed, which was good because Mary had a tendency to pick at her incisions and often had to have her hands restrained for the first couple of weeks after surgery.

"I healed up great and I haven't eaten anything bad for months now," Mary said proudly. She was as genuinely proud of this accomplishment as a normal person might have been for having graduated with honors or having completed their first marathon.

Mary's x-rays were also famous at the U for the number and variety of objects that she had swallowed. Jim remembered a particular flat plate of her abdomen that revealed three pens, sixteen bobby pins, an open safety pin, and a child's pair of scissors. These were sprinkled liberally along the length of her small intestine. As they were well beyond the reach of an endoscope, she had to go to the OR to be opened up where they could be retrieved. As it was, the surgeon was only able to remove the pens and scissors, which wouldn't pass. The bobby pins and even the open safety pin could not be retrieved but she was monitored with repeat x-rays for a few days and eventually everything made it through. The biggest surprise at the time of surgery was the retrieval of two hotel size bottles of shampoo that were not visible on the x-rays due to their lack of radiopaque metal. This was just one of many such surgeries that dated back to Mary's childhood when she first began eating inedible items.

It was true that more recently Mary hadn't been swallowing dangerous things as often. She had a pretty rocky course after her last surgery, so she had apparently changed her tactics. The last time Jim had seen her at the U she had presented with a pair of audio headphones in her vagina. They were the older style small over the ear type with an adjustable metal band between the ear pieces. Jim remembered the experience with a shudder.

Mary had an interesting combination of mental illnesses. She seemed to suffer with pica, an unusual appetite for non-nutritive objects, as well as Munchausen syndrome, a pathological predisposition to seek medical treatment and interaction with the health care system by inducing or faking symptoms of illness even to the potential detriment of one's health. Most often she just seemed bored. She wasn't particularly bright and had little of interest in her life. She had been abused as a child and had been in and out of group homes, psych wards, and the state hospital throughout her life. She was never unpleasant and was often jovial. She apparently derived some real enjoyment out of going to the ER and challenging the physicians with her shenanigans.

When she put the headphones in her vagina she bent them over on themselves in such a way that the metal headband acted like a spring and she was able to slide the entire unit inside but once it passed through her introitus and she let it go, the spring action of the bent metal lodged it tightly against the walls of her vagina. Nothing was visible from the outside, but there was no way to insert a speculum to see inside. Jim had to be creative to get the headphones out. He had her up in the stirrups in the lithotomy position, and then he had to slide both of his index fingers into her vagina one on each side. Mary never let on about what she had done or how she had done it. That was part of the game, the part that the unwilling participant, the doctor, had to figure out. All Jim knew was that she had headphones in her vagina. He had no idea how they were in there or how big they were. He also didn't know if there were any sharp edges that he would potentially cut himself on or if he moved it the wrong way would injure Mary. He couldn't use instruments to remove them because he couldn't see them. He needed to blindly do it by feel.

It was a very unpleasant, intimate few minutes for Jim. The nurse had stood next to Mary unable to really help and unwilling to sympathize with her. But Mary didn't care, because this was her opportunity to perform, in her bizarre way. She lay there with her legs up and open. She kept her head propped up on several pillows so she could watch Jim as he struggled to deliver the headphones. She coached and cajoled and cracked jokes as the procedure unfolded.

Jim remembered feeling his way around inside of her with his index fingers. It was an uncomfortable position to be in with his hands just inches apart and his broad shoulders squeezed between Mary's knees. Finally he was able to feel in the deep recesses of Mary's pelvis how the metal dug into the folds and side walls of her vagina, and he was able to squeeze the entire piece together as one unit between his two fingers thereby relieving the spring loaded pressure and slowly extracting the headphones through her vaginal opening.

Once they were out, Mary clapped and cheered loudly and congratulated Jim on his expertise and gentleness. For a second, Jim felt a swell of pride and relief. He briefly appreciated the accolades of his patient, but then he remembered that she was crazy, and the entire procedure, the whole production, was totally unnecessary. It was entirely self-inflicted in some strange attention-seeking scheme, acted out by a very lonely, sad, and damaged woman. Mary wasn't bright but she wasn't developmentally delayed either. She knew exactly what she was doing, and she did it all with deliberate intent. The entire experience played into her twisted notion of odd secondary gain. This was the payoff for her. This was her ticket out of the state hospital for a few hours. She got to ride in an ambulance and be the center of attention for the paramedics, nurses, and doctors for a little while. It didn't matter that for the most part they either loathed or pitied her. She was the star of her very own medical drama.

Tonight, was a similar such episode except this time the foreign body was in her rectum. This was apparently new territory for Mary.

"All right Mary, what have you done this time?" Jim said.

"I put broken glass in my butt," replied Mary, as she smiled with a look of satisfaction.

"Where did you get the glass?" Jim said.

"I snuck it back to my room from the cafeteria after lunch," Mary said.

"And then what?" Jim said.

"Then I smashed it in my pillow case and shoved the pieces up my butt."

"Mary, why do you do this kind of stuff?" Jim said, shaking his head.

"You know, I just get bored," Mary said, seemingly equally baffled by her own behavior.

"How much did you put in there?" Jim asked.

"I don't know, most of it. You know it was one of those regular cafeteria type glasses," Mary said.

"How big were the pieces?"

"I don't know, about like that I guess," Mary said, holding her thumb and index finger up about two inches apart.

"Didn't that hurt?" Jim said, genuinely interested in what kind of discomfort Mary was willing to endure in order to relieve her boredom for a few hours.

"I don't know. It wasn't too bad," Mary shrugged.

"You do like to make things interesting for me don't you, Mary?" Jim smiled.

It was hard to be angry with Mary. She was an enormous unnecessary drain on the medical system. All of her hospitalizations, operations, ER visits, and psychiatric care had undoubtedly cost the taxpayers many hundreds of thousands of dollars over the years. But she was pleasant and childlike. Which was more than Jim could say for many severely mentally ill patients who could sometimes be quite nasty.

"Well, let's get an x-ray to see what's going on in there, OK?" Jim said as he entered the order on the computer and left the room.

JIM WENT BACK to the nurses' station once again. The electronic track board showing the waiting room revealed that it had filled up once more. He scrolled through the triage notes quickly to see what there was, and to get labs or imaging tests ordered based on what he saw and what he expected they would need. This was another efficiency; to quickly scan a patient's chart to check for their "chief complaint" and review their age and vital signs. Based on these few bits of information Jim could determine what he would likely need to order, and that way the nurses could get started and get those orders underway. This allowed Jim to see other patients or circle back on the ones he had already seen whose results were back. He didn't always do this, and sometimes he was misled and would find out when he actually spoke to the patient and examined them that their problem was totally different from what the triage notes suggested. This occasionally led to the ordering of incorrect or unnecessary tests. Or in some cases once he saw them and had the full story, he would have to add additional tests. However, in general it was a good practice when it was busy in order to speed up the flow of patients, which made the patients happy, the nurses happy, and Jim happy.

Most of the new patients who had arrived were fairly simple "fast track" stuff. These were cases that required only a very focused history and physical examination. At the U they would have been triaged to the fast-track or urgent-care area of the emergency department. In many places these cases were managed by physician's assistants or nurse practitioners. However, one of the reasons that Jim liked working at Libertyville was that he got to see these cases. They were quick and fun and required limited thinking. These low-acuity types of cases included simple lacerations, sprains, and other uncomplicated injuries. The patients were usually younger and healthier. They were sometimes referred to as the "walking wounded" and they provided a nice break from the complex, chronically ill patients with a million problems, who were on a million meds, who filled up so many ER beds around the country.

Jim actually imagined that at some time in the future he would like to wind down his career by working in an urgent care area where the pace was fast but the mental and emotional stress was remarkably less. The first three charts were a finger laceration, a child with a cough but no fever and an eye injury that sounded like it was probably a corneal abrasion. The fourth one was a forty-eight-year-old man named Malcolm Johnson. The chief complaint simply read "suicidal." This patient was in the quiet room. This room and the gyn room where Mary resided currently and where Melanie had been earlier were the only rooms that actually had walls and a door. Now that Melanie's exam was complete, she had been moved to another area to make room for Mary. The other so-called rooms were actually just one large room divided by a series of curtains. Jim quickly saw each of these cases in succession. He injected the finger wound with local anesthetic and then Marcie took over and began irrigating and cleaning it to prepare for sutures. He saw the coughing child who had a cold but otherwise looked great and nontoxic. "Toxic" was a term used for a kid who looked seriously ill.

Because children in the first few years of life get sick every few months with a variety of upper respiratory infections and viruses, the real key to treating them was to be able to recognize those who were sick (toxic) versus those who just had another typical childhood illness. Jim found pediatrics to be challenging because it was easy to become lulled by seeing child after child after child with the same symptoms and presentation. Almost all of these children simply had viral infections that would run their course in a week or so. In the constant parade of "same old, same old," the problem was inadvertently overlooking and failing to recognize a child who was becoming seriously ill with sepsis (an overwhelming and potentially deadly bacterial infection), pneumonia, meningitis, or some other significant illness.

Pediatricians made their living in the first few years of a child's life. Most pediatric cases in the ER were infectious disease cases. Most were simple. The advent of immunization programs had dramatically reduced the incidence of many serious infections that in the past had claimed the lives of so many children and had caused parents to live in constant fear. Nowadays, really sick kids were rare and sometimes difficult to sort out from the masses of children whose brand-new immune systems were simply experiencing the usual childhood infections that had rotated through the population for millennia, but were of course new and novel to the individual. It took a few years to encounter all of those infections and for the inexperienced immune system to ramp up and produce antibodies to fight them off.

The immune system was just one of so many remarkable things about the human body that allowed it to repair itself and to correct problems when they were encountered. Unlike man-made machinery, the remarkable ability of the body to heal itself without any outside help had sustained the species. However, in the last couple of hundred years the explosion in knowledge of disease processes and the advent of sanitation, good nutrition, vaccinations, and modern medicines to help bolster the body's own innate regenerative capacity had allowed the human species to dramatically enlarge and expand.

Naturally this was a good thing, but it was also evident that in some cases the pendulum had swung too far. Jim spent much of his time during his medicine and critical-care rotations keeping people alive who frankly had no business still being alive. In seemingly harsh terms they had outlived their usefulness and even their ability to understand or appreciate their surroundings. Everyone in health care understood this was a problem. Everyone knew that it was a colossal waste of money and time and resources. But no one seemed to have the wherewithal to simply stop treating these patients and let nature take its course. It seemed that no one on any level was willing to just say no and to say that there is simply no point in keeping this person alive, let them go. Politicians wouldn't say it because no one could be elected on such a platform, and no one could stay in office with such a stance.

On an individual basis, doctors often tried to reason with patients' families and explain the futility of their efforts, but usually those conversations only took place several days and tens of thousands of dollars into a patient's care. Gradually over time the cost of providing health care to an aging and/or incapacitated population had continued to grow and expand until it was consuming all of the resources of the country, like a spreading cancer. This cancer, seemingly unstoppable in its progression, had now weakened the patient irreparably. Naturally, as the population ages and as the birth rate declines, there are more people to care for with fewer people to do the caring and fewer people to generate the income to pay the bill. Therefore, unless something were to change dramatically it appears that this cancer will continue to gradually strangle and bankrupt the country. Of course, this is not just happening in this country, it is happening everywhere in the developed world, and as the rest of the undeveloped world catches up, it will happen there also.

It has been said that the worth of a human life directly correlates with the GDP of the country. Because nobody wants to go down individually, we will all go down collectively. We will spend and spend and spend fighting to keep people alive right up until their final breath rather than allowing them to die with dignity. This approach has led to a revolving door of medicine in the emergency department where patients are repeatedly sent in by ambulance from nursing homes with recurring infections and other issues. When they arrive at the hospital they are worked-up with expensive tests, treated with expensive medicines, and admitted for a few days to an expensive hospital bed. Then they are discharged back to their nursing facility only to repeat the process a few weeks later. This process repeats over and over again and again until finally at some stage they ultimately can't be treated anymore and they die. The idea of hospice care and the use of "do not resuscitate orders" and POLST forms (Physician Orders for Life-Sustaining Treatment) have helped with some of this, but still far too many patients get too many expensive and ultimately unnecessary treatments, which effectively only briefly prolong their lives and postpone their inevitable deaths.

This is a problem for the aging population, but in some respects it seems even more absurd when it comes to babies. This is where the value placed on a single life correlating to GDP of the nation seems most extreme. A baby born prematurely at twenty-two or twenty-three weeks has a very slim chance of surviving even with heroic and incredibly intensive and expensive medical interventions, and if that baby does survive it will invariably be with severe limitations often requiring lifelong care. It is highly unlikely that such a child will ever be a contributing member of society or ever pay taxes or help build the future of the society. Yet in children's hospitals everywhere there are babies like this on whom we spend millions of dollars to treat and try to save. Oddly, and in stark contrast to this, however, very similar babies in terms of gestational age, are routinely aborted and discarded. It's certainly true that most abortions occur earlier in pregnancy, but it is possible in some states to routinely have an abortion up to twenty-four weeks. What really is the difference between the baby with a team of medical experts in an expensive neonatal intensive care unit and the one unceremoniously pulled from a uterus and dumped in a medical wastebasket?

Twenty-four weeks is generally regarded as an age of viability. In other words, a premature baby at twenty-four weeks can, with intensive medical care and management, more than likely survive. This will often mean months in a neonatal ICU and the expense of hundreds of thousands of dollars, if not millions of dollars. Medical science continues to push the envelope, and now you hear about babies even younger surviving. However, the younger the baby, the higher the likelihood of death or severe limitations. The difference is that somebody apparently wanted that baby. Those parents are unlikely to be able to afford to pay for the baby's resuscitation and subsequent NICU care, but they want it. The ones in the trash apparently nobody wanted. Very similar, but vastly different. In the undeveloped world, in a country with a low GDP, a baby born prematurely will survive on its own with the most basic care, or it won't. It's that simple. Simple economics.

Truly sick children in the ED are relatively rare these days, but routinely sick children are as common as they always have been. Today's helicopter parents who only have one or two children simply don't have the experience with a large enough sample size to realize just how common childhood illnesses really are. Therefore, they take every sniffle to the doctor.

———————•———————

JIM DIDN'T MIND this. For the most part these were easy cases and an opportunity to inform and educate. However, with every kid he saw there was always a morsel of doubt, of concern, a question. Could that have been an early meningitis that now just looked like a sore throat but in twelve hours would be deadly. This was what made medicine and particularly pediatrics a crapshoot. There was simply no way to not miss some bad cases or cases that looked good now but would soon go bad. That was the natural progression of disease. That was the whole movie, whereas during the visit you were only given a snapshot and you had to extrapolate the movie's ending from it.

Jim wasn't concerned about the burden of people seeking care for themselves or their families, which was why there was a medical system after all. But the unsustainable portion was the inordinate amount of testing and the costs involved in order to avoid a missed diagnosis when missed diagnoses were an indisputable actuarial fact. They were going to happen. It was the "sand dollar phenomenon." It was like the man who was questioned why he was throwing the dying sand dollars from the beach back into the ocean when there were millions more on the shore and therefore it didn't matter. Looking down at the one in his hand just before he threw it back, the man said, "It matters to this one."

Jim and the thousands of doctors across the country just like him were there trying to throw the sand dollars back in the ocean one at a time because it mattered to "this one and this one's family." The unanswered question on a societal level, however, was how much did the man on the shore cost and what else was he neglecting while he was busy throwing individual sand dollars?

JIM NEXT SAW the corneal abrasion patient. This was a man in his thirties who had been doing yard work earlier in the day and was clearing brush when he was poked in the eye. He didn't think much of it at first but now several hours later he was in excruciating pain. His eye was tearing and he could neither keep it open nor tolerate bright light. These were easy and very satisfying cases. Often the patients had no idea why they had so much pain. Jim entered the room and took a brief history from the patient and then instilled a drop of a local anesthetic into the patient's affected eye. Within ten seconds his cornea was numb and his pain, which moments before had been unbearable, was now completely resolved. These patients were always so grateful. Jim next placed a drop of fluorescein in the eye. This was a yellow/orange dye that lit up the area of injury when examined using a cobalt blue-colored light. Jim had the patient sit down opposite him on a stool with the slit lamp between them. The slit lamp allowed Jim to magnify the eye and examine it closely. He confirmed the presence of a linear scratch directly across the patient's cornea (the transparent and convex tissue that covers the iris or colored part of the eye). He explained to the patient the source of his pain and outlined a treatment plan that included resting the eye, using a cold compress, pain medications, and some antibiotic drops to protect the irritated area from the invasion of bacteria. He also remarked on what an amazing structure the cornea was due to its ability to rapidly heal. The patient was discharged home, very pleased to be out of pain and able to see properly again. The child with the cough was also discharged with his parents, and Jim quickly sutured the finger and that patient was also sent on her way.

CHAPTER ELEVEN

Suicide Is Not the Answer

Jim checked the computer and found that no new patients had signed in. It was now after 1 a.m. and a welcome lull in the action had occurred. Mary was back from x-ray. But before he looked at the films or saw her again, he wanted to see the suicidal patient who had now been waiting well over an hour. Mary could wait a little while as this was like a field trip for her; she was delighted to be out of the state hospital and in a new environment with new people to interact with.

Jim reviewed the chart and entered the room where he found Malcolm Johnson seated on the bed. He was sitting quietly with his feet on the floor, leaning forward with his hands on the edge of the bed. He was thin, but not overly so. Although not particularly muscular, he appeared wiry and fit. He had a ruddy complexion and short dark hair with flecks of gray. He had a dense beard of perhaps a day's worth of stubble. He looked like one of those men whose facial hair was so thick and coarse that he could use a shave about every six hours. He was wearing neat jeans and a long sleeve plaid shirt that was tucked in. The sleeves were rolled up to the elbows revealing powerful forearms covered with thick dark hair all the way onto the backs of his well-manicured hands.

On the whole he was not particularly remarkable, except for his expression. He looked distraught. His tight face was filled with worry and angst. His eyes were dark with a hint of blue or green, it was difficult to tell because his thick, dark brow kept them in constant shadow. Around his eyes there was faint redness and puffiness suggesting this man had been crying.

"Hello, Mr. Johnson," Jim said. "I'm Dr. McCray. What brings you in tonight?"

"I need to kill myself," came the reply as Mr. Johnson looked up and directly into Jim's face, held his gaze for a moment and then returned to staring at the floor.

This was mildly unnerving to Jim. Of course, he knew from the triage note that Malcolm Johnson was suicidal, but it was unusual for patients to admit it outright as their opening statement. Most suicidal patients were not in the ER because they wanted to be. Often, they were brought in against their will by the police who had been notified by a friend or family member. These individuals may have been involved in a conversation with someone on the phone or over the internet, and while expressing their frustration with their life, family, job, relationship, or whatever else was their most potent and immediate trouble, had made some statement indicating suicidal intent. Often this was only in passing and was primarily intended to alarm or irritate the person with whom they were conversing.

However, if it was taken seriously, then the police were called and before long the individual who made the statement and may have already forgotten it, received a knock on the door or their door was kicked in by the police. The police are not counselors and they only have one objective, which is to resolve their responsibility for this person as quickly as possible. This is as it should be. They may assess the situation but no matter what the individual's excuse or explanation is, as far as the police are concerned, they are going to the hospital to get checked out. This tended to happen late at night and often involved an already irritable, depressed, and often intoxicated individual being hauled from their home or apartment. Frequently this unpleasant interaction between the individual and the police was observed by lots of curious neighbors and onlookers' wondering what was going on. There was often a lot of drama that had transpired before the person ever arrived in the ER.

Once in the ER, they were typically herded into a psychiatric holding room, which is bereft of any furniture, electrical outlets, or anything exposed from the ceiling that would be suitable for hanging oneself from. There may be a bed attached to the floor without sheets but with strong anchors at its base if restraints are needed. There is usually a closed-circuit TV system that constantly records the goings-on in the room, and this is relayed to the nurses' station.

That is what the psych rooms are like in most large ERs. But at Libertyville there simply were not enough beds or enough rooms to reserve one exclusively for psychiatric emergencies. The room Malcolm was in was essentially like every other room in the ER, and therefore it was filled with equipment that could be used to harm oneself if one were so inclined. Luckily the whole place was so small that it was fairly easy for Jim and the nurses to keep an eye on everybody at the same time.

JIM RECALLED THAT on one particularly busy night at the university hospital, his first patient had been an intoxicated, suicidal Native American gentleman who had been placed in one of the orthopedic rooms because all of the psych rooms were full. As this particular patient seemed too drunk or sedated with alcohol to cause much of a problem, the nursing staff had simply undressed him, placed him in the usual paper scrubs reserved for psych patients, and laid him on a gurney with the rails up to keep him from falling out of bed. He was then left to sober up for a while as he waited for the doctor. There was no closed-circuit TV in that room to keep an eye on him.

Jim had arrived for the night shift and went into the room to see this man, his first patient of the shift. When he entered the room, he found him sprawled out on the floor. His face was swollen and purple, and he had an Ace wrap that he had taken from a drawer tied tightly around his neck and then onto a cupboard handle on the upper cabinets. He was on the floor slumped against the lower cabinets with the elastic bandage stretched to maximum.

Jim remembered yelling for help and being aided by the nurse who had put the patient in the bed a few minutes earlier. Jim was able to remove the Ace wrap and lowered the man fully to the ground. He began breathing spontaneously, and within a few minutes after all of the excitement had died down, his color returned to normal and he was able to groggily get up and climb back onto the bed with its rails still up. This time however, all of his limbs were restrained to the bed with leather restraints applied by the somewhat embarrassed security guards and nursing staff. By the time he was discharged the following morning, the patient was sober and eating breakfast. He was no longer suicidal, or "drunkicidal" as this is affectionately referred to in the ER, and he had no recollection that he ever had been, or that he had almost been successful in killing himself in the ER the night before. If he had chosen to use the non-stretch bandages that were next to the elastic wraps in the drawer, he would likely have been successful. It is surprising how quickly one dies when the blood flow to the brain is cut off.

------------•------------

MALCOLM WAS NEITHER drunk nor was he there against his will. He was the sober, voluntary, suicidal type. He came to the ER because he knew he very much wanted to kill himself, but he wanted to explore his other options as well. Suicidal patients were a very challenging group. It seemed to Jim that every girl between the ages of thirteen and eighteen had tried to kill themselves at least once. Their preferred method was usually overdose, and they usually had second thoughts almost immediately after swallowing a handful of pills. Therefore, they typically showed up in the ER within an hour or two of the ingestion. The drug of choice on which to overdose was usually based on availability and proximity, which most often meant ibuprofen or Tylenol. These tended not to be too dangerous, although Tylenol had the potential for toxicity to the liver if taken in large enough doses. However, it could be easily measured in the blood to determine the potential for toxicity and treated if necessary. The damage to the liver from Tylenol could be deadly, but this took days to occur and most patients lost their resolve before that and told someone about their overdose.

Antidepressant pills, which many of those who considered overdosing were already taking to treat their depression, were also a favorite. Fortunately, most of the SSRI class of antidepressants, which make up the bulk of prescribed antidepressants, were also relatively safe in overdose. Many overdose patients were evaluated and their care consisted of simple monitoring and treatment with an oral dose of activated charcoal with sorbitol in an attempt bind the medicine in the gut and then speed up its expulsion in the stool. In the past, gastric lavage had often been used to "pump the stomach." However, this had never been particularly effective and it was exceedingly unpleasant for both the patient and the nursing staff. Also, it was potentially dangerous by leading to aspiration of vomit and lavage fluid into the lungs. It was still occasionally used, primarily it seemed, as a punitive measure under the guise of therapy. The sheer misery of the experience did seem to have excellent results in preventing further overdose attempts, at least in the short term.

Young men were much more likely to succeed in their suicide attempts, mainly because they tended to use more lethal means. Often these patients were not even transported to the hospital as they were already dead when they were discovered. Two of the most lethal methods used were hanging and of course gunshot wounds. To kill oneself with a gun, one had to have access to one. Hanging, on the other hand, was particularly disturbing as it was so easy to do. Everyone had access to a rope or belt or electrical cord. Jim had seen a number of suicides by hanging over the last three years, and there were always so many unanswered questions.

Suicide by lethal and almost instantaneous means was such an impulsive act. Did this person really intend to complete the act? Placing any constricting band around the neck led to a rapid decrease in consciousness and not because of a lack of air. One could remain conscious for several minutes without air; just hold your breath. Instead it was the lack of arterial blood flow and thereby oxygen to the brain that induced unconsciousness almost immediately. When the distraught person placed a ligature around their neck, did they realize that the point of no return was literally only seconds away?

Many hangings occurred with the person's feet still on the ground or even with the person sitting or leaning and using only a portion of their body weight against the resistance of the rope. Almost all suicides committed in jail were the result of hanging. Additionally, on some occasions there was the question of whether the act was one of suicide or rather sexual gratification through autoerotic asphyxiation. Sometimes there were clues such as a suicide note, but often there was nothing. Nothing left except for an emotionally devastated family with a gaping hole in their life and a tragic series of unanswered and unanswerable questions.

THE SUICIDAL PATIENTS who were the most likely to carry out the act and to die were depressed older men. Often, they had nothing in their lives such as family or work to give it meaning, and many had chronic health problems. They also often had the knowledge and experience to choose a lethal method such as self-inflicted gunshot. Only a few weeks earlier Jim had seen a despondent seventy-eight-year-old widower who was slowly dying of metastatic prostate cancer, which had invaded his spine and left him with constant pain. He had placed a gun in his mouth and pulled the trigger. This was certainly a serious attempt, but the only gun he had was a .22 caliber pistol and it was loaded with a round that contained bird shot. When he arrived in the emergency department, he had a very sore mouth and was spitting blood. He was maintaining his own airway however and on x-ray and CT his palate was peppered with shot, but none had penetrated through the base of his skull and into his brain. There was little to do for him other than to let it heal up and focus on his depression. Now in addition to having an empty life and painful terminal cancer, he also had a very swollen, painful mouth and throat.

———•———

ALTHOUGH WOMEN, PARTICULARLY young women, tended to choose less lethal means, two recent patients that Jim had treated were young women who had chosen very lethal means and both had ultimately, unfortunately died. One had overdosed on a large number of tricyclic antide-pressant pills. These were older antidepressant medications that were rarely used for depression anymore, but were still prescribed for other conditions such as migraine preven-tion and to help with sleeping. Overdose on this class of medicine was treatable if recognized early. In this patient's case, she had delayed coming to the ED long enough that she died of a fatal cardiac arrhythmia despite aggressive resuscitation in the ED.

The second was even more disturbing as it was a twenty-nine-year-old woman who had not shown any signs of suicidality or depression. She was on the phone with her mother who was in a distant city. She described how she'd had a particularly bad day, and then expressed to her that, "Maybe I should just kill myself." She handed the phone to her roommate and left the room. The roommate and the patient's mother continued speaking on the phone, neither suspecting anything after this flippant remark. Within a minute, a gunshot rang out. The roommate ran to investi-gate and with the mother still on the phone found the young woman lying on her bed with a .38 in her hand and a hole above her right ear.

By the time she arrived in the emergency department she had been intubated by the paramedics. She had only agonal respirations and a Glasgow Coma Score of three. This is a score used for assessing brain function in trauma patients. It is based on three measurements of higher cortical brain function including motor function, or the ability to move, as well as speech and eye opening. A normal conscious and alert person is able to respond to commands to move, open their eyes, and speak. This results in a maximum score of fifteen. With absolutely no movement, speech, or eye opening of any kind despite even noxious, or painful, stimulation, a patient scores a three, the same score as a rock or a tree stump.

The CT scan of this woman's brain revealed a bihemispheric injury pattern. The bullet had fragmented and exploded into the right hemisphere with pieces of bullet and bone distributed throughout the right hemisphere of the brain and across the corpus callosum into the left hemisphere where it had stopped. There was no exit wound but a bihemispheric injury was, by definition, universally lethal. The remaining breaths, or agonal respirations, the patient took on her own were mediated at the base level of the brainstem. She had killed herself, but with the exception of her brain, her organs were in pristine condition and were ultimately harvested for transplant.

It has oft been said that "suicide is a permanent solution to a temporary problem." There was actually good data that when people used serious lethal means to attempt suicide and subsequently survived the attempt, they got a new lease on life and were often no longer plagued by suicidal thoughts.

THE MOST HORRIFIC suicide attempt Jim had helped to treat was a thirty-five-year-old man who had been crushed by a subway train as it pulled into the station. The man had apparently been standing patiently with dozens of others, but as the train approached he calmly climbed down off the platform and lay down face first on the tracks. The train was already slowing down as it approached the station and rather than running him over and instantly crushing him to death, his body became caught up in the train's undercarriage and he was dragged along the tracks for about two hundred feet. His head and chest were spared so he was actually alive and conscious under the train. It took almost an hour for paramedics and fire department personnel to extricate him.

When he arrived in the ER, his injuries were assessed. They were catastrophic. He had a series of large gaping ragged tears across the entire width of his abdomen. These were several inches deep and several inches wide, but owing to his obesity they had miraculously only lightly penetrated into his abdominal cavity. Each of these wounds and the remaining abdominal wall was caked in thick, black axle grease from the underside of the train. Below his abdomen the damage was more severe. As he lay on the tracks the train approached him from his left side and when it hit him his body was rolled from the prone position ninety degrees to his left. Then as the train slowed this forced the right side of his body to be abraded along the tracks. His right leg, from the hip to below the knee, had been completely ground away. All of the skin, fat, and muscle of the lateral hip, thigh, and knee were gone. The bones of the hip and knee and the entire length of the femur were partly and roughly abraded and exposed. Jim estimated that about 50 percent of the proximal leg was missing and left strewn in ragged, bloody fragments along the tracks. Although he had lost a lot blood from all of this open and missing tissue, the bleeding was fairly easy to control with compression dressings and as most of the major arteries run along the medial aspect of the thigh, he did not exsanguinate or bleed out.

Perhaps the least life threatening, and yet in Jim and his male colleagues' estimation the worst of this man's injuries, were those that had occurred to his genitalia. He had a complete degloving injury to his penis. This meant that in the similar fashion to the way a glove is removed from a hand, all of the skin of his penis had been circumferentially peeled away. His scrotum, although present and for the most part intact, was empty. His scrotum had been opened just below the base of his penis and his testicles had been unceremoniously yanked out along with their tethering spermatic cords. Almost comically, fifteen minutes after the ambulance arrived at the hospital with the patient, a second ambulance arrived and a paramedic rushed in with a bag of ice. Inside the bag wrapped in gauze were the missing testicles, which had been located by a firefighter next to the tracks. Needless to say, reimplantation was not an option.

This man ultimately survived his suicide attempt but he required dozens of painful, complicated reconstructive surgeries. He spent months in the hospital and in rehab facilities, and he cost the health care system close to a million dollars. After all of that, his injuries left him severely debilitated and with chronic, recurrent infections and intractable pain. If he didn't have a good reason to kill himself before he lay on the tracks, he certainly did now.

Although many suicide gestures, attempts, or even contemplations were nothing more than a passing phase or a cry for help, they also had created some of the most devastating injuries and the most devastated families that Jim had ever seen.

———•———

"WHAT MAKES YOU feel like you need to kill yourself?" Jim asked Malcolm, trying to sound genuinely empathetic.

"I can't go on like this anymore. I can't go on living a lie," Malcolm said, beginning to open up.

"What is the lie you are living?" asked Jim.

Malcolm looked up carefully at Jim and studied him. It was evident from his expression that he didn't really want to talk, and yet he had an overwhelming urge to do just that. He had kept his feelings suppressed for so long that he could no longer contain them. He felt that he would explode. He looked at Jim and wondered: Why this man, in this place? Is this the setting where I confess my greatest secrets, in the middle of the night in a tiny obscure emergency room to a man I have only known for sixty seconds?

"I am not a man." The words seemed wrenched from his throat and after speaking them, Malcolm turned away violently and tears were flung from his eyes and landed with a splash on the cold tile floor.

"Do you mean that figuratively or literally?" Jim asked.

Malcolm appeared defeated, but a tiny crack in the dam of his emotions had begun to open and leak. The leak was soon followed by a torrent, and as the pressure was relieved it became evident on his face.

"Ever since I was five years old, I have known that I was

a woman. At that time, I was a boy who knew inside I was really a girl. I have fought this knowledge for over forty years and I just can't do it anymore. I have done everything a good *man* is supposed to do. I played sports; I joined a fraternity in college, and majored in mechanical engineering. Did you know that mechanical engineering is one of the most male-dominated professions there is? I got married after college, and I have been married to the same woman for almost twenty-five years. We have two beautiful daughters who are in college now. I have been the perfect prototypical American man and the whole time I have been a woman. A woman trapped in a man's body."

Jim listened intently as Malcolm poured out his soul. He didn't want to interrupt him while his catharsis was underway. By this time, Jim had known lots of people who were gay or lesbian and he had treated many transgender patients who were in various stages of transformation both surgical and nonsurgical. Despite their relatively small numbers the LGBTQ community now seemed to be everywhere, all the time. Growing up, Jim had never really encountered people with gender-identity challenges. As he began to pursue his career in medicine however, he had begun to see many patients with so called alternative lifestyles and had come to a greater understanding of their unique view of the world and how the world, including the medical world, viewed them. Most of those patients were well into their journey and had dealt with the "coming out" about who they were to themselves and those in their sphere. But Jim had never before been present at the very moment of realization, of transformation, and of emergence into a new identity. Others he had known had made the change at some point in the past and now were resolute and only recognized themselves in their new role. Although most gender-identity patients reported they had always known what they believed was their true sexual identity, there had to be a moment when they first expressed it to their family, their friends, and the rest of the world. This was Malcolm's moment.

Jim looked his patient over. He was as identifiably male as anyone he had ever seen. He was tall with broad shoulders. He had a trim, muscular physique and a dark, heavily bearded complexion. There was nothing feminine about him. This would be a challenging transition.

"About a month ago I decided I couldn't take it anymore," Malcolm continued, feeling a little more comfortable bearing his soul to this stranger in a white lab coat, as the torrent of words and emotions began to pour through the recently opened flood gates of his mind.

"So, I went online and I found a support group for people just like me. I can't even describe how good it felt after all of these years to find I wasn't alone. I mean I had always known there were freaks out there who had sex changes and that kind of stuff. I mean I've watched Jerry Springer enough to know that. But I didn't see myself like that.

"I went to a couple of meetings and met people, local people, who were going through what I was going through. It was so liberating you wouldn't believe it." Malcolm's affect was elevating now. He became enraptured as he described his experience and joy.

"We call ourselves T-girls, you know for transgender. Tonight, there was a meeting at a hotel. It was in the ballroom. They chose a hotel two hours from town so we wouldn't be so self-conscious. There were 150 people there. It was magical. It was the first time in my life I have come completely out as a real woman. I wore full make-up and fishnets and stilettos and a mini skirt. Some of the other girls helped me get ready because I didn't even know how to put on makeup. They were so sweet to me, so caring." Malcolm was in a frenzy now as he recounted his experience and his mannerisms and voice for the first time began to feminize.

"It was the greatest experience of my life. I have never felt so energized, so alive."

He paused and his countenance fell.

"Well, that all sounds wonderful," Jim said, trying to be positive and keep Malcolm's confidence, while at the same time reading his change of demeanor. "But how did you go from this exhilarating life-changing experience to being here in the emergency room and being suicidal?"

Malcolm suddenly looked and sounded like an aging male engineer again.

"After I left all of my T-girlfriends at the convention, I came home and there were my wife and my daughter, the one that is on break from college right now, and everything just came crashing down. I hid all of my T-girl clothes and shoes and make-up. When I saw them I just felt such shame. I was overwhelmed"

"Did you tell them?" Jim asked.

"No! Absolutely not. How could I tell them! How could anyone possibly do that to their wife and to their daughter? Especially their daughter, she is only nineteen years old. Can you imagine? She is barely becoming a woman herself, trying to make sense of the real world and college life. How could I possibly drop something like that on her? The father, who she has always loved and admired for being so strong and so supportive and being this great masculine role model for her. The kind of man she wants to marry, she always says. What would I say to her? 'Oh, honey, by the way, I'm really a chick, do you mind if I borrow your mascara?' It's an impossible situation. I can't be who I really am, but I also can't go back to being who I was." Malcolm sighed, looking both defeated and exhausted.

"So, the solution is to kill yourself?" Jim said.

"It seems like the only way out and the only way to stop the anguish," Malcolm said.

"If you didn't tell your family what was going on, how did you end up here?" Jim asked.

"When I got home and saw them and everything hit me, I just started to cry. I was sobbing uncontrollably. I have never done that before. Never. Never in front of another person. They thought I was cracking up. They thought that the pressure at work had finally gotten to me. They were worried, so they brought me here for you to fix me," Malcolm said.

"Wow, that's a lot of pressure," Jim said with a smile, trying to relieve some of the tension.

"Do you have a plan to kill yourself?" Jim asked.

"Not yet, this has all been so sudden and there have been so many emotional ups and downs, I haven't had a chance to think it all through. I need some time to figure it out. I may be a woman, but I am also an engineer so I need to make some calculations, but you can be sure if and when I decide to do it, I will do it right," Malcolm said.

"OK, I can see that this is a pretty overwhelming situation," Jim said. "I can't really imagine what you are feeling right now, but I certainly understand the enormity of it. Suicide is definitely not the answer. There is a way out of this but sometimes the only way out is through. We can work on this together. I am going to ask one of our mental health specialists to come in and visit with you to see what we can do to help you out. OK?"

Malcolm nodded.

"I am going to have to talk to your wife and daughter; I understand they are in the waiting room, to let them know what is going on and what the plan is. How much can I tell them?"

"Well Doc, please don't tell them what a freak their husband and father is," Malcolm said. "You can just tell them that I had a nervous breakdown or something like that."

"Malcom, let's say you don't end up killing yourself and you are somehow able to tell your family what's going on," Jim said. "Now that you have come to this point in your life, what would you do going forward? Would you go the full distance and live your life as a woman?"

"I'm not really sure yet," Malcolm said. "I know I will lose my family and I will lose my job so I won't really have anything anyway. I will be a pathetic, middle-aged societal outcast. Without a job, I won't have any insurance, so I wouldn't be able to have a sex change, although I doubt that is covered anyway.

"You're the doctor; I should be asking you, what would be the steps to turn a manly hunk like me into some nubile young babe anyway?" Malcolm said, gesturing by opening his arms to show himself.

"Well the young part is a non-starter; we can't turn back the hands of time and the rest is definitely out of my area of expertise, but the patients I have seen who go through this transformation usually start with large doses of female hormones to begin to feminize and soften their masculine characteristics. Then you can have breast implants and if you are in for the full meal deal, I think they lop of your penis and fashion you a makeshift vagina," Jim said in an intentional unceremonious fashion.

"Wow, you make it sound so enticing," Malcolm said, smiling.

"Well, I think it's easier to go from male to female than female to male, at least from the surgical perspective," Jim said.

"Yeah, I have heard the 'addadicktomy' procedure is a tricky one," Malcolm said.

"In all seriousness Doc, just 'man to…man,' what do you think of me?" Malcolm said, with an earnest plaintiveness that Jim had not seen in him before.

"Well…I am not really sure," Jim said. "I like you and I sense that you have a good heart. I don't really fully understand the whole gender identity issue, but I don't know how anyone could unless they actually lived it. I feel sorry for you because of the weight of this on you. Aside from this issue you seem to have a great life, but this 'issue' is a rather enormous one. I do know one thing though, and that is, that 'it is always darkest before the dawn' and I believe you can get through this somehow and I know that suicide is not the answer."

"Thanks Doc," Malcolm said and reached out his hand to shake.

Jim took his outstretched hand, shook it, and stood to leave.

"I have a question for you Malcolm, and I hope this won't offend you, as I ask this with clinical interest. With your condition, with this sense of being a woman trapped in a man's body, where do your sexual desires lie? I mean you have been married to a woman for almost twenty-five years.

Does that make you a lesbian, or when you are a dressed up in your true identity as a T-girl, are you looking for a man?"

Malcolm smiled a wry smile. "I think I have to be careful here, because depending on my answer, I suspect your next question may be to ask me on a date."

Jim smiled. "Actually, that wasn't where I was going. I'm sorry to disappoint you."

"I know," Malcolm said. "But I couldn't resist. In all honesty Dr. McCray, for me this isn't about sex. I don't know where my desires are exactly. I have never been with a man and I have never cheated on my wife. For me, this is about me, and being who I really am, and as you can see that is still a work in progress."

"OK. Well sit tight here and I'll have the mental health specialist come see you, and I will talk with your wife and daughter," Jim said.

"Thanks Doc," Malcolm said as he lay back on the bed. "And thanks for not judging me."

"No problem," Jim said as he left the room.

Jim wasn't sure if that last statement was an affirmation or a request. He returned to the nurses' station and asked Ginger to call in the mental health specialist to help evaluate Malcolm.

Jim spent the next few minutes doing some charting so he wouldn't get too far behind. Then he looked at Mary's x-rays.

CHAPTER TWELVE

More on RFBs

A bdominal x-rays usually consist of at least three or four individual films. One, sometimes called the flat plate, or KUB for kidneys, ureter and bladder, involves shooting the abdomen from the diaphragm to the lower pelvis with the patient lying supine or on his or her back on the x-ray table. A second, nearly identically positioned film is then obtained, but in this case the patient is in an upright position allowing for liquids and gases to separate out vertically with gravity and delineate air-fluid levels in the bowel. A third requires patients to lie on their side. This is referred to as a decubitus film.

Finally, there is often a film that includes the chest and upper abdomen, particularly focusing on the area of the diaphragm in order to identify the presence of free air that accumulates in this area when there is a ruptured viscus. A ruptured viscus means that there is a hole somewhere in the nearly thirty-foot-long hollow tube that is the digestive tract, somewhere between the mouth and anus. Essentially all organisms with a digestive tract are doughnut shaped. In other words between the mouth and anus there is hole or pathway that while being surrounded by the body remains effectively outside of the body itself. Free air or air that escapes from a hole or leak in the tube remains trapped inside the abdomen or sometimes the chest if the hole is in the esophagus. The presence of air outside of the digestive tract is an ominous finding. The digestive tract is directly connected to the outside world at both ends and as such is full of nasty bacteria and other even less appealing substances. A leak somewhere allows that material to enter and contaminate the otherwise pristine and sterile environs of the chest, abdomen, or pelvis. Once a leak occurs, the body attempts to wall it off, but the bacteria that spill out continue to grow and they fester in this new habitat, ultimately resulting in the formation of an abscess or even gaining access to the blood stream where they can then move around the body.

Left untreated for very long, the growth of this material continues to worsen, often leading to sepsis, organ failure, and death. Antibiotics are frequently ineffective in this situation because they can only go where the blood stream can take them, and therefore, they cannot penetrate an abscess that is essentially a non-vascularized ball of pus. Typically, drainage of the abscess is the only effective treatment. This means the patient needs a surgical procedure to open them up and drain the pus pocket to the outside world. Sometimes these pus balls or abscesses are not in easy places to get to and it is difficult to reach them without damaging surrounding structures. Fortunately, techniques have been developed that allow the use of CT scans and ultrasound machines to carefully guide a catheter into the area and drain it percutaneously or in other words from the outside through the skin. This means using a needle to puncture the skin and then snaking a small flexible tube into the abscess site. Both open drainage and percutaneous drainage are complex, difficult, and delicate procedures. So basically, the best practice is to just keep everything flowing through the doughnut hole and not allow it to escape into the doughy part of the doughnut in the first place.

———•———

JIM REVIEWED ALL of Mary's x-rays, but he paid particular attention to her lower pelvis area where he anticipated that he would see the glass. Because these were sharp pieces of broken glass inside the tube, he was concerned that they could have cut through or perforated the wall of her rectum and allowed the contents to spill out. He thought this was unlikely however, because typically such an injury would be painful and Mary showed no evidence of any discomfort. In fact, she was exhibiting the opposite of discomfort.

Jim could see on the x-ray that in her pelvis there were several small pieces of radiopaque material with a greater density than the surrounding tissue. These appeared to be in her rectum mixed with stool and gas and framed by the ring of her pelvic bones. There was no evidence of free air, suggesting that the glass had not cut through the colon wall.

Now the question was how to get them out. It was possible that the pieces could pass through with her next bowel movement. However, there was a significant risk that depending on the size and sharpness of the shards they could slice up her anus as they passed out, so that did not seem to be a viable option. It looked like the only option would be to go in after them.

———•———

RECTAL FOREIGN BODIES (RFBs) were, as a general rule, a relatively infrequent occurrence in the ER, but when they did show up, they were always a source of levity. Not for the patients of course, but rather for the ER staff. Generally, those who presented with something stuck in their rectum were male and they were almost always the result of overly vivacious sexual activity gone awry. The most common RFBs were, of course, sex toys of various shapes and sizes. These always made for great x-rays as the metallic mechanical working parts of the device showed up with excellent clarity against the back drop of the radiographic abdomen. Sometimes the device would still be running, vibrating away. Depending on how long the patient postponed coming in, their vibrations and motions would sometime cause them to travel up the descending colon, make a ninety degree turn at the spleen and begin heading across the transverse colon toward the liver. If such an object had migrated beyond the reach of fingers or instruments in the ER, the patient had to be referred to surgery or GI where they could be anesthetized and then a long scope could be placed up into the colon and used to snare the object and retrieve it.

The fleshy tubular nature of the rectum and colon created a natural vacuum effect around large objects so it was often very difficult to extract them unless they could be grasped very tightly.

JIM REMEMBERED ONE particular patient, a gentleman who had lost a favorite device that was about eight inches long. It had a metal nipple on one end that allowed for the attachment of tubing in order to instill warm liquids. The tubing evidently had come off and the implement had slipped past the anal verge and was lost into the rectum. In order to retrieve it, Jim had to place the man in an unflattering position on a gyn bed with his legs up in the stirrups as female patients are positioned for pelvic exams. Jim then had the patient hold his own genitalia up out of the way. He could just barely feel the metal nipple between the tips of his two gloved index fingers when he inserted them as far as they could possibly go into the man's anus. While in this position he could feel the device, but he could not grasp it or hold it tightly enough between his finger tips to extract it.

In order to get a better grip while holding this position, he had a nurse assistant blindly place a long-handled pair of ringed forceps (the same kind he had used to remove Melanie's miscarriage) between his fingers and into the rectum. When he could feel the ring forceps in the correct position around the nipple, he had the nurse close them. He had to continue to hold the dildo nipple with his fingertips in order to keep it in position and to prevent any of the patient's rectal mucosa or lining from being pinched in the jaws of the forceps. The nurse, who of course could neither see nor feel what was going on inside, clamped the forceps tightly, locking them in place over the dildo nipple as well as the tip of Jim's right index finger. Using the forceps, the RFB and Jim's finger were then gently, but successfully, extracted from the man's rectum to his great relief. Jim had a sore finger for a couple of weeks, but fortunately his glove did not tear.

A torn glove or a slice through the skin of his finger while inserted into the toxic microbial soup of the human rectum was not a consequence that Jim relished. That would be a real concern when attempting to retrieve glass shards from Mary's behind. Jim would try to use forceps or other grasping instruments with Mary, but sometimes the only way to actually find an object was by feel.

Jim roughly calculated that there were about 5,000 emergency departments spread across the country, and that they all had at least a few patients every year having lost a dildo or some other commercially manufactured sex toy in their rectum. Retrieval of these lost objects cost anywhere from a few hundred dollars for the easy ones, up to several thousand for those requiring general anesthesia and surgical consultation. Therefore, Jim thought, a simple design tweak providing each of these devices with a cord or strap like the ones on cameras or umbrella handles, would allow people to pull their devices back out when they went too far. This simple addition could not only save the health care system tens of millions of dollars, but it could also save patients even more in terms of embarrassment and humiliation. Of course, that would be at the expense of the mirth of thousands of ER doctors and nurses and their ability to tell hilarious stories during the cocktail hour.

Since a great deal of the expense of retrieving lost sex toys fell on the taxpayer-supported health plans, Jim thought that the federal government should mandate the string. How was this any different from requiring seatbelts and airbags in cars, or warning labels on cigarette packages? Of course this mandate wouldn't help at all with all of the other noncommercially manufactured items such as fruits, vegetables, shaving cream bottles, shampoo bottles, candles, toilet brushes, and various other roughly penis-shaped objects that might be readily available in the heat of the moment that Jim and his colleagues had fished out of people. But at least it would be a start.

Jim could just imagine the advertising now: "The Dildo String—For the one that got away." It could be a huge business, both for new, improved devices and retrofitting existing ones. Jim considered it as a side business, but suspected that something so simple would likely be considered public domain.

———•———

AHH...THE RECTAL FOREIGN body, fun going in, and even more fun for the ER staff coming out. Patients with RFBs were generally male, but occasionally female. Otherwise they didn't seem to fit any specific demographic and often didn't look like the kind of people one would suspect to enjoy such a sexual predilection. Recently at the university hospital, Jim had cared for a fit middle-aged executive who presented having lost his "butt plug." Prior to that encounter Jim had not been familiar with such a device, but apparently they are popular with a certain portion of the population.

The butt plug that had gone missing was roughly four inches in diameter across its base and the best way Jim could describe its appearance was that it had the shape of a three-dimensional "ace of spades." The base was not intended to pass through the anal verge, just the big bulky top portion of the spade shape. In the center there was a large hole that allowed for the placement of a vibrator. This particular patient was a vigorous and frequent user of such devices and he had effectively stretched his anus and rectum to the point where he could easily accommodate such an oversized contraption. Unfortunately, on this particular occasion he had lost the entire device well up inside himself.

Due to embarrassment and with a surprising amount of ingenuity, he had tried some rather heroic measures to extract it himself before finally giving up and coming to the hospital. He had found an eight-inch-long galvanized lag screw in his garage and had managed to use a socket wrench through his anus to actually screw the lag screw deep into the hard rubber of the butt plug next to the vibrator. He had then tied a piece of cord around the lag screw and for several hours made numerous attempts to pull on it while bearing down in a squatting position in order to expel the whole thing. Unfortunately, these efforts were unsuccessful, so by the time he arrived in the ER his anus was a bloody, swollen mess with a large screw, like the kind you would use to bolt a deck to the side of your house, extruding a few inches from his back side.

When Jim entered the room, he didn't know what he was in for. The triage notes only said "groin pain" as the patient had been reluctant to detail to the triage nurse exactly what was going on. Jim entered the room with a female nurse in her twenties and a nineteen-year-old EMT student who was doing her first day of ER shadowing. The patient was of course mortified and Jim offered to send the student away, but by this time the patient had accepted the fact that any remaining shred of dignity he had was gone and he would simply have to endure whatever was necessary to get this thing out. Jim tried for a while to position the patient in such a way as to open his bony pelvis and coax the apparatus out using the screw and cord. Ultimately the screw pulled free from the rubber of the plug. The patient's anus was so patulous that Jim could place his entire hand in the patient's rectum and could get his fingers around the base of the plug. In this position he could feel the whirring motor of the vibrator against his palm. But try as they could with the patient bearing down, he simply couldn't break the seal of the rectum on the plug. Eventually, Jim gave up and called the general surgeon for consultation.

The surgeon was even more determined than Jim to get the plug out. He worked on the man in the ER for another hour before he finally threw in the towel and took him to the operating room where under general anesthesia he was finally able to extract the entire vibrating mess. The patient was admitted overnight to the hospital as the surgeon was concerned about a perforation or ischemic injury to the walls of the rectum from the device having been lodged so tightly against the fragile tissue and the heroic and somewhat barbaric efforts required to finally get it loose. However, an hour or two after the patient returned from the recovery room, he signed himself out of the hospital "against medical advice" when his wife arrived and absolutely blew a gasket, loudly berating him and threatening to divorce him in front of all of the nursing staff and other patients on the unit. To Jim's knowledge the man never returned or followed up. It was also unknown if the traumatized EMT student ever completed her training.

The classic rectal foreign body was usually a sexually motivated situation. In Mary's case of course it was different, she didn't do this for sexual purposes. For her it was a "get out of jail free" card. Also, she wasn't very selective, sometimes she ate inedible things, sometimes she put them in her vagina, and sometimes in her rectum. For her it was all about the attention. She had undergone several surgeries to remove intra-intestinal foreign bodies that had passed far enough into her gut that they could not be retrieved with an endoscope. She had found those experiences somewhat unpleasant so more recently she had been using the vaginal and rectal routes.

THERE WAS A whole other world of patients who swallowed foreign bodies. Jim had recently presented a case in grand rounds of a sixteen-year-old girl who had swallowed a Popsicle stick. She was a very typical-appearing teenage girl who presented one night with complaints of intermittent right lower-quadrant abdominal pain, but really no other significant symptoms. Her story and exam were very unimpressive. Appendicitis was considered as the pain was in the right lower quadrant, the area where appendicitis usually causes pain. Jim suspected this was unlikely, however, because the pain had been coming and going for weeks for no apparent reason and without other symptoms.

Appendicitis, although notoriously difficult to identify on the basis of a "typical presentation," usually presented with constant pain that gradually progressed over hours to, at most, a few days. This particular patient had recently gotten over a case of mono so Jim suspected that the pain could be due to mesenteric adenitis, which is a fairly benign condition of swollen intra-abdominal lymph nodes. Lymph nodes are part of the immune system and they become enlarged and sometimes painful when they are actively involved in fighting an infection. Although the most prominent nodes are in the throat, armpits, and groin, that is because they are closest to the surface and most readily identifiable there. In reality however, lymph nodes are actually found throughout the body and as such are distributed liberally throughout the abdomen. They can become enlarged with different infections including mono and can cause pain that mimics appendicitis. In fact, mesenteric adenitis is probably the most common cause of pain that is misdiagnosed as appendicitis. In the pre-CT scan days, a large proportion of appendixes that were removed were actually normal. In some studies, this was as high as 50 percent. The logic was that it was better to operate and remove a normal appendix than to leave it when it could potentially rupture and spill pus and infected material into the abdomen and cause peritonitis, a much more serious condition.

Other obvious concerns in a sixteen-year-old female were gynecologic issues. Ovarian cysts were a very common cause of lower abdominal pain and pelvic pain in females during the childbearing years. Ovarian torsion was even more serious. This occurred when the ovary became twisted on the stalk on which it was suspended effectively cutting off its own blood supply. Although rare, these needed to be diagnosed rapidly so that the ovary could be surgically de-torsed or untwisted before the organ died. Pregnancy-related problems, such as ectopic pregnancy and other gynecologic conditions such as infections in the cervix and fallopian tubes, usually sexually transmitted, also had to be ruled out.

This particular sixteen-year-old female of course reported that she was not sexually active so pregnancy and sexually transmitted infections were "impossible." However, the reliability of a teenager's responses to questions regarding sexual activity, particularly when the question is asked when a parent is present, is essentially zero. So, a pregnancy test always needed to be performed on any female with abdominal pain in the childbearing years. On a side note, Jim did once have a young female patient who, when asked whether or not she was sexually active, earnestly replied, "No, I pretty much just lie there."

This particular young woman who had presented with the intermittent right lower-quadrant pain gave no indication that she may have swallowed anything, she simply complained of unexplained pain. Jim ordered labs on her, including the standard complete blood count to look for evidence of an elevation of her white blood cell count. Although not always reliable, an elevated white count can indicate that the body's immune system is actively fighting an infection. Her white blood cell count was normal. Her urinalysis was negative for evidence of infection or blood, which argued against her pain being related to a urinary process such as a bladder infection or an upper urinary tract infection such as pyelonephritis or kidney infection. Also, the lack of blood in her urine argued against the presence of a kidney stone, which can present with intermittent abdominal pain. Her pregnancy test was negative, which essentially ruled out ectopic pregnancy.

At this point Jim remained most suspicious of a gynecologic process. Most likely this was an ovarian cyst or less likely an atypical presentation for appendicitis. He was left with the question of how to proceed and image the patient in order to sort this out. An ultrasound was best for looking at the gynecologic organs, the ovaries and uterus, but was often not great for identifying the appendix. Ultrasound was great for looking at solid or liquid-filled structures and could allow for evaluation of blood flow into and out of an organ as well as real time movement of the structure. But air or gas are the enemy of ultrasonic waves and cause them to scatter, creating uninterpretable images filled with artifact. Therefore, ultrasound of the gut is typically not useful due in large part to the presence of gas in the bowel.

G. Scott McCreadie, MD

A CT scan on the other hand is great for identifying structures throughout the abdomen and pelvis, but it provides only static images like a snapshot photograph, and although CT gives a nice look at the intestine, it is not particularly good for looking at the ovaries. The other drawback to a CT scan is the amount of radiation involved. Ultrasound uses high-frequency sonic waves bounced off the tissues in order to create an image. CT or computerized tomography uses a series or x-rays reconstructed by a computer algorithm to create thin slices of the body in various two-dimensional planes. This results in several hundred images that can then be scrolled through much like a cartoon drawn on a pad of paper, which when rapidly flipped through creates a rudimentary film-like image. Because this involves several hundred images it requires the radiation of several hundred x-rays. This results in a lot of radiation penetrating the body. Protocols have been established to try to reduce the amount of radiation used for certain studies and in certain patient populations, but no matter what, certain tests simply required shooting radioactive energy into a patient's body.

Radiation is of course, all around us. We are constantly bombarded with small amounts of radiation from space and also emanating up from radioactive materials in the earth. However, the amount of radiation in a single abdomen/pelvis CT scan is roughly equivalent to five years of background radiation from our surroundings or five hundred individual plain x-rays. Although that sounds like a lot, a single CT scan is not a big deal, but some people with serious medical issues require multiple and frequent scans and the cumulative effect of numerous scans over time is not yet fully appreciated. Radiation's negative effects tends to accumulate over time and can alter the basic genetic structure of individual cells even though that effect may not be noticeable or discernible for many years. The concern in the medical community is that numerous CT scans in one's youth could conceivably lead to the development of malignancies such as solid organ tumors or leukemia or lymphoma decades later. The cause and effect would be difficult to prove, but the risk is real and little different from the accumulation of cancer cases found years later clustered around Hiroshima or Chernobyl.

Jim was particularly reluctant to do unnecessary abdominal CT scans in young females as the radiation was shot directly through their ovaries, which contained all of the eggs that could potentially become children at some point in the future. However, like so many things in medicine, it was the balance of risks versus benefits. Patients present with problems and are looking for a diagnosis and treatment. Sometimes the very process of diagnosis and treatment involved tests, procedures, and medications that cause new problems in the process of trying to solve the presenting problem.

The additional factor that went into this particular young woman's case was that she had been sent in from her pediatrician's office with the expectation that "she needed a CT scan to rule out appendicitis." Given this, the patient and her mother came in with a preconceived understanding and expectation of exactly the test their doctor, who they may have known and trusted for years, thought was indicated. This sometimes made it exceptionally difficult for the emergency physician to redirect a patient's work-up or suggest a different approach. The patient was bound to be wary of a new doctor who they had just met, if he or she was contradicting the doctor that had been caring for them for years.

In this particular case, Jim would have probably chosen the ultrasound but after weighing all of the different factors, he elected to go with the CT scan. As it turned out, this was the correct decision although for a completely unexpected reason. The CT scan revealed a normal appendix. There were no significant swollen lymph nodes and therefore no evidence of mesenteric adenitis. There were no kidney stones. The ovaries were small and no significant cysts were present. In fact, everything looked completely normal, the way it should, except for one strange vertically oriented unidentified object in the midright abdomen. It looked like it was in the duodenum, which is the first part of the small intestine where it comes off of the stomach. It was unclear what this was.

At first the radiologist thought perhaps it was simply an artifact, a glitch in the computer-generated images. But it appeared to be a real object and about four inches long. It looked like something was stuck in the duodenum where it curves in a C-shape around the head of the pancreas. Jim returned to the young woman's room and explained the unusual abnormality he had found on the scan. The patient stared up at him dumbfounded. As he was leaving the room he said to the patient and her mother that he had no idea what this could be, but it almost looked as if she had swallowed a Popsicle stick.

Ten minutes later, Jim was in the dictation room doing some charting on the computer when the patient's mother found him. She looked shocked as she explained to Jim that after he had left the room her daughter had remembered that three months earlier she had indeed swallowed a Popsicle stick. Jim called in the gastroenterologist who performed an upper GI endoscopy on the patient and was able to retrieve the stick. The patient went home with the problem of her abdominal pain solved. A Popsicle stick is not very wide but it is about four or five inches long. This stick had made it through the narrow part of the esophagus and passed easily through the stomach and then lodged vertically in the "C" of the duodenum. Unlike other areas of the intestine, that portion of the duodenum is relatively fixed against the posterior abdominal wall and was unable to straighten out enough to allow the stick to make it around the corner and pass further into the digestive tract. The pain was in the right lower quadrant because the lower end of the stick was poking into the psoas muscle, which helps to flex the hip. The pain was intermittent apparently because it only pressed on this area when food was passing through and the smooth muscles in the wall of the duodenum were contracting and squeezing on the stick.

Jim had no idea, however, how in the act of eating a Popsicle, she could have swallowed the stick. An astute nurse suggested a plausible answer. She suggested that a weight-obsessed teen might have been using the stick to gag herself and induce vomiting. This would explain how she might have gotten a four-inch-long piece of wood down her throat, by tipping her head back and effectively straightening the throat and esophagus much like a sword swallower does. However, while in the act of inducing the vomiting gag response by touching the stick to the back of her throat, she had inadvertently let go of it and in an instant, it was lost down her esophagus. Not wanting to confess to her mother what had happened, she had apparently hoped it would be digested or pass through.

There hadn't been any pain initially and she must have thought that she was home free, but after a while the stick began to irritate the tissues around where it had become lodged. She finally presented to the ER, but even under direct questioning from a doctor she would not give up her secret (the secret that would have provided the diagnosis) until after being confronted with the unexplained abnormality found on the CT scan. Perhaps the most telling thing was the fact that, although she didn't speak much and let her mother do most of the talking, the one question she had for Jim was about how many calories were in the contrast material that she had to drink for the CT scan?

Once the stick was out, Jim asked the young woman how she had come to swallow it in the first place, and he asked her whether or not she might have been trying to gag herself with it. He attempted to talk to her about eating disorders in a very non-judgmental way and gave her an opportunity to come clean, but she continued to deny everything and reported it was simply an accident and she had forgotten all about it.

A year later she returned. This time she was in for depression and suicidal ideation. Although Jim didn't see her on this occasion, while preparing for his grand rounds presentation, he had reviewed this second chart and found that in the year following the Popsicle stick episode the patient had been in two different treatment programs for eating disorders.

This was an example of how difficult it was sometimes in emergency medicine to make a diagnosis when patients wouldn't or couldn't be truthful or forthcoming with information. This young woman had deliberately avoided telling the truth of what she was there for in order to avoid the embarrassment and exposure that would result from revealing it in front of her mother. Most patients, of course, were truthful and forthright about their situations and were honest in describing their conditions, but unfortunately many others intentionally lied or attempted to deceive their doctor. Sometimes the endgame was to get drugs or tests or sympathy from family or friends. Often it was an attempt to avoid embarrassment. Jim was always amazed by how many patients he had met who had slipped in the shower and landed directly on a shampoo bottle that had gone right up into their rectum. Jim was also amazed that these people actually thought the doctor would be dumb enough to believe such a story.

Many other patients were altered by drugs or alcohol, or they were confused or demented and simply couldn't give any useful information. These were the so called "veterinary work-ups," where one simply had to rely on experience, physical signs, and test results, much like a vet would do with an animal.

Foreign bodies, if nothing else, were entertaining and interesting regardless of where they were or how they got there. Jim had removed things from every known orifice including the throat, ear, nose, eye, rectum, vagina, and penis. There was always a story, sometimes it was believable and other times, not so much. In researching for his grand rounds presentation, Jim had included pictures of the famous Frenchman who had made a career out of eating inedible material including bicycles, TVs, and even an entire Cessna airplane. He would cut them up into bite size pieces and eat a pound or two a day until they were gone. Undoubtedly this must have been quite taxing for the sewer system in his town.

Humans are not particularly good digesters. During his presentation, Jim had also included a picture of a huge snake with the outline of a human being inside of its stomach whom it had recently ingested, as well as a great white shark as it was in the process of swallowing a 200-pound seal in two or three bites. These animals could somehow digest the entire skeletal system of their prey. Why couldn't this young woman digest a small stick? Truth be told, no vertebrate has what it takes to digest wood. Wood is made of cellulose, a type of carbohydrate, the same basic material as in bread or potatoes but with different bonds between the molecules. Bonds that cannot be broken without the help of a very special enzyme. This enzyme is found in the bacteria that inhabit the gut of certain animals such as cows, goats, beavers and gerbils. Even termites and carpenter ants, whose entire diet consists of wood, can't digest cellulose on their own without the help of these bacteria and their cellulase enzyme. The digestive tract is a remarkable thing, but the human digestive tract is rather unimpressive when compared to others in the animal kingdom.

Jim had also come across a fascinating article from a major hospital that had looked at all of their ingested foreign body cases over the previous eight years. It had documented 305 cases, but remarkably those only involved a total of thirty-three patients, most of whom had a diagnosed psychiatric condition. In fact, in the chart review, just four patients had been responsible for 179 cases and one individual had a total of sixty-seven emergency department visits for ingested foreign bodies. Jim wondered if perhaps this person might have been related to Mary. The hospital in the article had calculated that the care of these patients had cost well over two million dollars.

WITH THESE THOUGHTS swirling in his head, Jim re-entered Mary's room where she lay on the bed looking delighted with herself.

"Did you look at my x-rays, Doc?" she said.

"Indeed, I did, Mary," Jim said. "It appears you have glass in your ass."

CHAPTER THIRTEEN

The Medical Record

Mary smiled. "I know that. What are you going to do about it? Are you going to put me to sleep?"

"No, I don't think so, Mary. We are just going to have to dig it out," Jim said.

Carol entered the room with a plastic vaginal speculum and a light source.

She closed the door behind her and set the equipment on the Mayo stand. She then went to the head of the bed and addressed Mary. "OK Mary, we're going to have you lie back and we will put your feet up in the stirrups just like you are having a pelvic exam."

She pulled out the stirrups and broke down the bed for a pelvic exam. Mary complied with everything Carol said without any complaint or argument.

Meanwhile, Jim put on two pairs of exam gloves with the hope, however unlikely it was, that this might protect him from being cut by the glass.

When Mary was in position, he lubricated the lighted speculum and slid it into her anus. It was a good idea in theory, but the rectum collapsed around the speculum and he could see nothing but the brightly illuminated walls of the rectum glistening red. At least this mucosa appeared normal and there were no signs of injury, but there were also no signs of the glass. Jim probed with a pair of ringed forceps but couldn't feel anything other than rectal tissue.

Realizing this approach was futile; Jim withdrew the speculum, detached the light, and dumped the disposable speculum in the trash.

"Well, I didn't want to do this, but it looks like I am going to have to use my finger to see if I can feel the glass," he said.

Carol grimaced and looked down at Mary who continued to lay there motionless. Jim slipped his finger into her rectum and immediately felt a small hard object. He bent the tip of his index finger over it and gradually pulled it back up and out through the anal sphincter. Mary winced a little as it passed through. Jim examined it in his hand. It was a roughly triangular piece of glass, but it had been carefully wrapped in toilet paper, which was of course now saturated in mucus and stool creating a disgusting, gloppy mess. However, the presence of the paper had nicely protected Mary from the sharp edges of the glass.

Mary was crazy, but she wasn't stupid. She wasn't about to shove raw, sharp shards of glass into her own butt. She had cushioned each piece with a protective covering of toilet paper. This finding gave Jim more confidence that he was going to get out of this without lacerating his finger. He quickly began working his finger in and out retrieving another piece each time and within a minute he had collected five pieces.

"There were five pieces, is that correct Mary?" he asked.

"I think so," she said.

He did one more sweep of his finger around her rectum and felt no more hard objects.

"Good, it looks like I have got them all," Jim said. "That

wasn't nearly as bad as I had feared. Thank you for wrapping them all up."

Mary smiled.

"Now, you and I have got to stop meeting like this or people will start to talk," Jim said. "How about you don't do this kind of stuff again for a while, OK Mary?"

"OK," she said sheepishly.

At least not for the next few months until I get out of here, Jim thought.

He pulled off his gloves and tossed them into the trash, washed his hands in the sink, and then left the room while Carol sat Mary up and reassembled the pelvic bed. Jim returned to Mary's chart and placed an order for a follow-up flat-plate abdominal x-ray so he could make sure there weren't any other pieces left.

Despite the time Jim had spent with Mary, no new patients had signed in to be seen, it was now 2:30 a.m. and most of the world, thankfully, had gone to bed. The ER, which had been bustling a few hours ago, had become eerily quiet now with only a handful of people left, including Jim and the nursing staff, Mary, and Malcolm. The mental health social worker had arrived and was in the room with Malcolm interviewing him. Malcolm's wife and daughter were the only two people left in the waiting room. This was a good time for Jim to try to get caught up on all of his charting.

CHARTING WAS THE worst thing about emergency medicine or medicine in general. Over the years the documentation directives from the federal government, driven largely by Medicare and Medicaid, had become more and more arduous. In the old days, there was a simple one-page paper chart that had the patient identifiers, vital signs, medications, allergies, and a series of spaces where tests could be ordered and a few simple salient notes about the patient's presentation and management could be jotted down in the doctor's sometimes legible handwriting. Those charts had been replaced by dictated notes that had become a much more involved narrative of the patient's presentation and care. The dictated notes had essentially evolved to become full "history and physical examination" charts starting with a one-line "chief complaint" followed by a paragraph or two comprising a narrative of the "history of present illness." The HPI would outline all of the patient's complaints along with modifiers such as duration, character, and position of the symptoms. It was then necessary to document the patient's "past medical history" as well as his or her "family and social history." The social history could contain information such as whether the patient was a smoker, drinker, or drug user. It also may include the patient's sexual preference and activity as well as his or her occupation and living arrangement, if this information was pertinent and often even if it was not, just to fill up the blank space. This was then followed by the most useless requirement of all, the so-called "review of systems." This was a point-by-point review of at least ten major organ systems of the body identifying any other additional history of problems. This was almost always a completely useless exercise, which rarely ever contained any pertinent information. In fact, virtually all clinicians had become conditioned to simply skip over it when reading through a chart.

However, it had become a major issue with regard to billing. If there weren't the mandatory ten systems reviewed, the coding for that chart was automatically downgraded or dropped to a lower level, meaning less payment for the case. Even if the case was complex and the chart was otherwise perfect and deserving of the higher code, if it did not contain some meaningless line about each of at least ten irrelevant organ systems, the lower code was invoked. This was simply a hoop to jump through imposed by the system, so clinicians diligently included it over and over again in their charts. Although this was often simply a "text macro" that was mindlessly imported into each chart. Next came the "physical exam," which also had a documentation requirement for billing. This required that a certain set number of exam points were covered. Built somewhere into that were the few pertinent positive features of the exam that included actual significant findings.

Finally came the most useful part of the chart, the "medical decision making" and "emergency department course." This was the real meat of the chart, which indicated why the patient had presented and what the clinician's thought process was. This also included a list of findings and a review of lab and imaging data as well as a final disposition regarding the case. When reviewing a chart, most doctors skimmed the history of present illness and then skipped to the medical decision making and ED course to see what the outcome was. When Jim started in medicine, all of these charts were dictated into a hospital dictation system and an army of transcriptionists typed up a paper document that was then placed in the patient's paper chart. Now, due to more federal mandates, the EMR or electronic medical record (sometimes referred to as an EHR or electronic health record) had gradually been implemented across the country.

The EMR was supposed to streamline things and create a standardized record. Unfortunately, there were numerous vendors that had come up with many different versions of this, and none of them seemed to be very compatible with each other. Most were large and complicated template programs that listed many different potential chief complaints from which the clinician would choose and then try to fit to an individual patient. For instance, if the patient presented with the common complaint of chest pain, the clinician would choose the chest pain template from the computer. There was then a series of check boxes to click through with scripted wording describing the various factors of the patient's presentation such as the onset of symptom, duration, quality, etc. The program would then stitch the selected phrases into a choppy pseudo-narrative. However, the result was a generic and nearly incomprehensible jumble of words and phrases. The human brain, or at least Jim's brain, had trouble making any sense of these documents. The information was there, but the way it was laid out by the computer removed the human element. Jim found that his brain simply shut off when reading these, and he found himself skipping ahead to the scant sentences at the end of the chart that summarized the findings in real human language. So, a chart that was many pages long was really only useful in its last few summary sentences that were typed in by a living, breathing person.

Part of the push for these electronic charts was by the hospital because it saw the opportunity for savings by getting rid of all of those transcriptionists. The charts were supposed to be faster and more efficient, but in fact because of the time it took to jump around between screens and make hundreds of mouse clicks, the length of time it took for the clinician to create a chart had actually doubled. Jim found that he could dictate a chart in five minutes so he knew that if he had a typical shift and came home with twenty to twenty-five charts to do, he was looking at a couple of hours of work to complete his documentation. However, with the click box chart, the time doubled and it took around ten minutes per chart, so twenty-five charts now meant over four hours sitting in front of a computer, reliving the entire shift in mouse click after agonizing mouse click.

The ultimate idea was to document in real time as you saw the patient, but this was only practical if there was adequate time between patients. That meant you had to slow down and see fewer patients, which in turn meant less efficiency, less revenue, and the requirement for more doctors to see the same number of patients. Also, more often than not, it simply wasn't practical anyway.

If you were the only one there to see patients and they just kept coming, you had to work as fast as possible to see them as efficiently as possible. This often meant no time for charting of any kind until the shift was over. As it was nearly impossible to remember everything that had to be included in the chart regarding twenty-some-odd different patients over an eight- to twelve-hour shift, Jim had devised his own system of carrying a clipboard with blank paper on it. On this paper he would place an identifier for each patient, usually a preprinted label that was produced for each patient, and next to that he would jot a few shorthand notes to trigger his memory when he sat down to complete the chart after the shift or the next day.

Because of the workload of residents at the U, this system had recently become even more arduous due to changes made by the residency director. Because some residents were leaving their shifts exhausted and going home to sleep before coming back later to complete their charts, they were sometimes not getting their charts done at all. Sometimes a resident might work five or six shifts in a row, and if they got behind on their charts they might be facing a hundred or more charts at the end of the run. At ten minutes per chart, this could mean a thousand or more minutes of charting to get caught up. In order to resolve this, the residency director had mandated that a resident could not leave the hospital after a shift until all of their charts were completed. This meant that after an exhausting night shift, residents had to sit in front of a computer for several more hours in the morning when they were at their least efficient, fighting the urge to sleep, in order to complete all of the documentation on all of the patients they had seen. Once this was completed, they had the remainder of the day to try to sleep before returning in the evening to do it all over again.

In the years prior to this change made by the residency director, emergency physicians and residents like Jim could call the hospital dictation line or access the hospital electronic medical record on their personal computers and complete their charts from home. In fact, this was the main work that Jim's children saw him doing. They knew he went to the hospital every day but didn't really understand what that meant. What they did understand was that for a couple of hours after he came home from work Daddy had to be left alone because he was dictating and Daddy couldn't play until after he finished his dictations. Their mother was constantly after them to keep the noise down because Daddy was "dictating." One time after a particularly hard day, a visiting neighbor had asked Jim's three-year-old Tyler why he didn't like preschool. He replied he didn't like it because there were "too many dictations." Jim and Susan had a good laugh about the fact that Tyler's reference point for boring, hard work was "dictations."

The doubling of documentation time, by switching to the electronic medical record, had saved the hospital the fifteen dollars an hour that the transcriptionists were paid, but had heaped this additional time on the physicians with no pay increase at all. The residents had no choice with this. For the attending physicians and community physicians, this increase in time simply meant that adjustments had to be made in staffing and they each ended up seeing fewer patients and the end result effectively cut their wages.

Even more recently, the advent of voice recognition software had allowed physicians to dictate the important parts of the chart directly into the electronic medical record. This had essentially been a step back to the same system as the formerly all-dictated chart. Because it was too cumbersome to use the click box template system, most physicians simply chose a generic blank documentation template and filled in the spaces using the voice recognition dictation. This meant that the enormous EMR program with hundreds of nuanced templates for almost every conceivable complaint was simply ignored and a simple blank template was used for all patients. In many ways this produced a better, more readable chart and the cost savings for the hospital remained because the voice recognition software had replaced the human transcriptionists. But there was no time savings for the physician as he or she still had to do the work of the transcriptionist and read over and edit the voice recognition document. Some physicians were too impatient to do this editing and just let the voice recognition dictation stand. However, this system was far from perfect and the charts were filled with mistakes and unintelligible errors where the voice recognition software, which has limited ability to decipher and understand context, simply inserted the words that it thought it heard. Therefore, the narrative was often punctuated with all kinds of completely meaningless words or phrases unrelated to the context of what was actually meant. This led to the production of some very unprofessional and sometimes downright silly-sounding documents.

One staff member of the medical records department had actually been keeping an archive of these random words, phrases, and sentences that had cropped up in many of the charts. Many of these were actually quite funny. They were posted on the wall in the medical records department and were sometimes sent out in e-mails to try to shame physicians into being more careful and editing their charts to fix mistakes before they made them a permanent part of the record and electronically signed them. This particular problem of nonsensical words and phrases in the medical record was one of Jim's biggest pet peeves. The presence of such distractions in a patient's otherwise well-crafted chart diminished it so much that the chart became an embarrassment. Although Jim had not actually seen it come up yet, one concern he had was that such a chart could be referenced in court and the doctor would be made to look like a moron in front of a judge and jury as he had to explain why his documentation in the chart made no sense.

With all of the problems the new EMR chart had created, particularly with the burden of increased time for the physician and the overall diminished quality of the documentation, there were of course some benefits. One benefit that

Jim could appreciate was the electronic date and time stamp. Every entry into the chart either by a physician or a nurse was documented as to exactly when it was entered. This was especially important for the nursing documentation to tell exactly when a medication was given or when a result was obtained. Also, the EMR allowed for directly placing lab and imaging results and sometimes even pictures into the chart. It allowed for rapid access to past results and charts of previous visits without having to wait for a paper file folder to be delivered from medical records.

Gradually, different hospitals with the same EMR system, and even some with different systems, were learning to communicate with each other and make records available at different hospitals in different cities and even in different states. As far as Jim was concerned, the jury was still out on the EMR. It had taken some time, but the promised advantages seemed to be finally showing up. Newly trained doctors had no knowledge or experience with the old system of paper charts and voice dictations so they didn't know anything else.

There was no question the EMR had slowed the process of patient care; it had also increased the workload of providers. It was a major reason cited in studies of dissatisfaction among clinicians with their jobs. But one thing that Jim knew for sure, it wasn't going away anytime soon. Electronic medical records were the future and they were here to stay.

Jim was lucky however, because tonight he wasn't at the university hospital, and like many small hospitals, Libertyville was behind the curve when it came to implementing new-fangled technology like electronic records, so Jim had the luxury of old-fashioned dictated charts. He was about ten charts behind for the night but he knew he could knock those out in about an hour. He settled himself at the desk to get started on them, but before he did, he remembered that Malcolm's wife had now been in the waiting room for several hours and had no idea what was going on with her husband. Jim would just go talk to her quickly and let her know what was going on and then he would get busy with the charts.

CHAPTER FOURTEEN →

Emergency Mental Health

Before going to the waiting room, Jim decided that he would check in on Malcolm to see how things were going with the mental health crisis screener in case they were close to concluding their interview and a disposition was pending. When Jim entered the room, he saw Malcolm sitting on the bed in the same place that Jim had left him. He was talking in an animated way to the mental health specialist who sat in a folding chair near the door to the room. She was a fiftyish woman, small and unimposing. She appeared studious, with a clipboard and a legal pad on which she was taking notes. She had her legs crossed to provide an elevated surface for the clipboard. She wore bifocals low on her nose with a chain that fell down and then rose up behind her neck and was covered by her ponytail of auburn-gray hair. She had on no makeup and was dressed appropriately for having been called out in the middle of a cold winter night. Her name was Nancy and Jim had consulted with her on a number of psych patients during his shifts at Libertyville.

She was no-nonsense and a little stiff, but she seemed to be able to develop good rapport with patients and she was efficient in figuring out a plan and disposition for them. The mental health specialists typically had master's degrees in social work. They provided some counseling but primarily provided assessments and were able to act as intermediaries between the patients and the various providers of mental health services. They understood the complicated mental health system from the private psychiatrists, counselors, and psychologists, to county and state mental health agencies. They also were connected with the drug and alcohol treatment service providers and had some understanding of the options for domestic and sexual violence services, as well as child and adult protective services. They could recommend the detention of patients by court order if the patient was gravely disabled by their mental illness, or was perceived to be a threat to themselves or others due to suicidal or homicidal ideation.

Trying to assess the myriad different people and presentations, with the added drama of the emergency setting and whatever dynamic situation led to their arriving there, was rife with problems. It was a bit like traversing a field littered with landmines. It was extremely difficult to gauge just how crazy or how dangerous a person really was when the patients, by the very nature of their disease, often lied and/or attempted to manipulate and deceive. Many of these patients were drunk or high, and there were often family members, friends, or police involved who had their own agendas as well. It was a tough job, thankless and inconvenient, requiring visits in the middle of the night. To top it off, it paid next to nothing. Jim was thankful that he had not chosen such a career, although he relied on the judgment of the mental health specialists, and he was glad they were there.

Jim's job when it came to psychiatric patients arriving in the ED in various states of crisis was primarily to diagnose and treat any acute medical illness that could complicate or even be the source of their mental health issue. He would also make a tentative diagnosis of the mental health issue, and if possible, begin to formulate a treatment plan. He would do whatever medical work-up was required, and he was expected to provide "medical clearance." This was a misnomer and really a farce, but it did mean that there would be someone to shoulder the blame if the patient subsequently had a medical issue. Blame the ER doc. "How could he or she have missed this?"

Two tests that essentially every patient presenting with a psychiatric complaint got were an alcohol test and a drug screen. Based on the alcohol test, patients could not undergo psychiatric evaluation until they were deemed sober. Sobriety was a hard thing to define, but generally it was considered to be achieved if the patient was at or below the legal limit of .08. After all, if you were safe to drive a car at that level then you should be able to have your mental state evaluated without it obviously being compromised by the presence of an intoxicant. The challenging thing was predicting this state of sobriety. Many patients presented with alcohol levels that were four, five, or even six times the legal limit. Many were chronic alcoholics who were at risk of developing symptoms of withdrawal if they ever approached the legal level of sobriety.

Drunk patients were notoriously uncooperative and were often angry and even aggressively violent. They frequently required the intervention of security personnel (of which there were none in the middle of the night in a tiny ER like Libertyville) as well as physical and/or chemical restraints in order to provide safety for them and the ED staff. Many patients who presented slobbering drunk and made suicidal statements were detained for their safety and then had no recollection of what they said or even an inkling of having been suicidal once they awoke in the morning in the ED after having slept it off. By the time these "drunkicidal" patients awoke in the morning, there had usually been a shift change, and there was a new doctor and nursing staff that would have to reassess them.

There were calculations for how rapidly a patient could metabolize alcohol. These were variable, as experienced drinkers metabolized alcohol faster than those with naïve livers. Sometimes when a patient's alcohol level was tested, it was still going up. An acceptable level of sobriety from the effects of alcohol was a very difficult and subjective thing to judge, and different ERs had different systems for how they would do this. One thing that was certain, however, was that the mental health specialist was not coming in to assess them until they were deemed by the doctor to be both sober and medically clear. Sometimes this seemed to be more of a delay tactic than out of a concern for providing good patient care.

If the alcohol issue was a problem, it paled in comparison to trying to interpret the results of the drug test. The urine drug screen, or UDS, tested for a large number of illicit substances including opiates, cocaine, amphetamines, and marijuana as well as others. However, a number of designer drug variants and other intoxicants did not show up at all. Additionally, the drug screen only detected the presence of a drug or its byproducts. It was not quantifiable and could not indicate how much was in the system or when it had been ingested. Some substances would show up positive on a drug screen days or even weeks after they had last been used and long after the effects had worn off. Even more frustrating was the fact that many prescribed and over-the-counter medications also showed up in the broad categories tested for as cross-reactants. In Jim's opinion, the drug screen was only helpful to provide some confirmation of suspicion, but it was not effective in identifying the acute influence of substances. Determining if the patient's behavior was or was not the result of drug intoxication was really more of a subjective finding after careful interview and examination. Frankly, many patients often exhibited both the signs of mental illness and drug intoxication at the same time as the two often went hand-in-hand.

Once Jim had the results of the drug and alcohol tests back and had provided the medical clearance, the mental health specialist was called in and he or she generally spent much more time with the patient. They collected all of the little details in order to help determine if the patient needed to be hospitalized or could be discharged with follow-up. If hospitalization was thought to be necessary, they would also help determine if it would be voluntary, with the patient agreeing to the plan, or involuntary, where the patient would be admitted against their will or for their safety because they did not have the capacity to make the decision.

Involuntary admission required taking away patients' rights because they were deemed unsafe. This was a legal issue that sometimes required a second evaluation by another county-or state-authorized mental health professional, who could invoke what amounted to a court-ordered detention in a mental health facility. Generally, Jim and the mental health providers tended to agree in principle on the plan for most of the patients. Occasionally, Jim found himself disagreeing with the plan to discharge someone who he felt was a real danger or who was so acutely psychotic that they simply couldn't safely function in society. When this impasse occurred, there was a real problem because Jim knew that if the patient was discharged and then went out and killed themselves or someone else, the lawsuit that was sure to follow was unlikely to focus on the mental health provider who sent them home, but rather on the doctor who had the deep pockets of malpractice insurance. Therefore, the relationship between emergency physicians and mental health specialists was sometimes an uneasy one as both tried to evaluate these complicated and impulsive patients. This essentially boiled down to trying to accurately predict the future actions of a deranged mind, a tall order and a crapshoot at best.

At the university, mental health professionals were stationed in the ED twenty-four/seven, and there were psychiatrists available on call for consultation. Additionally, there was an inpatient psychiatric unit in the next building. At Libertyville, on the other hand, there was Nancy, who was called out at all hours of the day or night to come to the ED to evaluate and help place patients with acute psychiatric emergencies.

There were no inpatient psych beds at Libertyville, so anyone she and Jim felt needed admission required her to get on the phone and plead the patient's case to the various hospitals with psychiatric beds around the county and state until finally a bed could be procured and the patient could be transferred. Due to the disorganized nature of their minds, these patients rarely held jobs and were either uninsured or had only Medicaid or Medicare disability coverage. The lack of insurance meant the whole system of care for these patients was woefully underfunded and under constant strain. These and other factors had created massive backlogs in the system, which had resulted in patients often being detained and boarded for days or even weeks in ERs around the country.

Emergency departments and emergency physicians were neither equipped for nor interested in managing these patients long-term. But unfortunately, that had become the default system. If a bed was not readily available, then detained patients were held, often against their will in the emergency department. Their clothing was removed and they were placed in paper scrubs and then were secluded in sparse rooms with bare walls that had been stripped of anything that they could use to hurt themselves or the staff. They were observed by sitters or on closed circuit TV. They had limited human interaction and almost nothing to do to occupy their time. If they acted out in a way that was dangerous or they were threatening and likely to hurt themselves or others they were placed in physical restraints or medications were used to try control their behavior. With every shift change they were passed off from physician to physician and nurse to nurse. With every passing hour they became more detached from the physician who knew their story and agreed to their initial detention. Community mental health workers and crisis screeners would generally round on them daily and check to see if a bed had opened up somewhere so they could be transferred. The process broke down even further and delays were longer if they presented on a weekend or near a holiday, or if the patient was a child, pregnant, elderly, or had any number of other complicating issues.

Despite all of these issues, Nancy and others like her continued to show up in the middle of the night and showed real compassion for the challenging psychiatric patients they saw.

Malcolm of course was unusual, in that he had a job, he had insurance, and he had lived his entire life without any substance abuse issues and without ever needing any mental health-related care. That was until tonight.

Jim smiled at Nancy as he entered the room.

"Hi Nancy," he said. "I just wanted to check in and see how things were coming along in here"

Malcolm spoke before Nancy could. His mood was elevated and he appeared even more manic, but some of the distress was gone from his voice.

"We're doing great," he said. "Nancy is really helping me see things a lot clearer. In fact, she wants me to face my demons. She wants you to tell my wife."

Jim glanced at Nancy who looked surprised. He then looked back at Malcolm and said: "I thought you didn't want me to tell her anything. That's what you said before."

"I know, but as we have been talking about it, I realized that this has all happened for a reason and I have been so scared to tell her all these years, but she needs to know and she deserves to know and I can't tell her. But you Dr. McCray, you are so cool and calm and clinical, you could explain it to her."

Jim looked back to Nancy. "Was this your idea?"

Nancy twisted in her seat, but smiled. "Not exactly, we sort of thought of it together and figured maybe it would be best coming from you."

There was no real tension here. Jim had been telling people terrible, gut-wrenching things about their loved ones for years now. He had become accustomed to it and felt that he had become quite good at it. He couldn't even remember the number of times he had met with family and friends at the bedside or in the "quiet room" to tell them that their father, mother, son, wife or whatever the relationship was had had a stroke or a heart attack or had a brain tumor or was dying or had in fact died. The singular moment of receiving news of this magnitude was one of the most emotion-packed and raw experiences in any person's life and Jim had become accustomed to playing the leading role in this drama by being the one who delivered the news. It was never pleasant, but it was important, it was monumental, and it needed to be done right, with the right words and the right explanation, by the right person.

The very hardest, most painful ones were telling any young vibrant person that their equally young vibrant spouse had died, or even worse telling parents of any age that their child was dead. There were no adequate words to describe the overwhelming pain and emotion that coursed through the room at the very moment when those words were spoken and the realization hit. It could only be felt and physically absorbed to be understood. Although Jim had become accustomed to delivering such news to others, deep in his soul he knew that being on the other end of those words was his greatest fear in life.

Of course, Jim had also delivered good news plenty of times, but it wasn't the same. Nancy, or others in her position, were also part of this drama but their role was different. Jim would deliver the news and answer questions and then excuse himself to go care for other patients, and then the Nancy character would take over and hold hands, dry tears, and provide a shoulder to cry on.

Jim was not being asked to tell Malcolm's wife that he had died, although in a way that's exactly what had happened. This revelation would in many ways mean the death of her husband, the one she knew, the one she had built a life with for the past twenty-five years.

"So, this is it, huh. You guys wait until I'm out of the room and then you nominate me for the job," Jim said jokingly.

The levity helped break up any tension, and Jim could see that Malcolm was visibly relieved.

"OK, I will tell her," Jim said, his tone becoming more serious. "I will tell your wife and your daughter and I think it will be OK. They need to know and now is as good a time as any."

Jim began to move toward the door, but as he did so Malcolm reached out his hands and clasped them around Jim's.

He looked up at Jim and said, "Thank you."

CHAPTER FIFTEEN

The Family Meeting

Jim left Malcolm's room and peered in on Mary. She wasn't there, nor was the gurney she had been on, which meant that she had to be in x-ray still. He would go see Malcolm's wife and then discharge Mary after that. He stepped up to the large door that swung open automatically with a motion sensor on both sides. This was the door through which all of the ambulance patients entered the ED on stretchers. To the left through that door was the covered ambulance bay and another set of automatic doors, which were made of glass and slid together. To the right was the waiting room with perhaps ten chairs lining three walls, the fourth side being open to the entrance that led to the ambulance bay. If, after coming through the door as Jim had, you were to keep walking, there was an area where there was a snack vending machine and another door that led into the hospital, as well as a hallway to the radiology reception area.

Jim turned to his right and with one step was in the waiting area, which was empty except for Malcolm's wife and daughter who stood up with worried expressions as Jim entered wearing his scrubs and white lab coat.

"Hello, you must be Mrs. Johnson," he said as he reached out his hand.

She shook his hand and then straightened the bottom of her dark pullover and crossed her arms.

"Yes, I am Connie Johnson and this is my daughter Darcy," she said while motioning to Darcy who stood just behind her and wore the same weary and worried expression. Jim shook Darcy's hand also. She was young, not long out of high school. She had a studious conservative look about her and had pretty features, which were clearly downplayed tonight.

Connie appeared to be approaching fifty. She had a small frame, but appeared fit and well-groomed. She had an air of economy and intelligence.

"Shall we sit down?" Jim said and motioned to the chrome metal-framed chairs with plastic seats. They all sat. The waiting room was empty and the whole hospital was quiet. The snow was falling softly outside and was shining as it came down in the bright lights visible through the ambulance bay doors.

The room was relatively tidy with the chairs against the walls and a low table with a few paper cups and magazines in the middle. Jim sat across from Connie Johnson and Darcy with the table between them. He looked at them for a moment while thinking briefly about what he would say and how he would say it. This was a tense and pivotal time, and Jim had no idea how they would react to what he was about to drop on them. They knew that Malcolm was alive and safe so this wasn't like the many times when Jim had to deliver the news that a loved one had died. Sometimes that kind of news was met with weeping, wailing, and hysterical behavior, and at other times with quiet disbelief. It was never easy. But death was inevitable, and everyone on some level knows it is a possibility at any time.

This was considerably different. A lot of people at various times receive news that blows their mind and upsets their world view. This could occur when infidelity is revealed, when a child or parent announces they are gay or joining a cult, or perhaps for some, the army, or whatever else it is for you as an individual that upsets your apple cart. Sometimes these revelations are not a big deal, or were anticipated, or the person receiving the news is open to such things, but Jim had a feeling this would not be the case tonight.

"So, how is Malcolm?" Connie asked leaning forward and pre-empting Jim.

"Well, he is OK," Jim said, smiling. "He was pretty upset when he got here but he is much calmer now."

"What exactly happened tonight anyway?" Jim asked.

"Well, he just came home and he was very agitated. He was upset and was crying. He was rocking back and forth and wouldn't allow me to touch him or console him. I have never seen him like that before. I mean, sometimes he gets stressed out at work and I know he is working on a big project, but I thought he was enjoying it and it was going well. He wouldn't tell me anything. He wouldn't tell me what was wrong. He looked like a caged animal. It really scared me."

"Me too," Darcy said.

"Did he say where he was tonight?" Jim asked.

"No, I just assumed he had to work late. He does that a lot," Connie said.

"I didn't know what to do. It went on for half an hour and then I called the ambulance. The ambulance guys couldn't get anything out of him either, so they just loaded him up and brought him here. Do you think he's having a nervous breakdown?"

"Well I think that may be a good description, in a way, of what he is going through," Jim said. "He certainly is very emotionally distraught, even to the point of considering taking his own life, so I think it was a very good thing that you called the ambulance to bring him here tonight."

Jim didn't like the term "nervous breakdown." It was not a medical term and was vague and not quantifiable, but laypeople seemed to understand it, it had been around for decades, and it was useful as a starting point to describe a certain emotional state.

"Really? He said that? He said he wanted to kill himself. Why, why would he say that? Was it something I did to him?" Connie said as she searched her mind trying to think of something she may have done, trying to take responsibility for what she couldn't understand.

Jim marveled that so many people did this, particularly women, immediately questioning their own role and trying to take responsibility or even blame upon themselves for the inexplicable behavior of others.

"Not at all Mrs. Johnson, in fact Malcolm remarked to me what a wonderful wife and mother you are, and Darcy, he also said how much he adores you and your sister," Jim said trying to provide reassurance before he dropped the bomb.

By the way, where is your sister? Jim asked.

"She is away at school still. We are on different semester tracks and she is a senior while I am a freshman," Darcy said.

"Well, you will have to tell her what's going on then," Jim said.

"You see Mrs. Johnson, your husband, and Darcy, your dad, is experiencing some tremendous emotional distress in his life right now because of some issues that have been bothering him for many years. These issues have come to the surface recently and have really thrown him into a tailspin."

Jim searched their eyes for understanding.

"For whatever reason, Malcolm believes that he is a woman," Jim said, letting his words hang for a second before explaining further.

"He feels, in the deepest part of his being, and informed me that ever since childhood, he has always known that he has been a woman trapped in a man's body.

"Recently for the first time in his life he stopped fighting these feelings and quit trying to suppress them. For the first time he has begun to accept them and even act upon them. Tonight, he wasn't at work, rather he was at a meeting with many other people who share similar feelings and have the same concerns about their gender identity. He went to that meeting dressed as a woman. He said that the meeting was a remarkable and liberating experience for him, and he was as happy as he has ever been in his life. But when he came home and saw you both, he didn't know what to do. It overwhelmed him. He has a great love for you and for your whole family, but he feels like he just can't go on living as a man."

Jim paused, then continued. "Malcolm was so over-whelmed by all of this that for a while he thought the best thing that he could do to escape would be to kill himself. Fortunately, I don't believe he is thinking that is a solution anymore at least."

Jim looked at Connie who was leaning forward listening intently. When he stopped talking and their eyes connected in understanding she dropped her head into her hands and began to sob. Darcy, looking bewildered, reached over and began to gently rub her mother's back.

"Can we see him?" Darcy asked.

"Not just yet," Jim said. "He is finishing up with the mental health specialist and then I will need to check with him to see if he is ready for that."

"I can't believe this," Connie said, looking up, suddenly defiant. "He never let on. I never suspected anything like this. I mean you hear about this kind of thing on the internet and on lowbrow talk shows, but not Malcolm. My Malcolm. I have known him for twenty-five years. He has always been a 'man's man.' He likes to hunt and fish and go to ball games. It's not like I ever would have suspected him of sneaking around wearing my underwear or shoes when I wasn't home."

Darcy gave her mother a confused look. This family was being torn apart and put back together in a different form. Jim was watching this evolution. Roles were changing before his eyes. There was great grief and pain beginning to emerge. Reality for this family on this night had been turned on its head.

"What am I supposed to do now? You are basically telling me that for the past twenty-five years, I have been married to a woman. I guess that would make me a lesbian, wouldn't it? I have spent the better part of my life with that… that…*man*. I have raised his children; we have shared everything, and now this. This is worse than anything I could have imagined. I don't even know what to say or how to react," Connie said, her voice rising and falling in desperate gasps. This once very put-together woman was beginning to unravel, just like her world.

"Darcy, what are we going to do?" she said, turning to Darcy and beginning to sob again. Darcy, the faithful daughter, instinctively reached out for her mother and pulled her in. Darcy's face was thoughtful yet strong. In this instant, the parent became the child and the child became the parent. This was not a role Darcy wanted or liked. Her older sister was usually the strong one, the one who could be depended on in times of crisis. Darcy was the baby; she had never had to be strong in a family of strong people. But at this moment she was rising to the challenge.

It reminded Jim of his own experience. When he was in college and still single his parents went through a bitter divorce. His parents, whom he had always admired and looked up to, suddenly transformed into bickering, idiotic children. Jim unwillingly had become both a mediator and source of parental guidance and counsel. It was a very uncomfortable and unpleasant situation and for a time Jim felt like he lost his bearings as the foundation of his life, constructed by his parents, crumbled beneath him.

It is never an easy transition when your heroes and examples turn out to be surprisingly weak and shallow and human. But Jim came out of that situation stronger and better prepared to rely on himself, and he was ultimately able to find and follow his own compass. He felt confident in just the space of this few minutes together that Darcy would as well.

Jim spent more time with Connie and Darcy and talked through some of the logistics of what had transpired during the evening and what might happen next. They also talked a little about transgender people and the pathophysiology and psychology of the condition. Jim spoke about this as best he could knowing his education, like that of almost all doctors except for those very few who worked with these types of patients regularly, was extremely limited. In fact, he knew little more than the layperson and much of that came from media images and exploitive and sensational TV shows.

Jim's job was to make sure Malcolm stayed safe and didn't kill himself, and to deal with any treatable medical conditions, which Malcolm fortunately did not have. There wasn't much else he could do. But the most important thing was what he had done; which was to explain the situation the best he could in a straightforward, nonjudgmental way. The same thing could have been done by a social worker, psychologist, minister, cop, or anyone for that matter. But this time and almost every day he worked; it fell to Jim to deliver life-altering news to people. Jim felt this part of his job was an honor. To be there with people he barely knew, and to work to develop an instant rapport with them in order to be able to share some of their most intimate and life-altering experiences, was an honor. To be able to educate them, commiserate with them, and console them in such a time of great need, pain, and anguish and to do it in a professional, thoughtful, and caring manner, was an honor.

But this was just the beginning. The news about Malcolm was delivered; the cat was out of the bag. Now Darcy, her mom, dad, and sister would spend the next several years, in fact the remainder of their lives, managing the fallout. Tonight, the course of all of their lives had been irreversibly altered by Malcolm's revelation. That of course didn't necessarily mean any of their lives had been made worse by this, just different. Jim hoped that perhaps at some distant point in the future they would look back and think that different was actually, in some ways, better.

As Jim got up to leave Connie and Darcy, the ambulance bay doors, which were the only access to the hospital at night, slid forcefully open, shattering the quiet of the waiting room with a mechanical grind followed by a blast of cold winter air.

Through the doors came a teenage girl stooped over holding her abdomen in obvious pain. An older woman, presumably her mother, strode with her holding her up by the shoulders. Jim thought he recognized the older woman.

CHAPTER SIXTEEN →

In the Family Way

Sure enough, the woman was Barbara Sinclair, the daytime house supervisor at the tiny hospital. Jim interacted with her occasionally when he worked day shifts. As house supervisor, she was the head of nursing but primarily managed from the floors. Although the ER staff spoke with her on the phone routinely to arrange for patient admissions, she rarely made an actual appearance in the ER. Tonight, she was dressed in a heavy winter coat over clothes that she had either been sleeping in or hastily threw on after being awakened by her ailing daughter. Her daughter was nineteen-year-old Rosie, who was just finishing her freshman year at the nearby state university. Rosie was small, and hunched over as she was with obvious abdominal pain she looked even smaller despite her baggy sweatpants, sweatshirt, and oversized winter coat. She didn't say anything, but held her lower abdomen and walked clumsily with her mother's assistance. She had a grimace of pain on her face, and her mother spoke for her as the mother was in her element in the hospital.

"She's been complaining of intense, intermittent pain for the last few hours," Barbara said. "It seems to come and go in waves every few minutes. I kept thinking she would vomit or have diarrhea and that would relieve it. But it just didn't seem to be going away, so I thought it was best to bring her in. She thinks she ate a bad burrito tonight."

Carole, who was about the same age as Barbara and had known her for twenty years, came to Rosie's other side and together she and Barbara helped Rosie to the pelvic room. Rosie still said nothing and kept her head down, concentrating on the pain, while Carole as well as Marcie, who had now also arrived in the room, began to undress her and put her in a hospital gown. After the heavy winter coat came off, Rosie was noted to be wearing baggy sweats that appeared several sizes too large. It was a cold night and the sweats looked warm, and it was not unusual to see young women wearing bulky warm sweats such as these in winter.

Carole sat Rosie on the gurney and brought up the head of the bed. She systematically and rapidly removed her fluffy winter boots, socks, and sweat bottoms. Rosie's legs were thin and belied the bulk of the sweats. Carole then began to pull up Rosie's sweat top while Marcie held up the hospital gown to place over her as the top came off. It was just at this moment that Jim entered the room. As he did so, Barbara turned to greet him. Jim was facing Rosie who was not resisting as the nurses efficiently undressed her.

As the sweat top came off of Rosie, her arms were raised in the air and this exposed an impressive protuberant belly with a brown line running lengthwise down the middle from her sternum through her umbilicus and then disappearing into her underwear. Additionally, she had noticeably oversized voluminous breasts streaked with purple stretch marks suggesting recent expansion. The appearance of her abdomen and chest looked comically juxtaposed against the backdrop of her thin teenage arms and legs.

In the split second between the sweats coming off and the gown going on, Jim, Marcie, and Carole all immediately saw the cause for Rosie's intermittent abdominal pain. Their eyes met with recognition. Apparently, Barbara, and for that matter Rosie, still seemed to be in the dark and had missed the obvious.

Jim said hello to Barbara, grabbed his stool and rolled it next to Rosie's bed. With his clipboard on his knee, he began to ask her questions and take notes.

"Rosie, when did your pain start?"

"Right after supper. At first the pains were every five or ten minutes but now they are every couple of minutes and they are very intense," Rosie said.

"Have you had any other symptoms such as fever, nausea, vomiting, diarrhea, or vaginal bleeding?"

Carole looked at Jim incredulously.

Jim lifted up the edge of Rosie's gown and took another look at her bulbous abdomen.

He knew exactly what was going on, as did Carole and Marcie. Only Rosie and perhaps Barbara didn't seem to have a clue. He also realized that he may not have that much time. He took Rosie's hand in his and looked into her eyes.

"Rosie, I am worried that you might be pregnant. Is there any chance that you might be pregnant?"

Rosie looked back at him and said in the most sincere and innocent tone.

"No, that's impossible I haven't had sex for nine months."

Jim stifled the laugh that wanted to burst forth and looked at Carole who was at the head of the bed and was smirking silently.

"Rosie, I would like to do a quick pelvic exam to check your pain. Would that be OK?" Jim said.

"Sure, I guess," Rosie said, looking confused.

Carole and Marcie quickly broke down the bed to make it ready for a pelvic exam and put Rosie's legs up in the stirrups. Jim put on a pair of sterile gloves and lubricated the fingers on his right hand with sterile lubricant. He put his left hand on Rosie's bulging abdomen and slipped the index and long fingers of his right hand into her vagina. He could feel only a thin lip of her cervix posteriorly, which was soft and pliable. Above that and all around, filling her entire vagina and pelvic opening was the convex surface of a firm spherical object about four inches across.

Jim looked up at Rosie and said, "Rosie…you are about to have a baby."

Just at that moment a gush of warm fluid and a small amount of thin blood washed over Jim's hand and onto the floor.

Barbara stood up from where she was sitting with a stark look of shock and bewilderment.

"You've got to be kidding me," she said.

Simultaneously a look of understanding and recognition began to sweep over Barbara's face as she mentally recounted the changes in her daughter over the preceding months. She had noticed changes in Rosie's body but had just attributed them to her maturing and putting on the "freshman fifteen." She thought the predilection for sweats and bulky sweaters was just a college thing and that Rosie was just too busy with schoolwork to worry about dressing nicely.

Rosie, on the other hand, still didn't seem to get it. Whether this was simply an act or whether she really didn't know what was going on, Jim never did figure out. She swore she had no idea that she was pregnant. Not only had she not had sex for nine months, but she hadn't had a period for that long either. Rosie was normally a thin teenage girl. At nine months pregnant she had the look of a malnourished child with twigs for extremities and a huge pot belly. How could a typically self-conscious college freshman have seen that body every day in the mirror and not have noticed it or become concerned about it? But Rosie stuck to her story. She was just as surprised as everyone else that this could be happening to her.

———————•———————

JIM HAD SEEN one previous case like this. But that had been a thirty-seven-year-old attorney. She was already heavyset and hadn't really noticed a significant change in size or dimensions. Any changes she had simply written off to unchecked weight gain due to age, lack of exercise, and poor eating habits. She was single and rarely sexually active. She had had irregular, intermittent periods throughout her adult life and thought the lack of a period for nine months was either good luck or the early onset of menopause. She had never had any children and not knowing or expecting to be pregnant, she had easily rationalized and dismissed every symptom she experienced, including the breast swelling, expanding girth, lack of menses, nausea, and voracious appetite. She even dismissed the sometimes-violent kicks inside abdomen in the middle of the night as being gas-related.

She went to the university hospital ER late one evening with intermittent abdominal pain, expecting to be told she had a kidney stone or appendicitis or constipation. Jim actually suspected the same thing based on her story, until the obligatory pregnancy test that was routinely performed on every woman of childbearing age who entered an ER with abdominal pain turned out to be positive. This was followed by an ultrasound. It was then up to Jim to inform her that he knew the source of her pain, and by the way, she was about to become a mother.

This, of course, wasn't a pronouncement of someday in the future when she had married and planned her family, but rather that she would have a new baby in a couple of hours. In her case, there was more time than there was with Rosie, she was early in her labor and she was moved up to the labor and delivery floor where she was subsequently attended to by the on-call obstetrician.

When Jim first told her his findings, her incredulous response was, "Don't tell me I am like one of those freaks on Jerry Springer who has no idea they are pregnant until they drop a kid in the toilet."

In reality that was pretty much her situation. At the end of his shift the next morning, Jim went up to the Labor and Delivery to visit her. He found her sitting up in bed, nursing a beautiful newborn baby boy with dark curly hair. Her hard-driving, big city, single female attorney features had softened and her life had been irreversibly changed.

ROSIE'S SITUATION WAS similar, but her labor was much more advanced and in a matter of minutes in the middle of this cold winter night a baby was about to be born and preparations needed to be made.

"Carole, Marcie, let's get the OB kit and a warmer and call the OB floor and find out who's on for OB tonight and give them a call," Jim said, trying to remain calm.

In his mind, Jim began rehearsing what to do in an emergent and potentially precipitous delivery. These didn't occur often in the ER and when they did, they were usually in multiparous women, or in other words those who had previously had numerous babies and labored so quickly they simply didn't have time to get to the hospital and to the labor and delivery area. Sometimes these women delivered at home, in the car on the way to the hospital, or in the back of the ambulance. If there were no subsequent emergent issues, they were taken along with their new baby directly up to labor and delivery. Because these were women who had previously had multiple babies, their labors went precipitously fast, but they were also usually uneventful and they had been through the experience before, although usually in more controlled circumstances. Billions of babies have, of course, been born around the world for thousands of years without the intervention of modern medicine.

Childbirth is generally a very simple and natural process that, although painful and unpleasant from the perspective of the mother, generally proceeds without any major problems. That being said, when it does go wrong, it usually goes disastrously wrong, often with dire consequences for both mother and baby.

Rosie's case was definitely unnerving as she was a primip, in other words she had never had a baby, so it was unknown if she was even capable of a vaginal delivery both from an anatomical and emotional perspective. In addition, nothing was known about this pregnancy or about this baby. Rosie had had no prenatal care so the baby's size and true gestational age weren't known. For that matter, it was unknown if the baby was even alive. She had never had an ultrasound and she had been laboring all night without any kind of fetal monitoring. It was unknown if she had gestational diabetes or pregnancy-induced hypertension, which could lead to eclampsia and seizures. It was also unknown whether she, and by default the child inside of her, was addicted to drugs. It was unknown if she possibly had an underlying infection such as HIV, hepatitis, or even sexually transmitted diseases such as gonorrhea or active herpes lesions, which could infect the baby as it passed through its mother's birth canal.

Jim's mind began to race with the possibilities. Emergency physicians always felt woefully inadequate when it came to precipitous deliveries in the ER. These cases were generally just like this, with patients presenting in the late stages of labor with minimal prenatal care, with numerous unknowns, and they happened right now with almost no time to prepare. The stakes were even higher, of course, because one patient suddenly became two, mother and baby. These weren't like an unsuccessful code on a ninety-year-old where if the resuscitation failed it could always be said: "Well they were ninety after all. They had lived a full life." These cases involved a young woman and a newborn baby. A failure here was a major loss.

As these cases were so rare, there was no good way to train for them. Jim had more training than most. He was interested in OB/GYN and had even considered it as a residency choice. After ultimately deciding on emergency medicine, he had arranged to do an extra month on the OB/GYN service in order to learn more. Between his time in medical school and residency he had delivered upwards of forty babies. Plus, he had even been privileged to deliver his own two children. He had scrubbed in and assisted on a number of C-sections. But all of these situations had been in very controlled settings with healthy, low-risk women and low-risk pregnancies and had always been under the watchful eye of a seasoned obstetrician. All except for one case, one case that still gave him nightmares from time to time.

————•————

IT HAD OCCURRED while he had been working the night shift at the university hospital. It had been a busy night, so when Jim got a call from a paramedic who informed him they were bringing in a woman in labor, he was happy to direct them upstairs to the labor and delivery area. It was about 4:30 a.m., the absolute dead of night. No one was around in the hospital except those who absolutely had to be. Jim was a senior resident and was all alone. He was the only resident scheduled for the overnight and his "attending," or supervising physician, had just gone downstairs to the cafeteria to get something to eat. The other attendings and residents had left a little after three. Jim was providing medical control so he had the medic phone for all of the local paramedic rigs that were covering that part of the city in the catchment area of the hospital. Jim had received the call from a medic unit and a medic he knew well. The medic showed no signs of distress in his voice and informed Jim that they were bringing in a thirty-two-year-old woman who was gravida three, para two. That meant she had had three pregnancies and two previous live births. The third pregnancy was the present one and she was now in labor. However, the medic had checked her and felt confident that they had time and indicated that they planned to go directly up to labor and delivery. He asked Jim if he could have the charge nurse call the L and D unit to let them know of their impending arrival. Jim did so and moved on with what he was doing. He had taken many similar calls in the past and never saw the patients involved as the medics bypassed the ER on their way to L and D.

Ten minutes later Jim was standing at the nurses' station in the main hallway when the ambulance bay doors down the hall burst open. Jim looked up and saw two very disturbed looking paramedics racing down the hall, one of them the medic he had just spoken to on the phone. They were rapidly pushing a gurney on which sat a woman who was unclothed from the waist down. She had her legs bent at the hips and knees and her legs were spread wide apart. Protruding from her crotch was the wrinkled head and face of her unborn child. The child's face was pointing down, its hair was dark and it was covered in a cheesy white material called vernix. The baby's facial features were smashed together, and all of the visible skin of its face and forehead were a deathly blue color that contrasted sharply with the white/pink color of its mother's thighs and perineum.

This baby was stuck and everyone instantly knew it. The mother had a look on her face that she couldn't believe what was happening. Both medics looked entirely overwhelmed and unsure what to do. In a split-second, Jim and the nurses who had been relaxed in idle conversation sprang into action. But they had received no forewarning and therefore had no time to prepare. No equipment was set up. Judging from the look of the head and face of this baby as it protruded from its mother, it appeared dead. The gurney with mother and baby was quickly wheeled into a major trauma room and the medic Jim had spoken to earlier began, in exasperated sentences, to recount how after he had gotten off the phone with Jim, everything was fine, and then the woman had given a push in response to a contraction and the next thing he knew the baby's head was out.

This is when a strange thing happened to Jim. He knew exactly what to do. Everything around him was moving so fast and yet it all seemed to slow down. In a split second he looked at the blue smashed, dead face between this woman's legs and then up at her face. He read the plaintive look in her eyes, desperately pleading with him to do something to save her child. He looked past her to the child's father and then to the two paramedics, both of whom looked utterly confused with the ultimate uncertainty about what to do.

Jim knew that the baby's head was out, which is almost always the biggest part, but the shoulders were stuck. He reached his gloved hand down and in a single deft maneuver reached around the baby's neck, which was tight against the mother's swollen groin. He felt the umbilical cord around its neck and slid it up and over the moist, blue head. He then rotated the head so the face was pointing toward the mother's right thigh and then lifted up on the child's head in order to deliver the lower shoulder and then pushed it down again to deliver the upper shoulder, after which the baby slid easily out onto the sheet on the gurney in the space between the mother's legs.

Jim had handled lots of newborns in his time, including all of the babies he had delivered, as well as his own two vibrant, squirming newborns. He had examined sickly babies in the neonatal ICU and on his pediatrics rotations. But he had never seen one that looked as bad as this. This child's entire body was a pasty blue/gray hue. It was soaking wet with blood and amniotic fluid and vernix, which is similar in consistency to bacon grease and covers babies' skin in utero in order to waterproof them during their nine-month long immersion in liquid.

The child's color was alarming enough, but what was even more disturbing was the complete lack of movement, the lack of tone, the lack of any signs of life. This baby, which a short while ago had been moving around in its mother's uterus with all the anticipation and excitement of its parents and siblings and extended family regarding its impending birth, now appeared have ended its short life in a bloody, blue, watery mess on an ambulance gurney.

Jim knew exactly how to deliver this baby; it had been easy. He couldn't understand why an experienced paramedic hadn't done exactly what he had just done only ten minutes earlier when the child's head had first emerged and the baby was still alive, still had a chance.

What was he supposed to do now? Now he had two patients. Triage. Jim did whatever he could, whatever his skill and training allowed him to do in order to take care of his sickest patient. Mom was fine, emotionally spent, exhausted, slowly bleeding, crying, and with a placenta that needed to be delivered, but she was OK. She was in no imminent danger and she only wanted one thing and that was for Jim to save her baby, her floppy, dead, blue baby. Jim barked out to every nurse in the room. To get a warmer, to call OB, and the NICU, to get the respiratory therapist, and to get ready to intubate. Finally, exasperated, which he almost never was, he called out, "We have got to resuscitate this baby!"

A packet of OB instruments had been opened and he grabbed a large pair of hemostats and clamped the cord. The cord. The cord. The cord was what kept this baby alive, it was what fed this baby. The cord was the problem. The cord had already been clamped before Jim did it. It had been clamped around this child's neck and between the child and the tight, bony, tunnel-like walls of its mother's pelvis. That tunnel also clamped the carotid arteries in the child's neck prohibiting blood from flowing to the child's head and brain. The tunnel compressed the child's chest restricting any useful function of the heart and lungs. With no freshly oxygenated blood able to flow through the cord from the placenta into the heart and from the heart to the head, the cells of every structure in this new human began to starve. Every molecule of oxygen was used up and became uncoupled from every molecule of hemoglobin in every red blood cell and in turn from every cell in the body. When oxygen became uncoupled from hemoglobin, the very structure of the hemoglobin molecule changed and with that change came a change in its color. That change occurred in the bright red oxygen rich blood that flowed through the arteries and arterioles and capillaries of the skin and produced a living, vibrant flush. Without oxygen, the blood darkened and the skin changed to a sickly, pale, blue shade of death. It was all about oxygen. In pediatric resuscitations it was always about oxygen. *ABC.* This baby was blue because its cells had been starved of oxygen. A: Its *airway* was open. B: It was not *breathing*; there was no exchange of oxygen. C: *Circulation*; its heart was fully capable of pumping blood but the heart cells couldn't effectively contract in the absence of oxygen.

This baby needed oxygen. No equipment was set up, there was no warning. This wasn't supposed to happen. This hospital had millions of dollars of equipment and many highly trained people to provide lifesaving care but none of it in this split second was available. There was no time to intubate this baby; there wasn't even time to time to get a simple bag-valve-mask device to push air into these new lungs. In the five seconds it had taken for Jim to deliver this child and look around the room at all of the expensive equipment and the nursing staff that was frantically trying to get it out and set it up, he knew he had to do the most basic thing that could be done. He needed to give oxygen.

Jim bent his head down right then, right there in between the mother's legs and her bloody crotch, and he placed his mouth over that dead blue baby's mouth and nose. He could feel on his lips the slippery mixture of blood and vernix and amniotic fluid and God only knows what other bodily secretions were dripping from these two total strangers, and he gave OXYGEN. Jim poured the air that he had taken into his body and flooded it down into those tiny collapsed lungs. The cascading first molecules of oxygen spread deep into the alveoli and were picked up by the red blood cells, and the darkened hemoglobin molecules were reanimated and the firelight of life was reignited. The tiny heart, which had been slowly spiraling down with its last beats, suddenly began to quicken its cadence, and each new ensuing heartbeat was strengthened and began to push forward red blood cells filled with fresh, vital, life-giving oxygen to deliver to each starving cell.

Jim had no idea what to expect; he had no idea if it would work or if this life was too far gone. He anticipated a long struggle; he expected that this resuscitation might go like so many others. That he would need to intubate this baby by placing a tiny straw-like breathing tube into its lungs and then attach it to a ventilator to mechanically continue the breathing process he had begun with his own lungs. Next would be the question of circulation. Would there be a consistent heartbeat? If not or if it were too slow, CPR would be started, compressing and squeezing the tiny heart violently between the bony sternum in the front and the rigid spine in the back. Then he would need to administer drugs to stimulate the heart even more, and that would require accessing the circulatory system. Tiny newborn veins were exceptionally hard to find and access with IV needles. The large umbilical vein could be used, or an intraosseous line could be drilled into the bone of the lower leg and fluids and drugs could be pumped into the bone marrow space and from there find access into the vascular system. All of these thoughts washed over Jim as he continued to rhythmically puff tiny amounts of air into the baby's lungs.

Then something happened. She (the baby was a little girl) began to change. Her skin began to change from pale blue/gray to white and then to pink. She actually began to move and her leg muscles went from floppy and lifeless to energized with muscle tone. Next, she began to actually breathe on her own. Jim laid her back on the bed and pulled his mouth away. By this time, a tiny plastic mask with oxygen flowing to it had been set up by the nursing staff and Jim placed it over her tiny face and the pace of her recovery quickened. Her skin color rapidly normalized and she began to cry, quietly and weakly at first, and then with more vigor. This was the sweetest music ever heard by her mother. Jim looked up at her and her husband who was next to her at the head of the bed. He smiled. They cried.

The nurses wiped the baby down and stimulated her skin and warmed her. Jim cut the cord and the baby was moved to the warmer. No IV would be necessary, no intubation. Within a few minutes she was breathing and moving on her own with good skin color, vigorous movements, and a strong cry. Jim turned away and a nurse behind him reached up to wipe his face with a clean towel. She was beaming with admiration. As she wiped, she said in jest to defuse the seriousness of what had just happened: "It looks like you've got a little dead baby on your face there."

Jim laughed.

Mouth-to-mouth resuscitation is one of the most basic tenets of first aid. Every schoolkid who takes swimming lessons or a basic first-aid course learns how to do it. But almost nobody ever gets a chance to try it out. Nurses, doctors, and paramedics—who deal with airway and breathing issues in patients all the time—rarely if ever actually perform mouth-to-mouth because they almost always have equipment such as a bag-valve-mask available. In fact, mouth-to-mouth is the very last thing any medical person wants to do. But it can be lifesaving, as it was for this tiny newborn. There was no warning, there was no pediatric/neonatal bag-valve-mask immediately available, and this was a case where every second really did make a difference. Even though Jim had been a lifeguard at a swimming pool during his summers between years at college, this was the only time he had ever actually performed mouth-to-mouth on a real human being in an emergency situation. He hoped he would never have to do it again. It was better for everyone if the right equipment were available. But Jim had no regrets about what he had done. Without a doubt, his actions, his willingness to do it, had saved a life.

When Jim finished his shift a few hours later he went up to labor and delivery to check on the family. He entered the room and found the mother quietly nursing the newborn he had resuscitated a few hours earlier, while the father was wrestling with the two older siblings who had now arrived. As Jim approached the bed, tears began to stream down the mother's face. The father came to Jim, shaking his hand vigorously and thanking him profusely. This was one of the most emotionally exhausting cases Jim had ever had, and it was made even more poignant by his thoughts about his own wonderful children. He spent some time with the happy family because he wanted to see how everyone, particularly the baby, was doing, but also, he had some important questions to ask. Having to put his mouth on this bloody newborn, Jim needed to know more about the mother's health history. Fortunately, she reassured him that she did not have any history of HIV, hepatitis, IV drug use, or other known communicable diseases. The hospital still required that they both be tested, given the body fluid exposure, but Jim left the hospital that day knowing without a doubt that he had saved a precious new life.

It was still too early to tell what would be the quality of that life. Although the baby looked great at that point, she had spent a considerable period of time without sufficient oxygen to her brain. Children like that may ultimately suffer severe developmental delay or cerebral palsy or other problems. Many months later Jim received a Christmas card from the baby's grandparents thanking him again for their beautiful granddaughter, whom they reported appeared perfect and was developing completely normally.

JIM DESPERATELY HOPED that Rosie's baby would not require any extensive resuscitation because here in the middle of the night at Libertyville he had essentially no backup and considerably fewer resources than at the university hospital. The good news was that Jim knew at this stage that the baby was head down. He could tell this because he could feel the head. If he were feeling the baby's bottom or an extremity as in a breech or extremity presentation, the chances of major complications would skyrocket given the limited resources and lack of time. Another plus was that there was not marked bleeding, as is often seen with placenta previa where the placenta is low in the uterus and a portion of it is over the cervix, and as the cervix dilates open, the placenta begins to detach and bleeds profusely.

Rosie began to groan again as she experienced another contraction. Her water had broken and she was almost fully dilated. It was nearly time for her to start pushing. She was well beyond the point of no return. Jim placed his gloved hand back into her vagina and could feel the baby's head was very low in her pelvis. He ran his fingers around the baby's head where it was tight against the walls of Rosie's birth canal. The remaining thin lip of her cervix, which he had previously felt along the posterior portion of the baby's head, was now gone. Rosie's vaginal opening was now beginning to bulge open and Jim could see the baby's dark, wet hair and the scalp, which was wrinkled from the pressure.

By now the baby warmer was in the room and the OB kit had been opened and the instruments were laid out on top of a drape on a Mayo stand. Rosie was lying on the gurney with her hips and knees bent and her feet up in the stirrups. Her mother was at the head of the bed stroking her daughter's hair, which was damp with sweat. Jim thought for a second if there was anything else he should be doing. It was too late for much. He wondered if he should try to empty her bladder with a catheter to make more room and reduce the risk of damage to the bladder, but he wasn't even sure he would be able to find her urethral meatus, the opening to her bladder, at this point. There was really nothing left to do but to let this baby come, the same way babies had been coming for countless generations. It was a natural process that was about to happen whether Jim was there or not. All he could do was to help it along and then hopefully try to fix any problems that might result.

"OK, Rosie," Jim said with a calm voice. "This baby is ready to be born, and you are doing awesome. You have almost done this whole thing by yourself. Now all you have to do is a little pushing and this will all be over. Are you ready?"

Rosie said nothing, but nodded in the affirmative. She was ready. She had arrived at the ER a short while ago with the most severe pain she had ever experienced in her short life and whether or not she had any inclination as to the source of the pain, she was now ready to be done with it.

At that moment Jim could see Rosie's face begin to knot up; she bent her head back and began to moan as another forceful muscular contraction swept across her uterus.

"Push, Rosie!" Jim said.

Rosie bore down with all of her might forcing herself to exhale all of her breath and squeezing her core.

"Excellent job, Rosie," Jim said. "This is going to be easy. This baby is going to slide right out. You are doing amazing. You are in great shape and you're so strong. Get ready to push again with the next contraction, OK?"

Rosie responded to the coaching and encouragement, and Jim continued to act as cheerleader. With each new contraction, she gave a mighty push, and her perineum would bulge outward and her vaginal opening would widen. Each time more and more hair and wrinkled head became visible. Rosie's mother continued to hold her around the head and shoulders and wiped at her sweaty brow with a cool, damp washcloth. Marcie and Carol were standing on either side of Jim where he sat on a stool in between Rosie's leg. The nurses were mesmerized, even though both were mothers themselves, as they watched Rosie's body slowly open up and push out a new life. Jim thought about how exciting a birth was. He remembered the unspeakable joy that he felt when his own children were born. The mixture of cascading emotions that he had felt at those times was so overwhelming and so unexpected—the love, the pride, the happiness—especially with the first when it was all brand new.

Jim wondered if Rosie would feel any of that. Her circumstances couldn't have been more dramatically different. Jim knew his children were the overriding purpose of his life. They had been planned months or even years in advance and they were conceived in love. He and his wife wanted nothing more than to start a family and raise their own offspring, their own genetic material mixed together and made incarnate in this wondrous process of having a baby.

Rosie on the other hand…A few hours ago in Rosie's mind she simply had abdominal pain, intestinal cramps. She thought that if she could just have a bowel movement or vomit, it would probably go away. She wondered if it was due to something she ate. Now here she was a teenage college freshman about to become the mother of a child she neither wanted nor expected. Her only planning was a one-night stand with a drunken frat boy at a frosh week party. Of course, that was a plan for nothing other than having a good time. The situation she now found herself in was a million miles away at the time.

Rosie groaned and grimaced again as another contraction began to swell and crescendo in her abdomen. Instinctively she began to push again. With this push the baby's head turned the final corner, passed through her introitus and began to tilt up slowly. Jim held his fingers tightly against Rosie's forchette, the lower part of her vaginal opening to try to control and slow the emergence of the baby's face and avoid a tear of the tissue from the forchette toward her anus. The baby's face burst forth. It was wrinkled and squashed and wet and bloody, just like it should be.

"Great job, Rosie, we've got a head, we've got a face, you're almost there," Jim said.

For the first time Rosie managed a hint of a smile. Jim ran his fingers around the baby's neck and felt no cord. He took a bulb syringe from the OB kit and quickly suctioned the baby's mouth and nose to remove any amniotic fluid or meconium. He then gently began to rotate the baby's head and pulled up to release the left shoulder and down to release the right shoulder and then the rest of Rosie's baby slid out into the world. Jim held her briefly and then clamped the cord and pushed the infant up onto her mother's abdomen while the nurses began rubbing her pink skin with towels to dry her off and stimulate her. She cried a delightful little cry and everyone smiled and laughed.

Rosie had delivered a beautiful, dark-haired girl who weighed six pounds and six ounces. She was checked over completely and, for all intents and purposes, appeared perfect in every way. Jim next set about to deliver Rosie's placenta. He applied gentle pressure to her abdomen massaging her uterus and gently pulling on the knurled umbilical cord until he could feel the placenta gradually release from the walls of the uterus, and then it slipped out and into a waiting basin with a wet thud. Placentas always fascinated Jim. It was an amazing disposable organ that grew incredibly rapidly and completely sustained all of the needs of the growing fetus by transmitting nutrition and oxygen from mother to baby. It removed waste and it produced hormones. It also protected and insulated the fetus from both infections and attack from the mother's immune system. Jim spread it out in the basin to make sure it was intact and that it had all come out in one piece. He then again massaged Rosie's abdomen to promote her uterus to contract and thereby shrink down all of the engorged blood vessels that lined it in order to reduce bleeding.

Everything seemed to have gone perfectly for which Jim was very grateful. No resuscitation was necessary. Everything that could go wrong and turn such an unplanned precipitous birth into a disaster hadn't. This natural process had gone exactly as it should. Despite the circumstances of it being a surprise, the actual birth had been perfect. The nurses, who were thoroughly enjoying this opportunity to have a new baby in their midst, had bathed the baby and had located a diaper, a onesie, and a tiny cap from the nursery. Rosie had sustained a small tear in her perineum during the delivery so Jim worked to quickly sew that up. This had been a fairly small baby and he had done a good job of controlling the final push as the head emerged, so this was a typical small tear that was easy to close. Jim was always amazed at the healing ability of this area of a woman's body. If a similar-sized gash were to occur on the face, the patient would have a noticeable scar for life. But the perineum seemed to heal remarkably well to the point that initially nasty looking lengthy tears appeared almost undetectable a few months later. Fortunately, Rosie's tear was small and did not approach the anal sphincter, which when torn could lead long-term problems of bowel incontinence.

Jim discussed the case on the phone with an on-call family practice doctor who did OB, and Jim made arrangements for Rosie and her new baby girl to be admitted and go upstairs to the nursery where the on-call doctor would assume their care and manage the ongoing medical needs of mother and baby in the first days after delivery.

———————•———————

JIM NEVER SAW Rosie or her baby again, but he heard later from the nurses who interacted with Rosie's mother that she had never bonded with the baby and wanted nothing to do with it. Rosie's mother, the baby's grandmother, wanted her to keep it and to help her raise it. But Rosie put the baby up for adoption as soon as she was able.

Because Rosie didn't realize she was pregnant and gave the baby up so quickly after the delivery, her daughter was really only a part of her life for less than twenty-four hours. Rosie told her mother that she just wanted to forget about the whole thing. It was difficult for Grandma to let her unexpected first grandchild go, but it was Rosie's decision. Jim thought about this situation often afterward, especially as he played with his own children. The decision may certainly have been the best for Rosie and was undoubtedly a wonderful blessing for the baby's new adopting parents and probably for the baby herself, but the whole experience was hard for Jim to wrap his mind around. He loved his own children so much, and although he applauded Rosie's decision as both reasonable and pragmatic, he knew that it would never bring about the desired effect. Rosie would never forget.

CHAPTER SEVENTEEN

Tidying Up and the Logistics of Sleep

Jim returned to the nurses' station where Ginger was sitting at a computer terminal. She looked up at Jim with a questioning glance.

"Well, that was fun," Jim said with a smile. "It's not every day that I get to deliver a baby."

"How did it go?" Ginger asked.

"It was awesome," Jim said. "Just like it is supposed to go, and what an adorable little baby."

Ginger shook her head. "What a surprise. I can't imagine not expecting anything and the next thing you know you've got a kid. That's insane."

"Crazy isn't it? Jim said.

Within a short time, Rosie and her newborn were headed upstairs to their room, and Jim worked on clearing out the remaining patients. No new patients had checked in, and Mary was patiently sitting up and waiting to go back by ambulance to the state hospital. Jim looked at her follow-up x-ray and could no longer see any glass in her rectum.

He stepped next to Mary's bed where she was flipping through a magazine.

"Well, Mary it looks like we got all of the glass out of your backside. I don't want to see you back here or at the university with anything in any of your orifices, OK?" Jim said playfully. "That's what pockets are for."

Mary nodded.

"I'll try," she said with a pleasant childlike smile.

Arrangements were made and Mary was loaded into a basic life support, or BLS, ambulance and transported back to her room at the state psychiatric hospital.

Next, arrangements needed to be made for Malcolm. Nancy had completed her assessment and was on the phone calling various psychiatric units to see if they had any open beds where she could send him. She remained concerned about his suicidal ideation and was concerned that he was still a threat to himself at this time. She was able to find an accepting facility and transfer arrangements were made. The paperwork was filled out, the nurse called in a report regarding Malcolm to the nurse at the receiving facility, and he was packaged up and loaded into the back of another BLS rig for the ride to the receiving hospital.

Prior to his leaving, he had briefly spoken to his wife, Connie, and daughter Darcy. They continued to appear a little shell-shocked and overwhelmed as it all had begun to sink in, but at least they were trying to smile and were cordial, if somewhat distant, in their interaction with Malcolm. Malcolm, on the other hand, appeared elated, and he shook Jim's hand vigorously and thanked him profusely as he was wheeled past on the gurney on his way to the ambulance. Jim often wondered in the months after this night how things had turned out for Malcolm and his family. But as was often the case in the ER, the interactions with patients were frequently intense but brief, and there was often no follow-up regarding the ultimate outcome.

Jim spent the next hour or so catching up on his charts. The night was almost over and soon it would be time for him to go home. It had been a memorable night with some interesting cases. Jim's shift ended at 7 a.m. and it was now well after 5. The end of a shift was often the worst part, mainly because exhaustion had set in and the focus became a matter of watching the clock with the hopeful anticipation of getting out on time. At the university hospital ED, the volume of patients was considerably higher and there were multiple doctors working, so the stream of patients was more constant with less variability. There was rarely any downtime, and the routine was just to see one patient after another right up to the end of the shift. However, as one approached the end of a shift, the triage nurses would try to funnel shorter cases to the doctors who they knew were going home soon and avoid sending them cases that would take hours and extensive work-ups. It didn't always work out that way, but it was supposed to.

At Libertyville on the other hand, there was no one else around so you had to see everyone regardless of how close it was to the end your shift. However, because this was an ongoing and anticipated issue, it was possible and even expected that you could begin seeing a patient, get the work-up and treatment started, and then turn the patient's care over to the oncoming doc when he or she arrived. Jim didn't like to do that, and in the ER at the university, the expectation was that once you saw a patient you would manage them until they were ready for either discharge or admission. It was well-documented in the emergency medicine literature that the "handoff" between physicians and nurses was a dangerous time for patients. This was the most likely time for important issues to be missed or neglected. Although handoffs could be dangerous, in a place like Libertyville it was impractical to do anything else. To pick up a complex patient who might require three or four hours to sort out within thirty minutes of the end of your shift and then be stuck there with that one patient was simply a nonstarter. Particularly if you had to go home to get some sleep before coming back again for another shift in a few hours.

The shifts at Libertyville and at many small, single-coverage ERs were twelve hours long, and either started at 7 a.m. and ended at 7 p.m., or started at 7 p.m. and ended at 7 a.m. Jim had found that those doctors who struggled the most in emergency medicine were those who didn't manage time well. It was vitally important to manage patients quickly and efficiently. It was important to use any downtime to complete charts and to finish all documentation and charting as quickly as possible after a shift and to not allow uncompleted charts to pile up. However, even more important than any of those factors was to manage sleep. Because of the weird hours and intense work of emergency medicine, which required maximum mental awareness, it was of utmost importance to get adequate amounts of quality sleep.

Sleep was the most important thing for busy emergency physicians, and there were none busier than an emergency medicine resident who, in addition to the many shifts he or she was working in their program, was also moonlighting on the side. The night shifts were the worst. They were unpredictable in terms of how busy they were, and there was less backup in terms of specialists and referral physicians. But the biggest factor was simply that they were at night. If an emergency physician was going to make multiple split-second life-and-death decisions, he had to be well-rested and have control of all of his mental faculties. The night shift was always the biggest challenge for emergency physicians and it worsened with age.

In modern societies, there are lots of night-shift workers, but often the jobs and the pace at night are slower and more relaxed. The night watchman or security guard, the night-time store or hotel clerk, even the night-time factory worker was less busy and harried than when doing the same job during the day. This was the opposite in the emergency room where the number of patients per doctor often increased and were complicated by drugs, alcohol, and violence, which were more prevalent in patients presenting at night. Because of this, it was literally life and death to be well-rested and get adequate sleep. This was a huge challenge for some emergency physicians who struggled with being able to sleep during the day. As humans are not naturally nocturnal and have slept in darkness at night for thousands of generations, it runs counter to our biology to be up all night in artificial light performing tasks and carrying out actions that require an intense level of mental awareness and acumen.

Some physicians struggle enormously to accomplish this. Others seemed to be naturally better equipped for it and in fact often gravitated to positions that were strictly night jobs. There were some definite advantages as they often were offered greater pay by their photophilic or rather nyctophobic partners who were more than willing to buy their way out of night shifts by offering night bonuses to those willing work "on the night train." In Jim's position as a resident he had to do a mixture of days, evenings, and nights. But because of the demographics of when emergency rooms were busy, he found that about sixty percent of the time he was in the hospital occurred after midnight.

This required a major adjustment for Jim and his family. Because sleep was so important, like many nightshift workers he had learned to black out the windows of his sleeping room. His wife, Susan, had to adjust her schedule and would spend long hours away from home with the children to keep the tiny house where they lived quiet so Jim could sleep. Despite his best efforts, Jim found that he was unable to sleep in long blocks of time, but instead would come home and go to bed after a night shift and sleep for a few hours to get what was referred to as "anchor sleep." He would then be up during the bulk of the day and would go back to sleep for a few hours in the evening before returning to work.

It was often difficult to get to sleep, and the sleep that he did get was what he would describe as poor quality, neither restful nor refreshing. He always felt a little hungover. With his resident's schedule, he was always bouncing between days, evenings, and nights. There was never enough time to develop consistent sleep patterns. Sometimes he would become so exhausted he would have trouble getting to sleep at all and had to use sleep aids. He was fearful of using prescription sleep products because of the potential for dependence or hangover. So, typically he used a combination of diphenhydramine (Benadryl) and melatonin. Additionally, he was careful to adjust his diet and to exercise to maximize his health. However, despite his best efforts he could feel the effects on his body and mind. As he analyzed his life, he calculated that the incredibly long hours of effort during the seven or eight years of medical school and residency had, in his opinion, aged him by twenty years. Studies had confirmed that working nights altered the body's chemistry and hormonal milieu. It led to increases in stress hormones, weight gain, and was even considered by some to be a carcinogen, weakening the immune system and increasing the body's susceptibility to cancer. Night-shift workers also tended to crave foods that were unhealthy, probably due to an excess of stress hormones.

Although emergency medicine was generally regarded by other physicians to be an attractive lifestyle-specialty because of its predictable work schedule and lack of call responsibilities, it was relentless. Whereas many physicians settled into predictable and reasonable work patterns once they were out of training, emergency physicians still routinely worked a significant number of nights throughout their entire careers. At least in part due to this, there were very few old ED docs.

As this night slowly ebbed away and a new morning gradually emerged, Jim sat musing about how many busy nightshifts he had already worked and how many more he had left before he was finally done. Breaking the silence and invading his reverie, the HEAR radio crackled to life.

CHAPTER EIGHTEEN →

Trauma

The medics were on their way in: Code 3, lights and sirens. They had a forty-four-year-old male with severe trauma to his left arm secondary to a broken window. Jim was surprised to hear the anxiety in Benny's voice. Jim had seen a lot of patients who had punched a window or fallen through one. They usually had pretty significant but generally fairly superficial cuts. There was often a lot of blood, which looked dramatic, but the bleeding was usually easy to control and the wounds were easily repaired. But Jim knew Benny well; he was an experienced and solid paramedic who was not easily flustered.

It was now almost 6 a.m. Jim was down to one nurse, and a new nurse would arrive at 7 a.m. along with Jim's replacement. The house supervisor was still in the hospital and could be called down if needed. Carol was the remaining nurse and so Jim instructed her to call a "modified trauma" for the incoming patient. This designation meant a lot more at the university hospital where trauma was a big part of its business. At the U, there were multiple different "activations" and "codes" that could be called. These were announced overhead by the hospital operator in order to notify those involved, or those who needed to be involved, that something was going down. The original code was a "code blue" or in other places a "code 99." This meant a cardiac arrest. In most places when this was called, the emergency physician had to stop whatever he or she was doing, respond to the code, and lead the resuscitation regardless of where it was happening in the hospital.

Cardiac arrests were relatively commonplace in the ER and did not always require a code being called overhead. The one person who was sometimes helpful and would respond to the ER when a code was called there was a pharmacist, who could help rapidly dispense medications, although most of the medications used during a code were stocked in the "code cart" in prefilled syringes. Code carts were basically large rolling tool boxes that were stocked with all of the medications typically used during a resuscitation. Frequently the code cart also contained other useful items such as IV bags, central line kits, airway and intubation supplies, and on top of the cart, most importantly, the cardiac monitor/defibrillator.

When codes were called for a patient on the floor, the emergency physician had to leave his or her patients in the ER, go to wherever in the hospital the patient was, and run the code. This was often very challenging as the environment was unfamiliar and the nurses and other staff on the floor were only infrequently involved in codes and were often very nervous and inexperienced with resuscitations. At the U, a large tertiary care hospital, often an ICU doctor in addition to the emergency physician also attended codes as did various residents, techs, and nurses from the floor and ICU.

A few of the many people who came running when a code was called were actually useful, but many were not and simply stood around taking up space while trying to give the perception that their presence was of some value. A respiratory therapist would come to help with airway management and to set up a ventilator. The emergency physician ran the code by assessing the patient and giving instructions to the other staff to perform CPR, administer medications, draw blood, etc. The emergency physician would intubate the patient and place central lines as needed and also confer with the patient's doctor and other necessary consultants on the phone. If there was family present, the physician would also speak with them to let them know what was going on.

At the U, the responsibility for codes on the floor was gradually being handed over to the ICU doctors as it was difficult for the emergency physician to leave all of the patients in the ER to go spend thirty to sixty minutes running a code on the floor. When this happened, particularly in the middle of the night when there might only be one ER doc working, the ER could go to hell in a hurry while he or she was away.

However, at Libertyville there were no other doctors or residents or anybody else around at night, so when a code of any kind happened, whether in the ER or on the floor, it was Jim who had to run it with the help of a skeleton crew of nurses. There was no help, there was no backup. Frankly, however, they often ran better that way.

The trauma code had developed out of this system for patients arriving in the ER with major trauma. This had been further subdivided into "full trauma activation" and "modified trauma." These were differentiated on the basis of a protocol for patients with certain injury criteria. In particular, this included patients with abnormal vital signs; evidence of obvious severe trauma such as multiple fractures, gunshot wounds, and stabbings to the head, neck, or trunk (known as penetrating trauma); or alterations of level of consciousness secondary to the trauma, particularly head trauma. Also, certain mechanisms of injury, such as falls from significant heights, and certain types of motor vehicle crashes, such as rollovers, triggered trauma activations. Additionally, an age factor was built into trauma activations because trauma was always much more complicated in elderly patients or pediatric patients.

The basic difference between the full and modified trauma was the presence of the trauma surgeon. The trauma surgeon was a general surgeon who primarily operated in the belly. In some major centers, these surgeons were dedicated to trauma only and had special training in critical care. They not only ran the trauma resuscitation, but operated on the patients and managed them in the ICU afterwards. However, in most hospitals that did not have a level-one trauma designation, the trauma surgeon was a general surgeon in community practice who spent his days taking out gallbladders and appendixes and performing other routine general-surgical procedures. The degree of desire to be involved in the care of complicated multiorgan trauma patients among these surgeons varied widely. Many wanted little or nothing to do with it and did so grudgingly due to their hospital call responsibilities. Also, many patients who had major trauma had no injuries that would benefit from the expertise of a general surgeon. Instead, the patient's trauma may be neurosurgical (brain and spine), orthopedic (skeletal), or urologic (kidneys, ureters, bladder and male genitalia). Therefore, involving a general surgeon who wasn't going to operate on them and wasn't comfortable managing their medical needs either in the ER or the ICU seemed somewhat pointless at times.

This particular patient who was coming in was relatively young at forty-four and therefore presumably healthy. The only other detail known was that he had extremity trauma from broken glass. This means he could be a construction worker installing a window or he could be an out-of-control drunk who had fallen or been pushed through a plate glass window. The concern in either case was the control of hemorrhage, potential for treatment of hypovolemic shock, and management or evaluation of other injuries. In reality it could mean just about anything, but these were the particular eventualities that Jim began to prepare for.

The patient arrived a few minutes later. The medics crashed through the doors with the patient on the gurney. He looked pale and pasty and was actively vomiting into an emesis bag. His clothing looked like that of a construction worker and was covered in blood. His left arm was wrapped from one end to the other in large, bulky, apparently hastily applied dressings. Only his fingers protruded from the end of the dressing and there was blood dripping from the ends of each finger. He was awake, and the medics had him sitting up semi-reclined on the gurney so he could vomit.

This was a favorable position for vomiting but not when he had lost so much blood and was obviously in shock. They rolled him over next to the ED bed that was prepared to receive him. Carol began hooking him up to the cardiac monitor and moving the bag of IV fluid from the pole where it was hanging on the medic gurney over to the pole on the ED bed. The two medics were on one side of the patient and Jim and Carol were on the other side of the patient and the

ED bed. In unison they began to slide the patient over on a sheet from the pre-hospital gurney to the ED hospital bed.

As this maneuver was accomplished, Benny began to give a report of what had happened.

"Doc, this is Franklin Mayer. He is a glass installer, and he and his partner were loading some large mirrors about eight feet long onto the side of their glass truck this morning getting ready for the workday. A gust of wind caught the mirror, and as they tried to steady it, it buckled and just blew apart. Franklin here was holding it with his left hand, and as the glass came apart it fell and all of the shards came down on his left arm and just shredded his arm to ribbons. That appears to be the only injury, but it is extensive. We just tried to get some pressure on it and then 'scooped and ran' with him."

Jim looked down at Franklin as Carol proceeded to cut off what was left of his shirt and draped a hospital gown over his chest and abdomen. The unaffected right hand and arm was pulled through the arm hole on the gown. The injured arm was left uncovered. The automated blood pressure cuff was placed over the biceps area of his good arm. The tubing from the cuff snaked up behind him and into the cardiac monitor. On the monitor his oxygen saturation was reading 100 percent from the probe applied to the index finger on his uninjured hand. His heart rate was 140 beats per minutes in a steady sinus tachycardia. Carol hit the button to start the blood pressure cuff and the pump began to whir as the cuff filled with air. Franklin looked pale.

People often refer to someone with this kind of pallor as looking white as a sheet or like a ghost. Even in people with darkly pigmented skin it was possible to recognize a marked difference in the appearance of someone with profound blood loss or anemia. The presence of blood in the skin adds a luster and vibrancy that is lost in the anemic patient. They appear washed-out, ashen or gray. Franklin was so pale his skin was almost translucent. He wasn't so much white but more of a diluted cream color, and there was little differentiation between the color of his skin and that of his lips. He appeared sallow. There were great beads of sweat forming in the center of his chest, coalescing and then running down to his waist. He held the emesis bag up with his right hand to his mouth. He had already filled it with the breakfast contents of his stomach.

The blood pressure cuff had filled and was now gradually deflating, trying to find Franklin's pulse to measure his blood pressure. It stopped deflating with a click and a whoosh, and green digital numbers flashed up on the screen. They blinked repeatedly and the alarm bell on the monitor began to chime. 70/30 was the pressure reading. Franklin was in shock, hypovolemic shock. He had lost so much blood from his injured arm that he didn't have enough left to fill his blood vessels and perfuse his organs. His heart was desperately trying to compensate by pounding away 140 times per minute to push what little fluid remained in his circulatory system around his body. Because he had so little blood remaining in his body, he had lost the normal color in his skin. He looked ashen and gray, lifeless, and pale to an extent rarely seen in the living.

A systolic blood pressure of seventy was just teetering on the threshold of being high enough to provide blood flow to the brain. Seventy millimeters of mercury, which was the unit of measurement, was generally only tolerable when lying in a supine position. When a person is lying down, the heart doesn't have to pump against gravity in order to perfuse the brain. It doesn't have to pump uphill. Imagine holding a garden hose facing skyward as the water pressure shoots up several feet and then reaches its apex and falls back to the ground. Slowly close the spigot and as the pressure drops the flow diminishes until it barely wells up out of the end of the hose. This kind of pressure is ideal for taking a drink from a hose on a hot summer afternoon, but similar low-pressure flow put Franklin's brain on the verge of unconsciousness. His head was swimming, he was confused, and this induced the vomiting he was experiencing.

"Let's get him in Trendelenburg and get some fluids into him," Jim said. "What's our IV status?"

Trendelenburg position placed the patient's feet above his head in order to use the effects of gravity to shunt blood away from the legs and toward the brain and vital organs. The medics had hastily tried to establish an IV, but as Franklin was bleeding so severely, they determined that when they were unsuccessful after one attempt, they would abandon further attempts. Instead they hastily applied a pressure dressing to the arm, loaded him in the back of the rig, and ran lights and sirens to the hospital. The IV bag hanging from the pole was not connected to Franklin.

Carol began working feverishly to establish an IV in Franklin's good right arm. The left arm was useless of course and although Franklin was thin and fit and normally had veins that snaked like ropes up and down his arms, now with no blood to fill them, they were flat and hard to find. Miraculously however, Carol found a good one and slid an eighteen-gauge angiocath or flexible needle into Franklin's antecubital fossa, the crease of his elbow. This was a start at least, and a bag of saline was rapidly connected to the line and a pressure bag was pumped up over the IV bag to rapidly force the fluid into Franklin's vascular system and begin refilling his empty tank.

But the fluid now running into Franklin's right arm was only salt water. The fluid pouring out of his left arm, and soaking through the dressing, was blood. Blood, that marvelous red liquid that flows like a river through all of the great arteries and veins and then snakes its way into every nook and cranny of the body along tiny tributaries and capillaries. Blood, the most remarkable liquid in nature, which transports oxygen and nutrients to hungry cells to fire and feed their tiny relentless little factories. After the delivery, that same complex liquid milieu carries away carbon dioxide as well as the cellular detritus and the byproducts of the cellular machinery thereby cleaning the system and maintaining it at peak efficiency.

Franklin was low on blood. The average-sized male, which Franklin was, typically has about five liters of blood circulating through his body. This is a little more than a gallon, plus a couple of pints. Think of a plastic milk jug plus a soda-pop bottle, or two-and-a-half two-liter pop bottles. That's all there is. That amount of precious liquid continuously circulates and enlivens each human body, depending on gender and size, a little more in some and a little less in others. Jim estimated that Franklin had probably lost at least half of his blood volume; he was dangerously close to dying from the hemorrhage. The solution was simple; stop the leak and replace what was lost. The saline would at least begin to replace some of the lost volume. It would provide a matrix for the blood cells to move in and would help to repressurize the system. But that would be only a very temporary stopgap measure.

"We need to set up the level-one infuser and start some O-negative blood," Jim said.

Ginger was already on it and had requested the O-negative blood from the lab. Hospitals have access to a blood bank that can rapidly provide blood products for patients. The blood bank provides blood that is compatible with a patient's own blood based on a type and screen, or type and crossmatch test. In addition to whole blood and packed red blood cells, the blook bank can also provide platelets, the cells primarily involved in forming clots, as well as plasma, the liquid portion of blood that all of the cells float in. Plasma isn't just a simple liquid matrix, it contains numerous complex proteins essential to clotting and other processes. However, for all of these "type-specific" products, it takes time to accurately crossmatch the donor blood to the patient's blood in order to ensure that it is compatible and to avoid serious transfusion reactions. In a situation like Franklin's, there was no time to wait for blood that was specific and compatible with his. Without blood right now he would be dead long before type-specific blood was available. For just this sort of emergency, ERs kept a few units of O-negative blood on hand. "O-neg" is a relatively rare blood type that is known as the universal donor. Anyone, regardless of blood type, can receive O-negative blood without suffering major reactions or compatibility issues. In a tiny hospital like Jim's, that was also all it had available. Storing blood products was a big and expensive proposition. So, Libertyville could only keep the most basic and vital blood, and it had to be turned over frequently if it wasn't used.

In addition to these basic blood products used in resuscitation, blood banks also provide many other more esoteric blood products for use in specific cases.

The rule of thumb in a massive resuscitation was to start with IV fluid such as saline (a simple saltwater solution with roughly the same concentration of salt as in the blood), or lactated Ringer's solution, another type of so-called crystalloid fluid. This could be used as a starting point to initially replace lost volume and support the blood pressure. But in significant blood loss, crystalloids needed to be rapidly supplanted by red blood cells, platelets, and plasma. Some facilities used a ratio of 2:1:1 (red cells, platelets, plasma) and others used 1:1:1. What Jim wanted now were red blood cells. A tiny ED like this had no quick access to platelets or plasma so Jim would have to try to control the bleeding, give Franklin whatever blood he had available and then get him to a trauma center where he could be further resuscitated and where a team of surgeons could try to save his arm and put it back together.

In order to deliver fluids a device known as an infuser could very rapidly warm the blood and deliver it through large bore IV tubing to an exsanguinating patient in a matter of minutes. Because blood products are organic compounds, they will go bad if kept for long at room temperature. Therefore, they are kept chilled or even frozen with preservatives in them in order to protect the fragile cells and proteins until they are ready to be transfused. This meant that blood had to be rapidly warmed from refrigerator temperature to nearly body temperature before it could be safely administered to a patient. This warming process was tricky however, because if the blood was overheated or heated unevenly it would essentially cook and damage the cells. The infuser device helped to warm the blood and then deliver it quickly using a pressurized system. This required good large-bore IV access in order to push a lot of fluid through quickly. Carol now had one IV in Franklin's right arm with saline running through it and was working on a second. Jim might have to place a large central line as well, but that would take time and right now it appeared that the peripheral vein access would work.

"Let's give him some tranexamic acid and Zofran as well," Jim said.

Tranexamic acid, or TXA, was an inexpensive drug that had actually been around for a long time, but was now seeing more use in the trauma setting. It could help to reduce clot breakdown thereby slowing bleeding. Zofran was an anti-nausea medicine, which might be helpful as Franklin had been actively vomiting. Surprisingly Franklin didn't seem to have a lot of pain, or at least hadn't begun to complain about it yet. Perhaps this was due to his overwhelming fear, shock, or the effects of adrenaline. In any case, Jim initially elected not to administer any pain medicine. Pain medicine would potentially lower his already critically low blood pressure and could make the vomiting worse as well. The tranexamic acid could also do the same thing so Jim elected to avoid pain medicine until the blood pressure had stabilized. He knew that once Franklin was feeling a little better, he would have time to notice the pain and it would become a priority, but for now pain could be ignored.

Now that the resuscitation was underway, Jim began to turn his attention to the injured arm itself. Carol and Ginger continued to work feverishly to secure IV access and administer the blood, fluids, and medications. The phlebotomist, who had just arrived to begin doing morning blood draws on the floor, had also helped out by collecting a blood specimen from the IV start in order to get the lab studies and cross-matching process underway.

Jim looked at the injured left arm. It was wrapped from just below the shoulder down to the finger tips in a large bulky dressing. The dressing material the medics had applied was a thick, absorbent fleece-like material that had started out white but now was almost entirely crimson. There was blood actively dripping from the fingertips and onto the bed and floor next to Franklin. The bright red hue of the blood on the oversized arm dressing created a stark contrast to the remainder of Franklin's pale white skin.

"Ginger, do we have a portable blood pressure cuff handy?" Jim said while looking at the dressing.

"Yeah, we have a couple of them in triage, we usually use the automatic cuffs but I know there are some out there," Ginger said.

"Great, can you grab me one of those?" Jim said. "I'm going to use it to tourniquet the arm while I take the dressing off and see what's underneath.

"Carol, can you call and activate the helicopter? We need to get this gentleman to the university hospital as soon as we can. Also, as soon as I get this new dressing on, can you get the trauma surgeon there on the line for me?"

"Will do," Carol said.

⸻

JIM KNEW THAT he was entering tiger country by taking the dressing off. In so doing he might further open the floodgates of bleeding in an already severely compromised patient. But he also knew that the current dressing was not adequately controlling the bleeding, and if it continued at this rate, he was unlikely to be able to keep putting blood in faster than it was draining out. Ideally the dressing would be taken off in the OR by a surgeon who had the skills and equipment necessary to gain control of the bleeding, and who also had the help of an anesthesiologist and nurses who could simultaneously manage the resuscitation and administration of blood. Taking the dressing off could be like pulling a nail out of a slowly deflating tire. You might still be able to drive on it with the nail in place. If removed the tire was sure to go flat in a hurry. This is why knives, nails, and other items that were found to be impaled into various areas of a patient's body were best left in place until they could be removed in a controlled setting after imaging was done and where bleeding could be controlled as they were removed. This is also why it drove Jim crazy that in the movies they were always removing bullets that didn't need to be removed.

As is often the case in the emergency department and even more so at night time in a small ED with limited resources and limited backup, Jim had to make life and death decisions in the moment. He could leave the dressing on with blood pouring through it and continue to infuse blood and fluid into Franklin's veins on the good arm in the hope that he could stay ahead of it until he got him to another facility, or he could remove the dressing and see if he could control the bleeding now. These decisions were some of the most difficult because although it could potentially save Franklin, or any other patient with any number of other life-threatening dilemmas, it could also lead to a disaster and hasten his death. If the intervention was successful, then Jim was just doing his job. If the decision was unsuccessful and the patient worsened or died, then there would be a cascade of onlookers pointing fingers and retrospectively critiquing the decision with: "What the hell were you thinking?"

SUCH WAS THE life of the emergency physician. They always worked in a fish bowl. It was these very types of issues and decision points that paralyzed some ED docs. But Jim knew that given the time it would take to get Franklin to an OR for definitive care, he would never make it unless Jim controlled the bleeding now. Ginger returned with the blood pressure cuff. With the saline running and the blood being hung in the infuser, Franklin was looking a little better. His systolic blood pressure was now up to eighty and his profuse sweating had slowed.

Jim took the blood pressure cuff and slid it around the uppermost portion of Franklin's injured arm as close to his armpit as it would go. He slid the dressing down a little in order to get the four-inch-wide cuff fully around the arm without having any of the dressing underneath it. Once it was secured with the Velcro, he began pumping up the cuff. His intention was to create a temporary tourniquet to completely shut off any blood flow into the arm. He could then take the dressing off with the bleeding controlled and assess how best to manage the bleeding and see the extent of the injury.

———•———

AT THIS POINT he didn't want to place a tourniquet around the limb for the long-term. Without a doubt, tourniquets could be lifesaving when used correctly. It seemed like such a simple thing to do, but unless they were done correctly and in the right circumstances they could also cause more problems than they solved. Tourniquets had fallen out of favor for many years but had recently come back into the mainstream due to the number of catastrophic extremity injuries that had occurred during recent conflicts, the result of IEDs, roadside bombs and terrorist attacks. The problem with tourniquets was that they worked by completely cutting off the blood supply to the extremity. Therefore, if a person had a serious arterial injury distal to where the tourniquet was applied it would indeed work to control the bleeding, but the problems arose if it was applied too loosely, if it was on for too long, or if the wrong material was used. Then it could do more harm than good, and the results could be disastrous.

The reality is that most extremity bleeding that occurred in the civilian world could be controlled with simple direct pressure at the site of the bleeding. Even with an arterial injury, which were actually relatively rare when compared to the number of low-pressure venous injuries, applying direct pressure at the site was often enough to control the bleeding and allowed for some collateral flow to continue to perfuse the remainder of the limb. Placing a tourniquet upstream from an injury meant that the portion of the limb below the tourniquet would be made ischemic. This meant the entire downstream area would have no blood flow, and if blood flow was not reestablished, all of that downstream tissue would be compromised.

Once a tourniquet was put in place, the pain in the extremity would often increase becoming severe and agonizing. All of the tissues and each individual cell downstream would scream out in pain as they were starved for oxygen and gradually began to die. That cell death would then result in a buildup of what were essentially poisonous waste products as the dying cells broke apart and their walls lysed. This would then cause these waste products and other cell contents to spill into the blood stream.

This is why every tourniquet has to be marked for the time it was applied. It should be on for as little time as possible if there is to be any hope of salvaging the underlying limb. Also, tourniquet pressure has to exceed the pressure in the arteries in order to completely squelch the flow of blood. If a tourniquet is too loose or loosens after its application, the pressure will not be high enough to fully impede the high pressure arterial flow into the limb, but it will impede the low pressure return venous flow back out of the limb leading to the extremity becoming even more engorged with deoxygenated blood and lead to worsening of the bleeding in general. Lastly, if a tourniquet is used that is too constricting at the site, such as when a wire or narrow string or rope is used, it causes the tissue directly beneath the constriction to be crushed and irreparably damaged. A poorly or inappropriately applied tourniquet can damage skin, muscles, and nerves, and if it is applied too far above the injury it may lead to damage or death to much more of the extremity than would have otherwise been affected by the injury itself. Many a hastily applied makeshift tourniquet that was used when it didn't need to be, or was on for too long, has permanently impaired an injured limb.

Of course, tourniquets are used every day in operating rooms around the world for elective orthopedic and other procedures on limbs to provide a bloodless field for the surgeon to work in. But these are wide and well-padded to prevent tissue necrosis, and they are strictly timed to make sure they are removed before permanent cell injury or death can occur.

JIM CONTINUED TO pump up the cuff, gradually filling it with air and constricting down circumferentially around the arteries in Franklin's upper arm. When the cuff reached a pressure that was well above that of Franklin's blood pressure, Jim stopped pumping and began to quickly remove the dressing to evaluate the injury.

As he began to unwrap the blood-soaked dressing, a loud bang almost like a gunshot sounded through the small emergency department. Everyone in the room including Franklin was startled by the sound and confused regarding its origin. Jim, however, knew almost immediately what had happened. The rubber bladder inside of the manual blood pressure cuff, which had obviously been sitting in the drawer for far too long, had degraded and weakened. When it had been pumped up to a high pressure around Franklin's arm as a tourniquet, the rubber had fatigued and violently ruptured, leading to an explosive pop. As the tourniquet/BP cuff rapidly deflated, blood flooded back into Franklin's mangled arm and as the dressing was now off and there was no back-pressure, blood began again to pour and spurt from the myriad lacerated veins, arteries, and capillaries of the arm.

Jim quickly reached his bloodied, gloved right hand up under Franklin's upper arm near his armpit. He placed his fingers over the area on the inner aspect of the arm beneath the biceps muscle and squeezed down as hard as he could on the brachial artery using the pressure point to squelch the torrent of blood now flowing into the arm.

"Quick, go and grab another cuff," he said to the tech.

She was already on her way. This tiny ER didn't have any of the commercially available tourniquets. Those were mostly used in the field by EMS and first responders and were not currently stocked in the hospital. For now, Jim's fingers squeezing the artery was the only thing keeping Franklin from rapidly bleeding to death. Franklin's head began to swim and beads of sweat began to appear again on his pale forehead. While Ginger looked for a new cuff, Jim was able to see for the first time the extent of the injury to Franklin's arm.

The dressing was now completely off. Jim maintained his iron grip on the artery with his right hand, already beginning to feel fatigue creep into his fingers. Looking down on the arm he noted that the injury started just above the elbow so where Jim was holding under the bicep and where the blood pressure cuff had been the skin was intact and normal appearing. However, from just proximal to the elbow and extending distally to the hand the arm appeared more like something one would see in a slaughterhouse than hanging at someone's side. There were long strips of skin and muscle and tendons all going in different directions and stripped away from the bones of the forearm, which were exposed and glistening white, speckled with blood. There was no rhyme or reason to the array of tissues that hung in long, thick ribbons from the upper arm all the way down to the wrist. At first glance it seemed it would be impossible to put this jigsaw puzzle back together. Despite Jim's iron grip on the brachial artery, there was still plenty of blood welling up from the shredded tissues. Using his free hand, Jim was able to carefully remove several large shards of glass that were loosely embedded in the muscles. He could see where the brachial artery entered the forearm just distal to the antecubital fossa, or front part of the elbow, and bifurcated into the radial and ulnar arteries. He could see each of these arteries had been lacerated in multiple places. Likewise, there were numerous deep and superficial veins in the arm that were cut at odd angles. The median nerve was visible like a pale worm snaking down the arm and diving into the wrist. The complex musculature of the forearm that controlled the fine movements of the wrist and fingers hung suspended from the arm like bloody rags. From the wrist onward into the hand and fingers, everything was remarkably anatomically intact. The hand and fingers essentially looked normal except for the fact they were pale and lifeless and no longer attached to the muscles by the tendons that animated their movements. The hand and fingers had apparently been protected by the thick gloves that Franklin had been wearing when he lifted the heavy glass mirror. Franklin groaned as he also surveyed what previously had been his strong and functional arm.

Wow, Jim thought, it will take hours and multiple surgeons to try to piece this back together if it is even salvageable at all. The hand surgeons at the U were exceptionally skilled and typically managed everything in the arm from the tips of the fingers to the shoulder. Franklin's injuries would also require the skills of a vascular surgeon to repair the major arteries and veins. Hopefully there weren't large pieces of these missing. There would be a need for microsurgery to repair the nerves if they were lacerated. If a lot of skin was missing, he may require skin flaps or grafts to cover it all up again.

Ginger returned with a much newer looking blood pressure cuff. She quickly slid it around Franklin's upper arm and around Jim's fingers. Once it was in place, she began vigorously pumping up the cuff. As Jim felt it tighten, he carefully slid his hand out from under it releasing the artery.

With a few more pumps the cuff was up and the circumferential nature of it cut off any more blood flow to the arm. This time the cuff held without any unexpected explosion.

Jim reached for a one-liter bottle of sterile saline with a special cap on it that allowed him to squirt a forceful stream of the fluid onto the arm to begin cleaning it. Ginger had set up two bottles like this and had placed several absorbent pads under Franklin and his arm to catch the fluid. Despite that, the sheer volume of blood he had lost, now mixed with the saline, soaked everything until there was blood and fluid running off the gurney and onto the floor where it created large puddles. The area around Franklin now looked like the most violent of Hollywood murder scenes.

———————⋅———————

IT REMINDED JIM of the first time he had flown on the helicopter and had done an interhospital transfer of a trauma patient. When he and the rest of the flight crew arrived at the outlying hospital and walked into the trauma bay of the emergency department, there was literally blood everywhere, extending in all directions from the gurney on which the patient lay. Additionally, the entire room and area around the patient was strewn with discarded equipment and packaging that had been used during the resuscitation. Jim was struck by the scene as the patient, who was now somewhat stabilized, bandaged and on a ventilator, was being quietly attended to by a single nurse and respiratory therapist. The ED doctor had apparently moved on to new patients, and the surgeon, if there had been one, had also already left. It all seemed so routine. The patient, despite severe injuries, had been stabilized to the point that he could be put into the back of a helicopter and flown back to the U for further care. The scene reminded Jim of a movie but without the dramatic music and fancy camera angles and shots. This was just life in the ER. A life that the public, comfortably at home in their beds, really didn't comprehend was happening.

———————•———————

JIM CONTINUED TO irrigate the arm from top to bottom, careful not to splatter himself in the face as he had not had time to put on a mask, face shield, or even a gown, for that matter. He only had on gloves and his scrubs. The same scrubs that he drove to the hospital in and intended to drive home in. Ideally all of the staff in a resuscitation like this would be wearing protective gear from head to toe to avoid exposure to blood and other bodily fluids. But sometimes there just wasn't time. Jim realized that his stethoscope and clothing were probably constantly contaminated by serious pathogens. He tried to be careful and use precautions, drapes, and barriers, but the reality was that despite everyone's best efforts, most hospital staff that had direct patient contact were probably colonized with all sorts of pathogens such as MRSA (methicillin-resistant *Staphylococcus aureus*), a source of serious skin infections and abscesses, as well as *Clostridium difficile*, a particularly nasty cause of severe, persistent diarrhea.

Jim knew that he probably carried these organisms home with him and exposed his children when he cuddled them or they climbed on his lap. Over the course of his training he'd had a few direct exposures to blood-borne pathogens as well. The very first time he performed a digital nerve block as a medical student on a patient's toe, he inadvertently pushed the needle right through the toe from top to bottom and directly into his own finger on the underside where he was holding it. Another time he was examining a patient who had suffered a complex laceration on the volar aspect of the ring and small fingers. As he pushed and prodded to determine if there were any tendon injuries, the patient, who was drunk and belligerent, took exception to the pain this caused and slapped Jim across the side of his face with the bloody lacerated hand. This particular patient was known to have both HIV and hepatitis B. In any other situation this would have been assault with a deadly weapon, but in the context of the emergency department it seemed that it was somehow excusable because, after all, he was drunk and he was hurting.

The cold reality is that in health care, caregivers are routinely assaulted. Certainly, there are instances of patients being abused, and these instances get a lot of press, but the frequency of these encounters is miniscule in comparison to the frequency with which caregivers are physically assaulted, groped, or verbally assailed in the vilest ways. It would be nearly impossible to find a nurse or physician who could say, in all honesty, that it had never happened to them, especially in the emergency department where the incidences are much higher as the patients are frequently drunk, high on drugs, or psychotic. Jim had experienced such episodes numerous times himself, but he also knew that nurses, particularly female nurses, dealt with this kind of behavior much more than he ever did. It seemed to be so frequent and so common that it had become just part of the job. The professionals had to be professional, but the patients seemingly could do as they pleased.

JIM CONTINUED TO work his way through the irrigation bottles, rinsing the damaged tissues of Franklin's arm in order to reduce the risk for infection. Over the years there had been numerous studies on how to clean wounds to lower infection rates, but it seemed that the conclusion of most of them was that the best thing to do was to simply irrigate with clean water under pressure. As Jim continued rinsing, Ginger threw more absorbent disposable towels on the bed under Franklin's arm and on the floor to control the runoff.

Fortunately, this wasn't a particularly dirty wound. Those were much more difficult to deal with. Many wounds had dirt or grease ground into them and they required vigorous, often painful scrubbing. Dirt and debris had to be removed as much as possible. Sometimes sharp dissection was used to trim away dead or devitalized tissue or tissue that was simply too embedded with dirt to ever get adequately clean. When trimming away tissue, it was usually safe to trim fat and skin edges, but it was important not to inadvertently cut away too much skin affecting the ability to later close the wound. It was even more important to avoid inadvertently cutting nerves, vessels, or other important structures.

As Jim cleaned, he didn't find much dirt, but he did remove more small shards of glass. This was nontempered mirror glass so it had broken with shards of varying shapes and sizes. It may be impossible to find all of these. They may or may not be visible on x-ray. Jim searched as best he could to remove them and he felt confident that he got them all, but he also knew that the hand surgeons would spend hours attempting to piece this arm back together and they may find more. Sometimes it was impossible to find all the foreign bodies in a wound. Occasionally, the skin was closed over them and they only came to light later when they caused discomfort or infection. Some gradually worked their way to the surface, and of course some foreign bodies such as shrapnel frequently remained in the body forever.

Jim stepped back and surveyed the arm. The bleeding was now well-controlled with the tourniquet. He could visibly make out all of the muscles that made up the forearm, most of which were cut at various angles and hung like shredded ribbons from the arm exposing the bones. The nerves, arteries, and veins were also visible. Jim began gently placing the cut ends of the muscles back into their anatomical positions as best he could. He also untangled the drapes of skin and laid those back down. Ginger helped to hold the arm up and they each laid their gloved fingers across the damaged tissues in order to keep them from falling out of place again.

Jim then began wrapping the arm with a long roll of sterile, clinging, absorbent gauze. This rapidly soaked up the blood and irrigation fluid, which was helpful because Jim wanted to keep the underlying tissue moist. Following the gauze, he wrapped the entire arm from top to bottom in four-inch Ace elastic bandages. This secured the dressing in place and kept the injured and damaged muscle tissue from moving around underneath. Jim applied this tight enough that he felt it would control the bleeding without completely tourniqueting the arm. The blood pressure cuff tourniquet had now been on for about ten minutes, but Jim knew that it would take some time to get Franklin to the U and into surgery. Although there may not be any blood supply to the arm just due to the injury, he wanted whatever perfusion of blood that was possible to be maintained. In the operating room a tourniquet would be necessary to complete the repair. If the tissue was already dead by that time there wasn't much hope for recovery of function in the arm. Jim had to weigh this against the fact that if he released the tourniquet and the dressing he had applied was not adequate to control the bleeding, Franklin would simply bleed to death.

Jim slowly released the air from the blood pressure cuff by loosening the thumb screw. As he did so he watched for the appearance of crimson working its way to the surface of the Ace wrap. To his delight there was none. The dressing was holding and Franklin's fingertips actually regained a little color, and there was only a mild delay of the capillary refill. Capillary refill is checked in the extremities to judge perfusion and blood flow by squeezing on the skin of a body part such as a finger or a toe and waiting to see how long it takes for the blood to refill the area. In healthy, well-perfused tissue, this takes only a second or two. In Franklin's fingers it was about four to five seconds, but at least there was some refill. Jim laid the dressing encased arm down next to Franklin's body on new clean, dry, absorbent paper drapes that Ginger had placed when she removed the wet, bloody ones.

Jim and Franklin's eyes met.

"Thanks, Doc," Franklin croaked.

Jim just nodded and then turned to Ginger.

"How long until the helicopter is here?" he said.

CHAPTER NINETEEN →

More on Trauma and Transfers

P art of the process of transferring a patient from one hospital to another involves a series of hoops that the transferring physician must jump through. First it has to be determined that the receiving facility has both the capacity to manage the patient being transferred and space (a bed) to take the patient. A physician-to-physician call is required, and the physician on the other end must be willing to accept the patient. Patients can only be transferred from a lower level of care to a higher level of care. Most major receiving facilities have a transfer line that is staffed by an operator who will accept the phone call and then get the appropriate receiving physician on the line. This person then generally remains on the line in the background and often will be simultaneously confirming that space is available to accept the patient. Usually these phone calls are recorded.

Within a few minutes, Ginger had the transfer center at the university hospital on the line. Because this was a trauma situation, Jim would be speaking directly with one of the attending trauma surgeons. He or she would accept the transfer and participate in managing the patient even though it would be a hand surgeon who would actually take Franklin to the OR.

Jim picked up the phone and spoke to the very efficient call center operator who took down the basic information about Franklin and his situation. She then put him on hold while she contacted the trauma surgeon on call. It was early in the morning now, but it may still be the surgeon who had been on-call all night. Typically, call ended at 7 a.m., at which time there would be a handoff from the physician who had been on call the previous twenty-four hours to the new physician starting his or her call day. Jim would be calling at the very end of the twenty-four-hour on-call cycle. This was often the time when physicians were most loath to accept a call or see a new patient as they were so close to being done and being able to go home and sleep, or at least get on with their day without any more call responsibilities and interruptions. Sometimes in the last half hour or so of a call cycle, physicians became unusually hard to reach, hoping that if they could just ignore the call and sandbag for another thirty minutes, they could pass the call along to the oncoming doc. However, when the transfer center was involved, they really didn't have that option, and one of the requirements of being a Level 1 trauma center meant that there had to be a surgeon available in-house twenty-four hours a day, seven days a week, 365 days a year.

The transfer center operator informed Jim that he would be speaking to Dr. King. Jim patiently sat on hold listening to an ABBA song and wondering what kind of mood Dr. King would be in this morning. Jim knew Dr. King only too well. After spending three years as a resident in emergency medicine, he had been involved in dozens of cases with him. He had always found the man to be an arrogant, self-absorbed, condescending dick. Unfortunately, this tended to be the norm for trauma surgeon personalities.

Male or female, black, brown, or white, they all seemed to have sprung from the same unpleasant DNA. The old joke—What do surgeons use for birth control? Their personalities—seemed especially true for trauma surgeons.

————————•————————

IN MOST SMALLER hospitals the "trauma surgeon" was simply a general surgeon, which Jim lovingly liked to refer to as a "stool and pus" surgeon. Once every few days they would be on call for twenty-four hours to come to the ER to help manage trauma patients.

Jim understood how miserable being on call could be. He had done it on all of his rotations outside of the ER. He appreciated that there were few things worse than the prospect of already being exhausted at the end of the workday and then being obligated to stay up all night in the hospital to take care of more patients. If, while on call you were able to sleep, either in the hospital call-room or at home, hearing your pager or phone ring waking you out of whatever low-quality, fitful sleep you were able to steal, to be told to come to the ER to see a patient was indeed at times soul-crushing. This was hard as a resident, but some specialties required physicians to continue to take call for decades or sometimes throughout their careers all the way to retirement.

In the distant past, call was considered a hospital responsibility. The on-call physician wasn't paid to be on call. They made money if they were called in and could bill a patient for their services. That had changed, however, and now essentially any attending physician who took call was paid a set fee by the hospital in addition to whatever they made by billing the patients they may or may not see. Unfortunately, the guarantee of money for being on call hadn't seemed to do much to make the on-call physicians any more pleasant. In some respects, knowing that the on-call physician was being paid to sleep had made it even more frustrating to ED docs who worked all night seeing multiple patients and who might not make as much as their surgical counterpart at home in bed. To be yelled at on the phone by some lazy bastard who was being paid to be home in bed and refusing to come in and help out with a patient when the ED doc was drowning was a powerful stimulus for malignant acrimony between the specialties.

If the drudgery of being up all night was the bane of the ER doc's existence, at least it was a scheduled and predictable thing. For the on-call doctor there was the added issue of trying to pretend to live a normal life while waiting for the inevitable ring of the pager or phone that would disrupt the normalcy. Seemingly because of this, surgeons and other on-call physicians developed during their training a defense mechanism that generally involved being remarkably rude and condescending to the person they viewed as the source of their pain: the ER doc. This was especially true for ER residents who, as they were still in training, garnered less respect than their attendings. In Jim's experience, no one group of physicians exhibited this characteristic more than the trauma surgeons. Jim noticed this in all of his interactions with them.

Trauma surgeons at busy Level 1 trauma centers such as the university hospital tended to operate less than their general surgery counterparts who scheduled elective cases. Instead, they had additional critical-care training and ran the trauma ICU. Additionally, they coordinated with the other specialty surgeons, particularly the orthopedic and neurosurgeons, who were also frequently involved in the management of trauma patients. Jim found that trauma surgeons seemed to regard all nonsurgeon physicians with contempt and disdain, but the greatest amount of vitriol seemed to be directed toward the ER docs and in particular toward the ER residents.

It was comical to Jim that this sort of tension could even exist in modern medicine, but it did. Oddly, classmates and peers in medical school, within weeks of graduating and starting residency training, seemed to already begin to divide into warring tribes involved in perpetual turf battles. The ER residents seemed to have the most insight into this due to the fact that because of the breadth of their specialty, they had to rotate on most other services and were constantly consulting and interacting with residents and attendings from those other services in the ER.

There was some distinction among medical students with regard to grades and performance as to which specialty they could reasonably hope to match into. But it was by no means cut and dried. There were plenty of top-notch medical students who chose, for whatever reason, to go into family medicine, internal medicine, or other specialties that were relatively easy to get into. However, there clearly was an unwritten hierarchy or pecking order among the medical specialties. If you were in a specialty that paid particularly well or had a particularly arduous or long residency and fellowship training program, you were generally considered as being smarter or better than your classmate who chose to do three years of family medicine and then go to work. This, of course, simply wasn't true.

Some specialties were clearly harder to get into than others, but generally if you knew what you wanted to do early on and positioned yourself appropriately, you could usually get into whatever field you chose. Emergency medicine was a popular specialty. It was generally viewed as moderately hard to get into and therefore attracted a high quality of medical student. However, anyone who manages to get into medical school is generally considerably brighter and more driven than the average person. The reality is that the specialties that required the greatest breadth of knowledge were actually those generalist specialties like family medicine.

Jim had worked with Dr. King and had rotated through the trauma ICU for a month as an intern and then for a month again as a senior resident. He saw the favoritism that Dr. King showed toward the surgical residents and the contempt he seemed to have for the ER residents. It was obvious to everyone; there was no attempt to conceal it. In fact, it seemed to be a point of emphasis. This was despite the fact that the ER residents were often more knowledge-able and more adept at trauma-related procedures than their surgical colleagues.

The reality is that the first physician most trauma patients anywhere in the world will encounter is an ER physician who will resuscitate, diagnose, and manage the bulk of their problems prior to their going to the OR. But if you aren't the doctor who takes the patient or at least the subset of trauma patients who actually require it, to the operating room, then you really don't understand trauma. This inaccurate perception created a disconnect between the emergency physician and the trauma surgeon and was pervasive almost everywhere. It was unfortunate because what seemingly should be a collegial collaboration often disintegrated into a pissing contest. Frankly, this was driven by the surgeons, not the emergency physicians.

To the emergency physician, in even the busiest of trauma centers, trauma made up less than 5 percent of the patients that came through the doors. Whenever they were sucked into the time-and resource-consuming trauma patient vortex, the rest of the ER went to hell as other patients kept on coming and backed up in the waiting room. There was no easy way around it, the management of trauma patients was and is a complex process often with multiple organ systems involved. It was messy, time consuming, and emotionally charged. It often involved patients who were drunk, stoned, violent, underinsured, too young, or too old. Trauma was never convenient. It was much more palatable for a surgeon to schedule a hernia repair or cholecystectomy than to be dragged out of bed in the middle of the night to come in and to help manage a complex trauma patient.

----------•----------

"HI DR. KING, this is Jim McCray. I'm moonlighting up at Libertyville and I have a trauma patient I'd like to send down to you," Jim said after the transfer center operator put the trauma surgeon on the line.

"I've got a forty-four-year-old man named Franklin Mayer who was loading some large glass sheets on his truck this morning when the glass shattered. It basically rained glass shards down on his left arm and cut it severely…"

"So, you're sending me a cut arm from a broken piece of glass," Dr. King interrupted, his voice dripping with contempt. "You're sure this requires a trauma activation and the resources of a Level 1 trauma center."

"Yes sir, it's pretty impressive, he basically shredded his arm to the bone from his biceps to his wrist," Jim said. "It was completely devascularized, he was in hemorrhagic shock when he got here. I'm not sure the arm will even be salvageable. I have resuscitated him and got the bleeding under control for now, but he needs to go to the OR with hand surgery and vascular surgery as soon as possible."

"Hmm. How did you control the bleeding? I hope to hell you didn't use a tourniquet," Dr. King responded.

Wow, this guy is such a piece of work. Jim thought. He is so clueless about what it's like to work alone in a small ER. I guess the tourniquet debate rages on.

Clearly Dr. King questioned whether Jim's training was adequate for him to decide on the appropriate use of a medical device that was literally thousands of years old. As much as his condescending tone irked Jim, he also understood that tourniquets if improperly used could be harmful, and let it pass.

"I did at first, sir," Jim said, trying to sound professional and not let any of the loathing he felt for this man seep into his voice. After all, he had a few more months of residency to get through. Also, he was asking for his help and wanted to get Franklin out of his ER ASAP so he could get the care he needed.

"I used a tourniquet to control the bleeding initially and to see what I was dealing with. His blood pressure was seventy when he got here. Once the bleeding was controlled, I washed it out, removed some glass shards from the wounds, laid everything loosely back in place and then put a big bulky compressive dressing over everything. I was able to let the tourniquet down and it's not bleeding through, but I don't think there is any good arterial flow to his hand as it looked like the arteries were cut in several places. While I did that, we resuscitated him with a liter of saline and he has had two units of O-negative blood so far, but I only have a total of four units here. I'll be starting the last two shortly. I gave him some TXA, but I don't have any other blood products. His blood pressure is up to one hundred systolic now and he looks a heck of a lot better, but I need to get him to you as soon as I can. Oh, I also gave him some Ancef (an antibiotic), some Zofran, and a tetanus shot. I've called for the helicopter and I recommend you have more blood products and an OR ready. Will you take him?"

There was a pause on the other end of the line. Then Dr. King came back on. "Transfer nurse; are you still on the line?

"Yes sir, I'm still here," she said.

"Do we have beds in the trauma unit?" King asked.

"Yes sir, we do," she said.

"All right, McCray send him down," Dr. King said with a sound of resignation in his voice. "I hope this doesn't end up being a case where I have the surgical intern sew him up in the ER and then send him home."

"I can assure you that won't be the case," Jim said curtly and then hung up the phone.

"Ahh, Dr. King. King of assholes," Jim mumbled to himself.

Jim was aware, however, that sometimes transfers were unnecessary and frankly inappropriate. He had himself been on the receiving end of such transfers while working at the U where he thought, "What was this guy thinking shipping this case?" He had seen a finger injury that literally required a few stitches and a Band-Aid arrive in a helicopter from a small rural ER. The quality of care at such facilities was very variable and he understood that since King knew him, he also felt at liberty to question him. Transports, particularly by helicopter, were expensive and they put the transport crew and patient at significant risk.

"All right, he's accepted at the U. Let's get the helicopter here and get Mr. Mayer packaged up and ready to go," Jim said. But as he looked up, he realized that Ginger had anticipated this and was already on the phone and talking to the dispatcher for the helicopter. She winked at him to let him know she was on it. The flight crew had already been notified and was standing by waiting for the moment when the dispatcher pulled the trigger on the order from Ginger and Jim.

In order to transfer a patient, it was necessary to have a receiving facility and a receiving physician. In this case that would be the university hospital and Dr. King. Accomplishing that sometimes created delays, but it was bad form to actually put the helicopter in the air before those items were checked off. There was paperwork to fill out, and federal regulations to follow that had been worked out years before regarding any kind of transfers. You put yourself at risk if you didn't do it by the rules. Generally, the system worked well, but time was a precious commodity and Jim had transferred patients who had died in transport, so he was mindful of how precarious the process could be.

Jim looked in on Franklin. He looked so much better. He appeared comfortable, the dressing was dry, his vitals looked good on the monitor, and the color had returned to his face.

"I just talked to the university hospital, we're going to send you there in a helicopter as soon as they get here to pick you up, OK?" Jim said. "Once you get there, they will take you to the operating room and see if they can put your arm back together."

"A helicopter? I've never been in a helicopter before," Franklin said, looking a little apprehensive but grateful. "Hey Doc, thank you so much for everything. When this first happened, I thought for sure I was going to bleed to death. There was just so much blood."

"No problem," Jim said. "You really did a number on that arm. I just hope they can fix it so that it works again"

Jim nodded to Franklin and then walked back to the nurses' station. In his mind, he reflected on the image of Franklin's arm hanging limply, shredded to ribbons. He just hoped they could save it at all. Franklin was far from out of the woods at this point. This was a truly life-altering injury.

CHAPTER TWENTY

Finishing the Night Shift

Seventeen minutes later, the crew had arrived, and Franklin was packaged and on the transport gurney, ready to be wheeled out to the helicopter waiting on the pad. Jim exchanged information with the flight nurses and pilot, the same crew he had interacted with a few hours earlier. Two helicopter transports in one night. That was unusual.

It was now 6:47 a.m. Jim's shift was scheduled to end at seven. The entire episode with Franklin, from the time he arrived by ambulance until he was loaded into the helicopter, had taken less than an hour. It had gone so fast because it was a basic resuscitation. Franklin only needed the bleeding controlled and some of the blood and fluids he lost replaced. He had required no real investigations or procedures. He had not had any imaging tests and only minimal lab testing, basically just a CBC, BMP, and type and crossmatch. Even the CBC, or complete blood count, hadn't technically even been necessary as Jim only required a baseline hemoglobin and hematocrit, or H and H, in order to monitor blood loss. The BMP, or basic metabolic panel, gave some basic information including blood glucose, basic electrolytes such as a sodium and potassium, and basic kidney function tests. The type and crossmatch results had been forwarded to the lab at the U so it could prepare crossmatched blood products more quickly.

The emergency department was now empty of patients, and Jim had a few minutes to reflect on the preceding twelve hours of the shift. He had for the most part kept up with his charting as he went along. That was a luxury when it wasn't too busy and the patients' arrivals were somewhat spaced out.

With the advent of the EMR or EHR (electronic medical record or electronic health record depending on the source), it often felt like there was way more time spent on the computer documenting the patient interaction than with the actual patient or patient care.

In order to try to make physicians more efficient when it came to documentation, some EDs had implemented the use of scribes. These were typically pre-med students or young people who were interested in medicine and were computer savvy. They would follow the doctor from room to room, usually dragging a computer on a wheeled cart, and would attempt to document everything into the EMR in real time. Jim had some experience using scribes, but he was not enamored with them. He wished, however, that they had existed when he was an undergraduate student. During that stage of his academic journey, he had very limited medical experience and exposure highlighted by shadowing a few doctors and volunteering once a week at the hospital. These kids who worked as scribes actually got to follow practicing emergency physicians into every patient room. They got to understand and document in real time the thought processes of the physician. They got to witness the procedures and observe all of the physician's interactions with patients, families, nurses, and consultants, and they got to do all of this while being paid. It was almost unthinkable for a pre-med student to get that kind of experience and exposure to real-world emergency medicine. Jim would have killed for that kind of experience when he was in college as he was desperately trying to make himself attractive to a medical school admissions committee.

Jim was especially fastidious about his charting. He felt strongly that, other than the patient's actual therapeutic outcome, the most important product he produced was the patient's chart. It was there that he told their story and described what he had done to diagnose and ultimately treat them and relieve their suffering. It was that chart that would be reviewed by the next physician they saw, and it was the words in that chart that would be laid bare before judge and jury should there be a bad outcome and subsequent legal action. Regardless of how good a scribe was, it was their words and their description that made up the chart. Sometimes the narrative they produced was incomplete or lacked the sophistication or understanding of what the physician was trying to convey. Some of the scribe charts just sounded amateurish or were simply wrong and had to be corrected. This was hardly the scribe's fault. They did the best they could with the knowledge they had. They could hardly be expected to have the fund of knowledge of the physician or be expected to "guess what I'm thinking." The other problem that Jim found with scribes is that they were just one more body in an already cramped space next to the patient's bed. He suspected that the scribe craze probably wouldn't last much longer, particularly as EMRs and voice recognition technology continued to improve.

JIM HAD ONLY a few things left to tidy up in his charting from the night and he quickly finished those off. It was now just after 7 a.m., and the hospital was becoming more active as the day-shift workers arrived and began their workdays. At shift change there was always a lull in patient care as nurses met to handoff patients and update the oncoming staff about each patient. Jim didn't have any patients to handoff this morning, the department was now empty. Two patients with minor complaints were being triaged, but they would be the responsibility of the day doc. The day doc was Dr. Jerry Franks. Jim knew him well as he had graduated from Jim's residency program two classes ahead of him and had been a third-year when Jim was an intern. Dr. Franks had stayed local, he worked part-time in several small community ERs and pulled occasional shifts at the university hospital. It was well-known that he was angling for a faculty position, and Jim hoped he got it because he was a good doc and a nice guy. The real reason he was still around, however, was more likely because he was dating one of the OB/GYN residents in Jim's intern class.

Jerry had now gotten his morning coffee and had signed into the computer.

"Well McCray, how was your night and what can I do to get you out of here?" Jerry said while sipping his coffee.

"Actually, I'm in pretty good shape. I just finished my last chart," Jim said. "I got the place emptied out and I'm leaving you a clean slate."

"Excellent, that's what I like to hear," Jerry said. "Was it an easy night?"

Jim smiled. "Actually no, I walked into a hornet's nest.

The place was jammed when I got here and Lindstrom beat it as soon as she saw me. I had some seriously sick patients. I transferred two by helicopter and I delivered a baby."

"No way, that's awesome," Jerry said. "You're a stud, McCray. All that and you're leaving me with an empty ED in the morning. I knew the moment I laid eyes on you as a baby intern that someday you would grow into a fine young ER doc. Your mother would be so proud."

Jim smiled back. "All right, wise guy. Have a good day. Call me if any of my patients bounce back or if you need my help. Do you remember my number? It's 1-800-try-and-find-me."

Jerry laughed. "Get some sleep man, and drive safe."

Jim enjoyed the camaraderie he had with other ER docs and with his fellow residents. Nobody except other ER docs really understood what it was like, and that created a strong connection.

Jim said goodbye to the nurses, gathered his backpack, put on his winter coat over his scrubs, and walked out of the ED through the ambulance bay doors. As he approached the doors, they slid open with a whoosh and he was hit in the face with a blast of cold winter air. He walked across the parking lot to his car. It was still fairly dark, and frozen mist hung in the air beneath the parking lot light posts. The air was cold and he knew his car would be even colder, but at least it hadn't snowed too much overnight. Jim climbed into the car, started it and turned on the heater. As he sat there waiting for the windows to defrost, he reflected on the preceding twelve hours.

He felt exhausted but alive. He was nearly overwhelmed with fatigue, but he also had a powerful sense of satisfaction about what he had just done, about the lives he had touched, and the people and patients he had helped. While most people were sleeping, he had been involved in some of the most intense, intimate, and at times painful moments that a small group of random unrelated people will ever have in their lives. He would likely never cross paths with any of them again, but he had been there during their moment of crisis when they needed his skill, his expertise, and his care. Jim mused that at that moment, all across the country there were ED docs just like him who were exhausted but exhilarated on their way home from their night shift with those same thoughts playing through their minds. As difficult as it had been, he was thankful for it and knew it was a great privilege.

EPILOGUE

Jim's drive home was uneventful and before long he was in bed and asleep. He awoke just after noon and spent the rest of the day playing with the kids. He was tired and felt the familiar hangover sensation from having been up all night. His lack of energy meant that he directed the kids toward sitting quietly on the couch where they cuddled up with him, and together they watched their favorite shows rather than engaging in typical rambunctious toddler play. By four o'clock he sat down to an early dinner with the children and Sue. In a small house and with noisy toddlers, Sue was used to making schedule adjustments to keep the kids quiet or take them away from the house so Jim could sleep.

Emergency medicine families got used to this way of life. The schedule was always all over the place. The doctor in the family was often at the hospital evenings, nights, and holidays. Because of that they missed a lot of important events and meal times were rarely consistent. The children needed consistency in their schedules, so it was a balancing act to make it work. Of course, there were advantages also. When the rest of the world was working nine to five Monday to Friday, emergency medicine families often had time off. This allowed them to do things and go places when those places were less busy. This worked well for the McCrays especially now while the children were young and not yet in school.

Jim and Sue put the kids to bed together between seven and eight. Jim then had a couple of hours alone with his wife. They talked about their family, and Sue updated him about the children's activities. She asked him about his work and about the patients. But he always had some difficultly talking about it right after. The shifts were emotionally draining and he found that he needed time to process them, and if he talked about it too soon it was like reliving the shift. Sue had become accustomed to this. Although she was interested, she didn't push and over time Jim would open up and talk about his experiences. When he finally did, he felt better and appreciated that although his wife didn't understand the medicine, she had a keen sense of the raw humanity in those patient interactions.

Jim had twenty-three hours off from work. His night shift at Libertyville ended at 7 a.m. and he was home by 8. He slept for a few hours and then tried to reset his clock back to a day-shift schedule by going to bed at a regular time that evening. Unfortunately, the sleep was of poor quality and he had to be up at five the following day in order to be back at the university hospital by 6 a.m. for a day shift.

This particular day shift was a good one. Shortly after four in the afternoon he had dispo'd all of his patients and had completed all of his charts. Although on his recent night shift at Libertyville he had seen a lot of patients, the one he kept thinking about was Franklin with his shredded arm and ghostly pale face. Perhaps this was because of the graphic nature of the injury, or perhaps it was simply because he had been the last patient of the shift.

He wanted to see how Franklin was doing. All of the other patients—the newborn, the morbidly obese febrile woman, the stripper with the broken wing, the conflicted middle-age transgender man, and all of the others—had run together in his mind. Over time they would all coalesce into the mass of humanity, lumped with the thousands of patients that Jim would see every year, year after year over the course of his career. At times, perhaps prompted by a conversation or an image in a movie, some of the more dramatic cases would rise to the surface, and he would try to recall the details of their particular presentation. There had been so many and there would be so many more to come.

Jim looked on the hospital computer system to see where Franklin was. He found him in Room 323 on the surgical floor. Jim gathered his backpack and headed to the elevator and to Franklin's room. He walked past the nurses' station on the third floor and found the room. He gently slid the door open and found Franklin alone and sleeping on his hospital bed, his head and upper body propped up at forty-five degrees. His injured arm was covered in bulky dressings but his fingertips were exposed. He had IVs in the other arm, and medications and pumps hung from IV poles next to the bed.

The lights were off but there was fading light from the winter afternoon sun filtering through the blinds. When Jim saw Franklin was sleeping, he thought about turning to leave, but then Franklin's eyes fluttered open and a pleasant smile spread across his medicated visage.

"Hey Doc, how's it going?" Franklin said, his voice quiet and raspy.

"I thought I would stop by and see how you were doing," Jim said as he entered the room and quietly made his way to the bedside.

"How was the surgery? How's your arm?" Jim said.

"Well, it's still there." Franklin smiled again, looking down at his bandaged arm. "The surgeon said he thought they got it all back together and he is hopeful that it will be pretty functional when all is said and done. He thought it might take a year or more to heal, and I'll have to go through a lot of physical therapy and stuff before we will really know for sure."

Jim looked from the arm to Franklin's face.

Franklin's chin began to quiver and his voice began to crack. "Doc, thank you so much for everything you did for me out there. When I saw my arm and all of the blood, I thought that was it. I've never been so scared in all of my life. I honestly thought I was going to die."

Jim nodded.

"I mean it Doc, if you hadn't been there and did what you did; I never would have made it here. I would have bled to death for sure. Thank you. Thank you so much."

"You're welcome," Jim said, and as he did so he could feel tears beginning to fill the corners of his eyes. "You're welcome, I'm glad I could help."

THE END

Made in the USA
Las Vegas, NV
31 October 2021

33459549R00164